OPERATION LIPSTICK

MISSION FOR MR RIGHT

OPERATION LIPSTICK

MISSION FOR MR RIGHT

PIA HEIKKILA

RANDOM HOUSE INDIA

Published by Random House India in 2012
1

Copyright © Pia Heikkila 2012

Random House Publishers India Private Limited
Windsor IT Park, 7th Floor, Tower-B
A-1, Sector-125, Noida-201301, UP

Random House Group Limited
20 Vauxhall Bridge Road
London SW1V 2SA
United Kingdom

978 81 8400 174 7

Typeset in Adobe Garamond Pro by Eleven Arts

Printed and bound in India by Replika Press Private Limited

For sale in the Indian Subcontinent and Middle East only

For
Joe and my Kukki

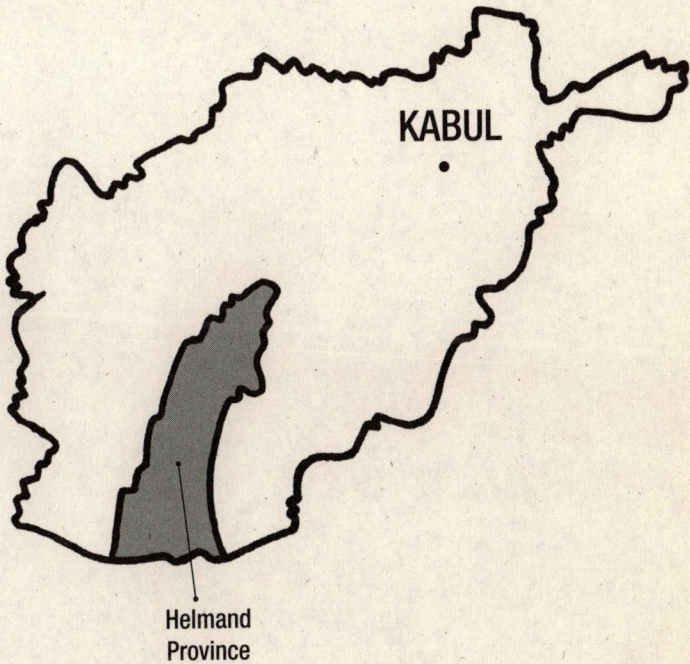

KABUL

Helmand
Province

1

'We are about to land, folks,' announced a cheery mid-Western voice.

'Say your prayers and fasten your belts. I'm turning off the lights now.'

Two weeks in bloody Helmand Province and I was ready to come home. Covering a story that turned out to be yet another bombfest was getting tiresome. The plane plunged into darkness but my head felt light and I was full of the joys of spring.

Kabul—dream base for a single female war correspondent. Not because it's beautiful, scenic, or otherwise culturally significant, but because there are so many single men. And so many parties to meet them in. Aid workers, embassy staff, private contract workers, and, of course, journalists congregate at guesthouses, makeshift bars, or embassies where the booze is free and about ninety percent of the partygoers are men. It is an intoxicating mix of international people—reckless, carefree boozing, with an added danger element. Want a taxi ride across town to a party? What you get on the way is a dozen checkpoints manned by armed men, and you're not quite sure whose side they are on. Want to get legless in a bar? Sure, but aside from a fiery tequila, you might also get blown up in it, since it's been the insurgents' number one target for a while.

It's a recipe for success, if you ask me—Anna S, thirty-two, single, and horny beyond belief.

After an uneventful landing at the Kabul military airport, I strolled out of the plane accompanied by about fifty battle-weary soldiers. My step was light despite the fact that I was still wearing my dusty blue body armour, which weighed a ton, and a rucksack full of camera equipment and survival kits. And a few pairs of frilly knickers.

Everyday life for a single girl in Kabul is the same as it is in London, Reyjavik, or Mumbai. We work, go out, and look for love. Admittedly, in a war zone there are challenges. Fashion is one of them. Sometimes we have to wear big padded blue vests and unflattering helmets. Not a good look if you ask me, but worth it if you like staying alive.

Everything looked as it should on my way back from the airport. Out of the taxi's window, the scene was soft focused and seemed far away…okay, so the window was filthy. Shabby little kiosks selling almost anything—from car engines to chewing tobacco; women hurrying around in their burkhas, with a gaggle of children trailing behind; an endless parade of gun-toting soldiers. This city was anything but easy, even its roads were like dirt tracks—bumpy and unyielding. The taxi inched past the sandy coloured walls which lined the street. Someone once said that Kabul is a city of walls and behind them, many stories lay hidden. It coulnt be more true.

Now, curfew or not, us single girls have to do a lot of mundane things, like going to the supermarket. So I instructed my taxi driver to stop outside the A1 Top Shop. All supermarkets in this town were aimed at the expat community and usually had fancy names, like 'Chelsea' or 'Number One', or 'Bestest'. Sadly, the locals could never afford their ridiculously inflated prices so they shopped in the bazaars instead.

A1 wasn't bad. The shelves were densely stocked with tinned Russian vegetables, chickpeas from Lebanon, and a breast enlargement cream called 'Lovely Bosoms'. It was clean, well lit, and the staff was always friendly. And it had only been bombed a few times.

Inside, Pakistan's top ten from 1988 was blaring. As I looked around, I was tempted to buy a tin of out-of-date Polish dried meat and 'Taschen-off' upper lip hair removal cream. Instead, I opted for a chicken that may only have been defrosted twice. Power cuts were commonplace. Try using your hairdryer with dodgy electricity and you'll be guaranteed a free perm.

I was picking up stuff from the shelves and had accidentally wandered off to the household items section when my tired eyes spotted something far more interesting than 'America tan popsocks' at the shaky makeshift counter. Hunched over the counter was a tall, good looking guy with a bad mullet and a quizzical look on his face. I quickly did the math—mid–to late thirties, ex-army (perhaps a contractor), very fit, completely yummy, and no wedding ring.

How. Hot. Was. He.

He turned around, as if sensing my stare.

'Excuse me, could you help me with something? What does "denier" mean?' he asked, as I stood there, rooted to the spot.

Among everything else, being a single woman alone in a war zone meant finding a man wherever you could. Even if it was in the household items section of A1.

Breathe, I told myself.

'It means the thickness of the tights,' I replied. 'So, for example, 20 denier is sheerer than, say, 50 denier. But if I were you, I wouldn't buy any tights from here,' I rattled on, searching for smart words that would snare this man.

Those eyes! Deep, brown, mystical, yet warm. Full of firm promises of things to come.

'And why is that?' he looked at me quizzically.

Think of something witty, Anna. Come on!

'Um, because they create a drop crotch…you know, the sort that hangs low in the middle, because they are not good quality.'

He thanked me politely and walked off with two pairs of 'Lovely Legs' 20 denier black tights.

I felt like an idiot. Drop crotch? Jeez. No wonder I was single.

Feeling disappointed, I watched his marvellous, firm backside disappear down the aisle. I realized that I must have looked like a mad woman with my greasy hair, dusty face, and filthy clothes. To top it all, I was wearing a pair of ancient, fraying jeans, which should have been thrown out long ago because a bootcut that hung low on the hips looked so last millennium! But they had been with me on several tough assignments, and I was superstitiously attached to them. I could only hope Mr Delectable didn't know his 'skinny jeans' from his 'boyfriend cut'.

I walked out into the busy Kabuli street clutching my shopping bag, and jumped into my waiting taxi. 'The English house, Share-e-now, please,' I muttered in my basic Dari.

A1 used to be a good place to meet men. There were always the random NGO boys in their multi-coloured hemp trousers and contractors in utility wear wandering around with shopping baskets. But it didn't seem to be the case today. How will I ever find a man when even my trusty pulling places were no longer delivering the goods? Hell, I was even prepared to make small talk about processed Iranian cheese.

But then again, come to think of it—thin black tights? Not a good look on anyone, if you ask me. Mr D can keep his tacky girlfriend.

My crawling taxi came to a sudden stop. The driver, a friendly looking man in a white turban, turned around and pointed at a convoy of armoured cars blocking the road ahead. A soldier jumped out of the first car and started to flag us down.

'Ma'am, the road is blocked, security alert. You must turn around, no taxis allowed past this point.'

I swore out aloud. I was tired after the long trip and wanted to get back home. A detour, which would add at least another hour to my trip, was not the thing I wanted now.

The driver started to reverse the car rather quickly. I didn't have a good feeling about it so looked behind to see if he was going to hit anything. And sure enough in another moment there was a screech of tyre and the car jerked and tilted on to its right, throwing me along with it. The car hung precariously over an open sewer.

Perfect! This was all I needed.

The driver had a look of panic on his face. 'Ma'am, I will have to call my cousin to come and help.'

I sighed and nodded. Judging from the traffic, it would be midnight by the time his cousin got here.

I tried to open the left passenger door, but it was stuck. The driver gesticulated for me to jump onto the front seat so that I could get out.

Now, Afghan taxis are small and I'm not. I am over 5 feet 10 inches and have wide hips. Hauling myself to the front seat would require serious acrobatics. The other option was to get out of the right door and jump into the sewer. Even though I was wearing my desert boots and not my Miu Miu platforms, the thought of wading through the sewer was enough to make my stomach churn. I guessed the sewer must have been at least knee deep, if not more. I could have made the jump, however, the brown layer of scum floating on the surface made me stay put in the car. The stench was unbearable.

A group of Afghan men had already gathered around us, to gawk at the foreign woman in a taxi. Anything foreign always attracted attention in Kabul, and a woman stuck in a car was a definite crowd-puller. Some even tried to help and pull the taxi out, but it seemed to be stuck good and proper.

I'm sure many of them would have wanted to help me out too, but in this city men do not touch women in public.

It was time to act before the crowd got any bigger. I gestured to the driver to step out, and then slung my leg over the front seat. I then tried to flatten myself so as not to get stuck between the seat and the ceiling. I had planned to twist my body so that I would land on the driver's seat and half way out of the door. Slowly I began sliding towards the driver's seat, legs first. I could hear the Afghans cheering. I turned my body so I could land on the pavement. I had managed to secure my left leg on the pavement but it was proving difficult to get the second one to follow. There was a ripping sound.

Damn! I had just ripped the crotch of my jeans!

I was annoyed and embarrassed, and glanced around sheepishly in case someone had seen my grey knickers that had survived multiple field washes and were now peeking through the rip. I tugged my tunic lower to cover my embarrassment, but every time I tried to move, the rip just got bigger, now showing almost half of my buttcheek.

Fuck. Fuck. Fuck.

I started to yank out my leg but it was stuck. The poor driver was beside himself. He wouldn't dare to touch me since I was a woman, but I could see that he was desperate to help me.

'Here, let me help,' an English accent cut in.

I looked up to see Mr D standing in front of me.

Fuck. Fuck. Fuck.

He grabbed me, and with one firm pull, my other foot was released.

The Afghan spectators broke out into loud cheers. This had turned into quite a spectacle. To think that I had just got into town!

'Thank you so much…you saved me…' I stuttered.

As an afterthought, I was immediately horrified that he had probably seen me in an ungainly acrobatic position, in jeans, torn at the crocth and ancient underwear to boot, trying to haul myself out of the taxi.

'Pleasure was all mine,' he smiled, a wicked gleam dancing in his eyes.

That smile! Enough to make my heart melt.

'Would you like a lift?' he asked.

Would I like a lift with a man who just saved me from swimming in shit and who was as hot as a pool of lava? Hell yeah!

Forgetting the fact that my smalls were on show to the world, I paid the taxi driver, wished him luck, grabbed my bags, and nervously climbed into the waiting four by four while trying to control my unruly heart from pumping too fast.

There was never a dull day in Kabul.

2

'Where to?' The driver asked Mr Delectable who was sitting in the front seat.

'Where do you live, Anna?'

Wait. He knew my name. This was getting better and better. Perhaps he had seen me on television? Or maybe he knew that I was a super-duper important war correspondent and not some helpless woman who got stuck in taxis?

'The English House in Share-e-now. Near Kabuli Kebabs, please.'

We started towards the car line up. The same soldier who had stopped us earlier, simply waved us past the road block. It must have been the vehicle we were in. Behind the barricade, the road was empty and it would take us ten minutes to get to my house. Damn! That was too little time to be charming. I had to act fast.

'Thank you again for rescuing me. It was a real tricky spot.'

'No problem at all.'

'What is your name?'

'Mark.'

'Hi, I'm Anna.' I held out my hand formally like I was interviewing a president. And then cursed myself silently for my stupidity. 'But you already know that.'

He took my hand and held it just a few seconds too long. Or was it my imagination?

'I know, I've seen your stories.'

His voice was deep, the kind I could listen to for a long time—manly but soft. That was another tick in my list. There is nothing worse than a hot guy with a high pitch or a nasal voice. It gives me a headache after a while. Can you imagine someone wheezing in your ear during sex—I am coooooming. No, nor can I.

'And what do you do here when you aren't rescuing damsels in distress?'

My poor attempt at a joke sounded corny even to me.

'I work in security, you know, like everyone else here.'

His job didn't surprise me. There were lots of these security 'babysitter' types around in Kabul, usually ex-military guys, who wanted the money and easy work. He wasn't very chatty, but I liked that. Men who talk nonsense just to impress a girl tend to have the opposite effect on me.

'So you've seen my stories?'

'And your face is on TV a lot.'

'Occupational hazard I'm afraid.'

'It livens up a report…your delivery is…engaging,' he said as if searching for words.

I wasn't sure if he wanted to pay me a compliment or was taking the piss, but it nonetheless gave me a nice warm feeling inside. To be honest, he could have said anything and I would have still smiled like an idiot. I had to try hard not to look too eager, too single. But I hadn't seen him out and about in Kabul before, so maybe he stayed cozied up at home with his tights-wearing girlfriend. Or maybe he wore them for a kinky sex game? I pushed the thought out of my head.

'Been here long?' I ventured to safer ground.

'Long enough to know where to get a mean drink.'

Was he asking me out?

'So where can I find this "mean drink"?' I allowed myself to flirt a little.

'L'Atmo, Bar 21, and Verandah.'

We had arrived at the English House far too quickly, before I had a chance to say 'Will you be going to any of those places this Thursday?' Thursdays were our Fridays, and the end of the week meant copious amounts of alcohol and general mischief around town.

The car drew to a stop and he jumped out and held the door open.

'Well…thank you so much, Mark.' I held out my hand again. I just wanted to touch him and since a kiss on the cheek was inappropriate, I settled for a handshake instead.

'No problem at all, happy to help. Have a good day.'

Firm, friendly, unflirty.

The car door slammed shut and they drove off. Along with it went my dreams of a future with a lovely, decent, unmarried guy. I had a momentary flash of a sixty-five-year-old, single, fat, eccentric, gin-reeking cat lady. Me, that is.

The sleepy guard came out of his shed to see me standing there, with my bags scattered around my ankles, and muttering to myself, 'Why, oh why, didn't you ask him for his phone number.' With a sigh and a half-hearted hello, I gathered my bags. Why couldn't I just get lucky? Why were all the best men so unattainable? I rang the doorbell and the housekeeper, Hassan, came to the door.

'Salaam, Miss Anna, nice to see you. Here, let me take your bags.'

The English House was named after its previous occupants—a British family that had lived in Kabul for over a decade. The house was a sprawling Afghan-style family home with two floors and a big south-facing balcony. The large windows ensured that the winter months were freezing despite the wood burners. My favourite part of the house was the quaint backyard—an unkempt garden where stray cats loved to sniff about and piss in. We didn't mind them, it made the rose bushes bloom. The house wasn't luxurious, but it was comfortable and felt safe in a city full of uncertainties. Most of all, it was my home. And, of course, theirs too—the two other journalists—my housemates.

'Anyone hooo-oome?' I called out as I made my way through the lobby.

'Over here, in the garden,' came a voice.

I walked to the back of the house, to the garden, where Tim sat enveloped in a cloud of cigarette smoke, on an ancient wicker chair, nursing a sweating beer. Despite it being September, the roses were in full bloom and added a gorgeous whiff to the air.

I hugged him and ruffled his hair affectionately.

'Miss Sanderson. Welcome back. How was your holiday in Helmand Province?'

'Good. One shag, two lead stories, and zero injuries. Oh, and I nearly fell into a shitty ditch on my way back home. The irony of it all. But, most importantly, I got saved by a hero.'

'Only one shag?' he grinned. 'Anyone interesting besides your usual ropey security blokes?'

'Naah, shagged a captain at the back of an armoured vehicle and managed to get a sneaky snog with that new *Times* correspondent who was at Camp Bastion last week.'

'All in all, a classic week for Anna. And who's the hero?'

'Just someone with a fantastic rear,' I said flippantly and laughed.

Tim. My best cameraman, my best friend, my best everything. In his late thirties, with a dimpled smile and a 6-feet-4-inch frame—most girls would call him attractive. A real catch. So why not? I had asked myself this many times.

Never really happened, I guess. And now we had ventured into the comfort zone, like an old couple who knew each others' smell too well. There had been some near brushes, mind you. Once, early in my career, we had been sent to Northern Iraq to cover the Kurdistan plight. But the only plight we experienced was getting captured by a bunch of rebels. Unlucky for us. We really thought that was it for us, the end, sitting in that murky little hut, surrounded by masked men with AK47s. We started to share things, intimate stuff. Everything about our childhood and people we had believed in, loved, and cared for. I can still recall that moment.

15

'I've always wondered what it would be like, you know, if you and I had got together,' he said. I didn't say anything. When he leaned over and kissed me, I didn't resist, but later I thought it was just something he felt he had to do since we were going to die anyway.

But we didn't die. We were set free and we never brought up that kiss again.

Tim got me a cold beer and I lit a well-deserved ciggie. 'Cheers, Anna, welcome back.'

I took a big gulp of my ice-cold beer. The evening was beautifully quiet. How I've longed to sit here, hand in hand, with a man of my own, in our pretty garden. Instead, Tim and I watched in silence as two stray cats jumped the garden hedge and played a horny chase-me game that seemed to involve both taking turns to bum one another.

'The cats have turned gay while you've been away.'

'And you? Still being Mr Picky?'

To be honest, it was odd that Tim hadn't met anyone. There had been the few giggly blondes that I had seen creeping out of the house in the wee hours, but not one that stayed for breakfast. He was so bloody eligible and sane that I had even tried to pimp him off to some of my friends, but he was just his cool and charming self, brushing off the suggestions with a laugh.

My thoughts came to a halt. An all too familiar wail from the kitchen broke the tranquility.

'Sounds like Kelly's in.'

Tim nodded.

'And she doesn't sound very happy.'

3

A teary-eyed Kelly burst into the garden.

'Fucking, Rich, he's gone off again. I can't get a hold of him, and he hasn't got his satellite phone on. He always does this. Gets me worried sick with his bloody hero antics.'

Kelly. My dear friend and confidante. Australian print journo par excellence. Intelligent, sexy, and the only person I knew who could rant, drink, and smoke simultaneously. Someone had called her Turbo-Kel because she talked so fast. She specialized in investigations on human rights, or human wrongs, as she called it. Today the 'wrong' seemed to be all about her boyfriend. A subject which turned the chilled out and fun Kelly into a jealous, incoherent beast. As a friend she was as solid as the Hindu Kush and I missed her madness when I was away. We laughed, cried, drank and smoked a lot together. We told each other secrets that no one else would ever know and shared embarrassements and annoyances. Adorable and only occasionally unstable—that's how I would decribe her.

I handed her a cigarette. 'Kellster, if I had a quid for every time you said "hesgoneoffagain" I wouldn't need to bother with this journalism shit. Remember, all men are bastards until proven otherwise. Except Tim, of course.'

Tim gave me a wink.

Kelly was in an on-off relationship with Richard, who we had officially christened 'Ropey Richie'. He was an unreliable rogue who promised the moon, but Tim and I were sure that he probably shagged anything in a skirt.

Although I could see why Kelly was hooked onto him.

Ropey Rich was dangerously charming and blessed with good looks. He was tall, with a rugged face and an incredible smile, and messy, salt-and-pepper hair. Sort of a cheap version of George Clooney. And, according to Kelly, he had the most wonderful cock known to womankind. It was a lethal combination.

Kelly, on the other hand, was the picture perfect ideal of an outdoorsy Aussie blonde girl. Tall, with long enviably tanned limbs, Kelly's good looks always turned heads wherever she went.

'What happened this time?' I asked.

'All I got was a text from him.' She pulled out her phone. '"Off tonight. A top secret job. No communication devices, will call you. R.X." What a load of crap. We had a date fixed to go out to that new Italian restaurant in Wazir. Plus, I got a new outfit from my last trip to Dubai and Fatima had waxed me, well more like skinning me alive.'

I sympathized with Kelly on many levels. First, the grooming—an ordeal for any woman anywhere in the world, but in a war zone the task took on gargantuan proportions. And getting Fatima to wax your pubes was not far from being humiliated. Her beauty parlour, if you could call it that, was a one-room den, decorated circa 1973 and reeked of ammonia and animal fat. Everything was makeshift. She made you get down on all fours on her desk, all the while shouting, 'Give me the doggie, give me the doggie.' But it worked. And she even did rudimentary shapes if you wanted. Usually, my on-the-road beauty routine consisted of using my fingers—both as a comb and toothbrush. And as a sex toy, of course. But definitely not at the same time.

The second and the most important reason was that Kelly was a good, warm person, with a big heart and did not deserve this crap from Rich. Well…none of us did. She was my best girl friend, even though she was far from being a girly girl. There had been numerous times when one of us was crying our eyes out for the fear of being left alone. Or when we cheered each other up with trips to Dubai, where all the glitz just made us laugh. Not that we didn't enjoy it. But after we would return to the war zone, we would be relieved for not having to fill our days with spa sessions, parties, and designer tags. Don't get me wrong, spas and parties are excellent. But every day?

Smoking and sitting on the wicker chair, Kelly completed our troika. We were made of the same stuff—we were wanderers who were constantly on the move, never settling down in a place for too long, sensing the shift in the wind, following its course to the next adventure. And even though we came from different parts of the world, in many ways Tim and Kelly were my family here.

'You know he can't live without you, that's just the way he is. He lacks emotional intelligence,' I tried to soothe her.

'He doesn't bloody lack any intelligence when he is trying

to woo other women to bed. This time I'm not letting him get away with it. I'm going after him, I'm going to bloody catch him at it, you know. And teach him the lesson of his life…not to mess around with Kelly Kellman.'

Tim flicked his ash into the bed of roses. The cats were still at it, but instead of mounting, they were now sniffing each others' rear.

'Oh do shut up. He'll be back here in a few days and both of you will be at it like rabbits again.' He lit a second cigarette off the one he was smoking.

'I'm turning thirty this year. I can't afford to have someone mess around with me like that,' Kelly grimaced and took a deep gulp of her beer.

Kelly was right. It was no fun being single out here, especially when the war zone was as unpredictable as heck. But despite Miss Kellman's rants and woes, it felt good to be back in our safe and comfortable Kabuli home. The lack of warm water and the uninvited cockroaches did not bother me; it felt like a five star hotel after Camp Dragon's Neck—my home for the last two weeks.

We sat outside for a long time, till it got too dark to see each other's faces. Hassan came and lit the lanterns in the garden, and we switched to whiskey. I finally felt relaxed, and mildly buzzed, after the long trip.

When I finally got up to unpack, Kelly, much calmer, was lying on the grass, singing 'Beat it' completely off tune.

It was bloody good to be home.

A shower later, I slipped into my crisp and clean sheets. There was such joy in details like this. I was asleep in a heartbeat and had a dream of Mr Delectable wearing his see-through black tights with nothing underneath.

It was 4 am when the mortars came to my dreams. Uninvited. It occurred sometimes—an occupational hazard I had gotten used to. I couldn't go back to sleep after that so I opened my laptop and began trawling through my emails of the past few weeks. There wasn't anything worthwhile. An invite to a reception at the British Embassy—something about welcoming the new Deputy Ambassador. It was an instant pick me up. The idea of an evening quaffing free champagne seemed like the perfect antidote to my singleton gloom. And there were a few emails from Match.com. I had placed an ad and put my base as Dubai. I had figured that there might be a better chance of me sounding less of a freak if I was from a saner place like Dubai and that I might actually find a man there. Plus there was a direct flight to Dubai from Kabul, which only took two and a half hours. As far as I was concerned, it was commutable distance. The first email was from a guy called Ali Baba.

Hmm.

Dear Missy A,

You seem like the kind of lady I would love to love, very beautiful and classy. I am very gentle with my hands. I also have a Ferrari. See picture. When can we meet?

There was a picture of a fat guy with a bad tash standing next to a red car.

I hit delete. Next.

My darling A

21

I love your breasts, they are boyant, boyncy like large balloons. I want to press them on my face and drown in your softness… will you float my way?

I wouldn't. Even if you knew how to spell buoyant and bouncy. Ugh. Delete.

Hi—my name is Duncan. I am originally from Brighton but now live in Dubai where I work as a surveyor. My job is to, well, to survey things. I collect maps and have an attic full of antique Ordinance Survey maps back in the UK. I enjoy bars and clubs but would love to find a partner-in-crime to explore the sandy city.

He had attached a picture of a nerdy looking man with button down collars and specs. He didn't stir my nether regions so I hit delete again. It seemed the odds were good online but the goods were odd.

Ever the optimist, I moved on to Facebook. Friend requests 21 and 11 messages mostly from men I didn't know. I got a lot of creeps stalking me. It seemed to be okay for a man to approach a woman who was on TV with lewd messages but God forbid if it had been the other way round. The *Daily Mail* would definitely label the woman a 'deeply disturbed lonely spinster.'

There was an email from CPTPeterACroftwswood@ mod.gov.uk. I perked up.

When I had first arrived at the Helmand base camp, Captain Pete had been distant towards me. Like most soldiers, he was deeply suspicious and wary of a reporter on assignment. But one night after a briefing, we got talking. He was friendly and interesting and we chatted late into the night.

'I'm lonely, Anna. This job is all I have.'

He was thirty-four, married, with two kids back in Surrey. His wife worked part-time, but when he was at home recovering from a tough tour, she wasn't interested in sex.

Or so he said. They always did.

'Join the Not-Getting-Laid club. What about your family?' I replied.

'I rarely see them, and they don't feel like my family any more. I don't think my wife really cares, she just likes to shop online for more and more stuff.'

And on he went. My shoulder was there for him because he was very very hot. And I was too horny to care about wives who preferred Boden Catalogue to bonking. Night had fallen on the majestic Helmad mountains surrounding us, our faces lit by a single candle. Shadows were soft and his hand had brushed against mine. It could have been quite romantic if it wasn't for the toilet smell wafting around us, and the fact that we were sitting on ammo boxes, drinking warm water, and eating a soggy imitation of Pringles from Iran. He smelled good. Soldiers always smelled nice. Soapy, yet sweaty. I always thought that's what courage smells like.

The rampant lovemaking with Captain Pete suddenly filled my mind with fleshy flashbacks. I remembered how hard he had been and how good it had felt—our bodies squeezed together in the back of the armoured vehicle. I had straddled him, riding him hard. He came very quickly, silently. We had had to be quiet so that the night patrol boys didn't catch us.

Darling Anna,

I hope you are safe and well back in Kabul. I must say I enjoyed meeting you and wished you could have stayed longer. I'll be in Kabul next week for training. Would you care to join me for dinner? It would be lovely to see you again.

Nice and polite, a bit too formal for my taste. But sane, which was always a bonus. I bit my nails. He was undeniably hot and a good prospect. Of sorts.

Should I? I thought it had been one of my 'get in, get out' jobs. But he was married, and it always led to some sort of a complication later on. My mind was already lining up the excuses—perhaps he was looking for a way out? Or maybe he had felt there was a connection between us? Or that he just fancied a bit on the side? Again, it wasn't easy being a single girl in the war zone despite all the seemingly available men—because most men seemed to want only one thing.

Which, deep down, was not what I wanted.

Although, a bit of it also helped.

'Yes' I typed out quickly, before I changed my mind, and hit send.

Damn, Anna. You'll never change.

4

'Wake up. It's cocktail hour.' Kelly's cheery voice accompanied by her knocking on my door woke me up.

I groaned. 'Kellster, it's not even midday yet.'

'Never mind, it's cocktail hour somewhere in the world and we could be dead tomorrow.' She walked over to my bed and handed me a perfect mojito.

A good start to a day off work. It was officially a weekend but correspondents are never really off duty because news won't stop just because you have a hangover.

My boss in London, Phil Spencer, was firm but fair, and gave me enough freedom to decide on the news agenda. In general, he did not harass me and Tim too much. I liked him but I knew many people who didn't.

A flirty silver fox with twinkling deep blue eyes (never mind the fact that he was in his mid-fifties), Phil was notorious in the newsroom for making researchers his 'protégés'. In the Eighties, he had been a bit of a hero of Fleet Street, snagging some of the best scoops for a Sunday rag, after which he moved to television. Some say it was probably to get close to glamorous women. He finally married a pretty young thing.

He had done the whole baby and family thing too, but I guess he got bored shagging the same woman for more than two years in a row, and was now back on the fanny chase.

Phil and I had an unwritten agreement, which meant that as long as I didn't miss a major story, I could decide how I went about my work.

Kelly stirred the drink with an expert hand, making the ice cubes tinkle temptingly in the glass.

'Where did you get the mint from?'

'Got it from the bazaar this morning after a good bargain. You know how it goes in a Kabuli market—early bird catches the perfect cocktail ingredients.'

Kelly threw herself on my bed.

'Any news from Ropey?' I stirred my drink and took a gulp. It was good, rummy.

'No. And I don't want to talk about the bastard. Now show me the outfits you've got.'

The party would start early and I didn't have much of a choice in my wardrobe, which meant careful planning was a must.

Dressing up for an embassy party was always a bit tricky. It had to be formal but not too formal, and if you didn't get it right everyone would think you had just stepped off the boat.

I pulled out a turquoise dress that I had worn at a party in Lebanon.

'Too revealing,' said Kelly, in between sips from her drink.

'What about this one?' I held out a bias cut silk dress that was one my favourites.

'Too formal. And a bit Ninties.'

I rolled my eyes.

'Okay, how about this?' A patterned wrap dress which I thought was surely up to the mark.

'Not formal enough; it's a bit home-counties.'

'Kellster, how do you know what home-counties is? You're from the buttfuck of Oz.'

'Actually I lived in London in my early twenties. Is that all you've got? Show me more.'

We went through nearly my entire wardrobe and several mojitos along with that. In the end, I ended up wearing my favourite lucky tunic, which showed off my cleavage and tight jeans that complemented my legs. A long scarf wrapped around my neck would cover the cleavage until I was inside the building. I didn't want unnecessary trouble coming my way. I slipped on my Jimmy Choos that I bought at a sale in Dubai—shoes that I absolutely adored but seldom had the opportunity to wear. After hair assembly help from Kelly, I looked at myself in the cracked mirror.

'Ta-da! Your Mr Delectable will not be able to resist you know. But you can't leave without the most important element,' she said finishing out a lipstick from her purse. 'I feel naked without my Sax. And so will you.'

I had forgotten that I had told her about my mystery man last night in our druken haze. So much for keeping him secret! I applied a bit of the lippy and was ready.

Tim was nowhere to be seen so I decided to leave. It's not a rare sight here for an expat woman to go out on their own, as most of us come to Kabul by ourselves and are forced to make friends by talking to random strangers. Also, this was a city with ample socializing opportunities for journalists. Not only were there the usual end of the week drinking fests, but also NGO lock-ins or diplomatic back pattings that we were always more than welcome to attend.

The party was already in full swing when I arrived at the embassy. It never ceased to amaze me how people in war zones could effortlessly pretend that it was perfectly normal to drink champagne inside the safe walls of a compound, while just a few hundred metres away there was abject poverty and suffering. I guess you train yourself to forget the bad things in the real world and live in this beautiful vacuum with fun parties, glossiness, and expat gossip.

And I admit I am one of them.

The party had congregated around the pool, which was beautifully decorated with little paper lanterns and sparkly floating star lights. Despite it being a September evening, it was still warm enough to be outdoors. Olive trees surrounded the thick exterior wall, disguising the ugly barbed wire. Many of the partygoers were already very drunk. The DJ was playing Phil Collins's Easy Lover. I laughed to myself. It seemed Collins was hip among the ageing diplomat crowd. Drinks and what could be classified as canapés were flowing. The place was full of smartly dressed men and women and if it wasn't for the armed men patrolling the garden, you would think it was happening in Richmond in London.

I spotted a diplomatic trophy wife sashaying around, dressed in a colourful Dianne von Fürstenberg wrap dress. And another in a garish Dolce & Gabbana. Generally, this lot played it safe with classics that showed no labels but were distinguishable enough—Ralph Lauren, Armani, and lots and lots of Jigsaw flowery dresses, and of course, the occasional Topshop. I had to give British High Street fashion a pat on the back. It had managed to find a space to showcase itself, even in war-torn Afghanistan. My outfit was elegant but not too show-offy and the shoes gave me enough confidence among the label-wearing blow-dried wives.

There was plenty of polite chitchat. These parties always made me feel awkward. I often suffered from a type of Gangsta Tourettes at formal events, probably because of my subconscious insecurity of never being quite rich enough or well taught, and always had to control myself from saying something inappropriate like—'Mrs Tannebaum, I really like your haircut. Where the fuck do you get it done around here, you piece of badass muthafucka?' Tonight I decided to keep my swearing firmly under control.

I was introduced to an American diplomat and his immaculately groomed wife. The husband had turned to talk to a group of men so I was left to entertain her.

'How do you do?' She shook my hand formally.

She was model thin and was wearing a tailored, light eau-de-Nile soft wool twinset with matching shiny shoes. Shiny, swishy, dark hair—extensions perhaps?

'How do you like Kabul?' I asked.

And I take it your botox isn't from the bazaar?

'Well, it's good for William, and I keep myself very busy organizing our social life. There are a lot of parties coming up, especially since we are approaching the holiday season.'

'And how is that going?'

'It's a challenge to be honest. There is no fresh produce, or even basic ingredients like olive oil available, so making Italian canapés is extremely difficult. William's last posting was in the UK, which made hosting parties in our Kensington town house easy peasy. But I manage,' she laughed dryly.

Gangsta Tourettes or not, I was suddenly gripped with a massive urge to swear. Did the woman realize that this was a war zone and that there were people dying out here? That she was lucky enough to to be alive? I took a deep breath, and continued to nod politely at the ageing beauty queen while taking huge gulps from my my glass of, now slightly warm and flat, bubbly. It was the only thing that ensured that I didn't end up strangling her.

My eyes began to wander around the garden and I spotted a familiar looking, tall, broad shouldered, delectable bearded man, even though his haircut smacked of a bad experience with the infamous barrack barbers. He was standing by himself near the pool, holding two glasses.

I suddenly recognized that mullet.

It was Mr Delectable!

He looked even better the third time around. My heart leaped at the recognition. Suddenly, this party wasn't as dull as it was turning out to be. Hell, even the music didn't seem such a drag any more. This was a textbook lust case for Anna S.

I kept stealing glances at him and in one instance our eyes met. I felt the blood rise in my cheeks and quickly turned my gaze away. What was happening? I never blush! I wondered about the second glass he was holding. Maybe he was waiting for his lady to come back. Did he recognize me? I turned to the extended brunette who was now on a rant about the exorbitant school fees in Switzerland. When I looked back, Mr D had disappeared. I felt a surge of disappointment. My glass was empty, and I took the chance to excuse myself for a refill and quickly made my way to the bar, hoping I would to run into him.

The volume of chatter was now drowning Phil Collins's voice. I found myself standing by the bar, trying to decide which drink would get me drunk the fastest. At the same time, I was also frantically thinking of something witty to say in case I bumped into Mr D, and began rehearsing the lines in my head.

'Hello. Thank you for saving me from drowning in shit.' Hmmm…not very ladylike.

'Hello. How's the babysitting going?'

Too bland.

'Is that a gun in your pocket…'

No!

As I reached out for my freshly filled glass of neat whiskey with a drop of water—my signature drink—a hand suddenly took my drink and passed it to me.

Mr D!

This wasn't fair. I wasn't ready yet. Not drunk enough, and sans repertoire of witty remarks. I felt my knees go weak and downed my drink in one shot. He held my gaze and without a smile said, 'Hello.'

'So did the tights fit?'

Oh dear. I regretted it as I soon as I said it.

He smiled, clearly out of politeness. 'I think so. I needed them to fix the broken fan belt in my car.'

Ah! So he wasn't buying tights for another woman. This needed further investigation. And what was even better, it was promising. A man who could fix things. I noticed he was towering over me, despite the fact that I was one of the tallest women there.

My heart rate quickened as I looked into his eyes. How could you tell if someone you fancy fancies you back? I hated the smug 'oh you just know it when you meet the right man' answer. Because you never really know.

I had met so many men who I thought were the 'right' ones—the bad boys, good boys, nerdy blokes, and the cool guys. Some felt right for a while until they suddenly stopped calling me despite us dating for several weeks. Some *seemed* right for about five minutes but when they started telling me about the character they played in online fantasy games, I didn't think they were so right after all.

Or there were those who I hadn't even met in flesh, who wrote lovely emails and made me *hope* they were Mr Right, but then, out of the blue, they'd send me a picture of their genitals. Why did men think sending a picture of their cock would be seductive? Then there were those who I straightaway knew would not click, but decided to shag anyway, just in case we found the magic. But most were just

Mr Right-aways. Honestly, I was never good at this game and usually just went by trial and error. A lot of times it ended nowhere. It was such a tiring game.

In my nervousness, I ordered another whiskey. In Kabul, the whiskey measure was about half a pint and I was hoping the drunkenness would mask my nervousness.

'How do you like it here in Kabul?' I tried my best to not let my hungry eyes wander over him.

'Not bad, still finding my feet. You know how the security business is. And you—you've been here for a while?'

I liked a man who asked me questions, who wasn't willing to stay at the receiving end of my questioning. 'It's been a few years now, I'm used to Phil Collins.'

He smiled. 'Any plans of staying here?'

Was he looking for something long term? This was getting promising, very promising indeed. 'Our postings are open ended; they let us decide when we've had enough. You?' I threw the question back at him.

'The same. I consult, which means I'll be here as long as there is work.'

He seemed to be ticking off all the right boxes.

'How is your security arrangement?' he asked suddenly.

'Are you offering your services?' I replied flirtatiously. The whiskey was definetly working its magic.

'No, there are rumours about journos being forced to stay in because of security, and wondered if there was any truth in it.'

'Oh.' Embarrassed about my obvious come-on. 'My security is one chowkidar at our house who has a couple of stolen guns and who smokes dope most of the day. So I guess my bosses aren't too concerned about my safety.'

He frowned. 'You should really be more careful…'

I was getting all warm and fuzzy about this nice man caring about me when I felt someone tugging at my sleeve.

'Tim! I didn't think you'd come!'

'Can I borrow her for a sec?' said Tim a bit urgently.

Mr D nodded, turned around, and walked off. Maybe it was me but Tim seemed to look pleased that Mr D had vanished.

'What are you doing? Ruining my chances of ever finding a steady boyfriend?' I started angrily.

'Sorry, Anna. But there's been an explosion and we have to go. Now!'

'Do we really? I was just getting started.' I pleaded, hoping that maybe there was a fraction of a chance that I did not have to go chasing a story.

'You know better.'

Argh. Bloody insurgents, always ruining my chances of having a half-decent love life. I followed Tim out of the party and into the night.

5

It was late and I was wasted.

'You should have called, Tim,' I moaned.

'I tried but your phone must have been on silent.'

He was right; it was exactly this kind of interruption that made me keep my phone on silent mode.

Tim kept steadying me ahead, past the security guards at the embassy. He sounded tired. 'Anna, they rang us from London and they want it for nine o'clock. There seems to be little other news.'

'That gives us around two hours. Crap.'

'You've done it faster than that, Sanders.'

I was annoyed. My body was in dire need of more alcohol and I really didn't want to go hunting for headless terrorists in my best heels. Plus, I had an awesome man on the boil. But a girl's got to do what a girl's got to do. Tim had already hailed a taxi and had managed to negotiate with the driver to take us as close as possible to where the explosions had taken place. I dialled the number of our Afghan fixer, Ali-Ahmad Massoud.

Fixers are people that foreign correspondents rely on when putting stories together. They are our eyes and ears on the ground. Often, it's a local journo with a wide knowledge of internal affairs and a thick contact book—they are the silent stars behind any major news story. Without them we wouldn't get anywhere.

Ali-Ahmad was in his mid-forties. Mild mannered and kind, but he never smiled or betrayed any other emotion. You could never tell what he was thinking.

I had once asked him why he never smiled. He replied that he had witnessed his sister and mother being tortured and raped in front of him by a group of Russian soldiers. Smiling didn't come easy after that.

And with that, it seemed, the subject was closed.

Ali-Ahmad was great at his job. Through him, we got access to people we would never dream of finding on our own. It was a good working relationship because we didn't ask too many questions, and when money changed hands, we closed our eyes and didn't tell our bosses in London. Kabul was all about having connections with the right people.

A few rings later Ali picked up.

'Hi, Ali, you've heard about the explosions I assume? Do you have any information about who was behind it?' I asked while slinging my bag over my shoulder and testing my pen on my tattered notebook.

'Hold on.'

I could hear him scrolling down his phone.

'Suicide attacks. Two targets I think—one at the Netherlands Embassy and another at the Ministry of Health.'

'Can you meet us at the ministry?'

It would be easier to get in because the embassy would be swarming with Afghan police.

'Okay. I'm on my way. And when you get there, try the east gate.'

The nocturnal streets of Kabul were oddly serene. It was impossible to tell that there had been explosions in one part of the city. The taxi driver, understandably nervous, refused to drive too close to the scene of the bombing. It would be more dangerous to walk to the gate because the security forces would not be expecting anyone, but we had no choice.

Blue and red flashing lights zoomed past us along the wide embassy road as we jumped out of the cab. A troupe of soldiers, mostly Afghans, were milling about but no one seemed to be in any major hurry, which spelt bad news—it was too late for the dead. A few ambulances were parked in front of the gates with bored looking medical staff standing around and smoking.

We tried to get closer but the army had already put up roadblocks in fear of further attacks, with two massive American soldiers standing in front of the concrete slabs.

'Those two meatheads will never let us through,' said Tim.

'Let's try the east gate. Ali said it might be easier,' I suggested.

We walked fast, out of the busiest spot, along the dirt road that went around the embassy. My heels had started to pinch my feet and I had to slow down.

'Here, take these.' Tim pulled out a pair of flip flops. 'I picked them up before I left. I know you and your party footwear.'

I wanted to kiss him. 'What will I do without you? Lucky will be the girl who'll win your heart.'

'Lucky indeed,' he snorted.

'Honestly, Tim, you could have your pick. I just don't get it.'

'I guess I'm just waiting for the right person.'

'Aren't we all,' I said.

As we approached the east gate, I spotted a familiar figure waiting in the shadows.

I greeted Ali Ahmad with a nod and we carried on forward. No soldiers, good. As the three of us walked on, a beam of light hit us.

'Hold your weapons. Hold your weapons or we will shoot. This is an order.'

Fuck, that's all I wanted. Getting shot in what was now turning to be a nasty hangover. I needed to think fast.

A voice boomed from the other side of the gate. We couldn't back down because they would shoot us; these guys didn't joke about such things. The metal gate stayed closed.

'It's your camera, Tim. Hold it up so the idiots can see,' I said. 'Ali, get your hands out in front of you so that they can see them.'

Tim held his camera high above his head while I had pulled out my press card and held it at arm's length. We stood there, bathing in the bright light, our hands above our heads.

Someone must have seen us because instead of gunfire, an American soldier, no more than twenty-five, came running towards us, his gun slung firmly over his right shoulder.

'Good evening, ma'am,' he said almost robotically. 'We are dealing with a security incident here. Can I see your papers?'

I nodded discreetly at Tim. It was our strategy to let me handle these kinds of soldier 'chat up' scenarios.

I gave him my card and letter from my channel that stated that the three of us were free to move around in the city without restrictions.

'Ma'am, you need to have a special permit to enter the area today,' he said in a nasal tone.

'And where can I get such a permit?' I asked him.

'Oh, inside the Diplomatic and Press Relations building, there is a bureau called "External and Domestic Staff Movement Temporary Passes" or EDSMP as we call it,' he said proudly, almost chuckling to himself at his cleverness for possessing such important information.

I should have realized this was the first sign of things to come. American occupation and its insanity in all its glory, right before my eyes.

'But how can I get a pass from EDSMP if I'm on this side?'

'Ma'am, I don't know, I'm just following orders. It's a special situation.'

I pushed my chest out and pouted ever so slightly. 'What is your name, sir?'

'Private Jack Marsden, ma'am.'

His ma'aming was beginning to irritate me but I had to get in, I couldn't risk losing the story since we were here first. The other channels would arrive any minute now because everyone must have heard about the explosions. Plus I was operating on auto-pilot, which meant the story was now number one priority.

I mustured up my sweetest voice. 'Now, Jack, maybe you can do me a massive favour…You see, I'm just a correspondent who needs to get on with her job.' 'I need to find out what happened inside the ministry so that I can tell all the folks back home that you and thousands of others are doing a great job. Do you think anyone can get me a pass from EDSMP if I give them my ID?'

Jack looked perplexed, but like all army men, couldn't resist a damsel in distress. 'Wait here, ma'am. I'm gonna call the HQ press people.'

'Don't bother with the press people; they're busybodies who know nothing about how real soldiers work.'

Besides, they will try to stop us from getting to the story, I thought.

'Find your duty officer and he'll let us in.'

With any luck, his boss wouldn't be too fussed about a couple of journos snooping around. After all, they must have been sent here on an emergency mission and had their hands full with 'security assessments' and 'emergency clearances'.

He came back five minutes later, grinning even wider—a smile of a pleased man who was able to show his power. We were in.

'It's okay, ma'am, you and your colleagues can go through, but just this once. You just have to go straight to the EDSMP desk first with your current ID and fill out some forms and then go to the emergency "Permanent Freedom Passes for Non-Essential Staff" issue desk or PFPNES, where you'll get a laminated pass,' he said.

And I thought the Afghans were bureaucratic.

'Thank you so much, Jack,' I said and winked at him as we walked on.

He looked very proud and waved us off. If that's how easy it was for suicide bombers, my life really wasn't worth much.

Needless to say we had no intention of wasting our time following his orders. We approached the inner section of the secure zone, which looked as if the ministry building itself had remained intact, but on closer inspection revealed that the surrounding security compound had taken a serious battering.

What unfurled in front of us, bit by bit, was a bloody carnage. I heard a sharp intake of breath from Tim. A body lying across the road, covered in blood, lifeless. A giant flashlight had been placed in the centre of the pavement, which made the scene even more macabre. There were corpses covered with white sheets lying haphazardly everywhere. Fresh blood was splattered across buildings, and dazed people were still crouched along the roadside, some with no arms or with fingers swaddled in blood-soaked bandages. It was immediately evident that the majority of the victims were, as usual, innocent local people. Few Westerners die in suicide attacks because they are so much better protected.

I looked around at the confusing array of bewildered

and stunned faces. A young Afghan woman lay lifeless on the ground, caked in blood and still clutching her shopping basket full of fresh goods. The eerie calmness was punctuated by sobs and high-pitched wails of grief and pain. Ambulances were still coming in, some too late. The dead could wait. Those who were beyond help were left to die there on the filthy ground. Tim picked up his camera and started to film the scene.

My thoughts went back to my first year in Iraq, nearly a decade ago. I was a greenhorn, but had got thrown right into the deep end. Back then suicide bombs would come with weekly, if not daily, regularity. We saw scenes like this one too often. Different country, same mindless devastation.

We walked through the rubble, looking for someone who could tell us what they saw. Tim pointed at a little boy crouched in a corner, sobbing in an almost trance-like state and said, 'He should do, he looks the part.'

I approached the boy cautiously. 'Are you okay? Can I help you?' I asked in my basic Dari.

He stared at me intently for a second and then started to cry again. I couldn't see any immediate injuries. The poor thing was in shock.

'Can you tell me what happened?'

He now started wailing. Ali spoke to him and tried to calm him down a little.

The boy spoke in between sobs. And Ali translated for us.

'I saw the explosion, I saw the bomber explode himself. My name is Farid Kohsar. I come here to clean the building every night. I had just come through the north gate to start my shift and was on the second floor of the building. Suddenly I heard an explosion and rushed to the window. I saw a young man who shouted "Allah Akbar" and then he exploded himself. First the top half of his body and then the rest of him collapsed. The head—his head flew off like a canon ball,' said Ali. 'By the grace of Allah, the most merciful, I was saved because I was on the other side of the bunker wall and because I came here earlier than usual.'

His face had a heavy shadow of sadness. I guessed his age to be about ten, but it was hard to tell. So many Afghan children had tough lives and looked older than they actually were. Farid was no exception. He was small and wiry with gangly arms and legs but was blessed with the wisest of deep green eyes. This young boy had witnessed the worst evils of the world today. Children of his age in the West normally see such violence only on a computer screen. If at all.

He told us that there had been several bombers. They had positioned themselves in the busiest part of the line-up, through the main gates in the embassy, at a time when most Afghans would leave work, and detonated their weapons, one after the other, at different gates.

Tim had stopped filming. He pulled the little boy up. Farid wiped his face and took Tim's hand.

While scenes of pure evil were routine to us, it didn't mean we weren't affected by them. Just because you see a lot of blood in your lifetime, doesn't mean its colour changes. Our hearts cried in silence and stored the images in drawers deep inside us, allowing them to surface when the pain got too much to bear. We could always walk away, while the locals didn't have the same luxury and had to carry on living and learn to smile again. The whole situation here was a mockery of human life.

Eight bodies in total. Six grown-ups and two children including the headless bomber. Sometimes they found the head, sometimes they didn't.

We caught up with a medic who was running past. 'Salaam Alaikum. I'm Anna from Global News Network, can I ask you few questions?'

He nodded. 'Be quick.'

So I fired off my usuals. How, when, what, and why.

As we were preparing to leave, I spotted a flash of pink velour from the corner of my eye. I took a deep breath and tried not to panic. It could only be the Barbie Doll of war zones—Shabita. And there she was, standing in the middle of the misery, all sequinned and glittered up. Like a human disco ball, spinning in the vortex of an inferno.

6

The sequinned dragon in pink strode towards me, perfectly made-up, leaving a trail of expensive perfume behind her. She looked like she had stepped into the set of the wrong movie in her tight jeans, far too tight for working in an Islamic country, pointy boots, and a very expensive looking flashy handbag.

This was her signature grief coverage look.

I forced a smile as she approached, mentally noting that the pink velour jacket was adorned with a diamante letter 'S'.

Tasteful.

'Hey, Annaaa, how lovely to see you back in Kabul. You look fantastic, so chic. Been to a party tonight?'

My headache came hammering back. My crumpled appearance, muddy flip-flops, streaked make-up, and sweat patches under my armpits did nothing to boost my confidence in front of her.

'Nice to see you as well. How are things?' I could hear the lack of sincerity in my voice.

'Great. It feels soo good to be back on the road. Love this city soo much. You know me, I get so bored sitting in a stuffy newsroom. Ha-haa. What's the death toll by the way?' she asked casually, while inspecting a chip on one of her immaculate nails.

'The figures keep changing; you need to check with the spokespeople.' I was not going to share my sources with her. She could bloody well do her own work.

'So what else is new, chica? Been up to anything fun lately? I hear you were in Helmand? Was it interesting, hmm?'

It wasn't just the way she said hmm that made me uncomfortable but she pronounced the word 'interesting', as if she wanted to ask me how many men I had fucked on my trip. I wasn't a fool. I knew camaraderie was just her act. She wasn't the one to have female friends, nor was she interested in small talk. Shabita was all business and took great pleasure in destroying other women in the business.

'Just work and more work,' I replied, helping Tim pack our kit and in the process busying myself.

'Gosh they like to keep you busy at GNN, don't they? And you poor poor little beaver, just carrying on non-stop. Don't you ever need a break? A sabbatical? A long holiday perhaps? Hmm. Must be exhausting to hang out with all those uniforms, you poor girl.'

Why couldn't she just disappear? The woman was like a scratch of nails on a blackboard, and she always knew how to get under my skin.

Our paths had crossed in Palestine in early 2000 for the first time. There was a high level summit going on between Israel and Palestine, and the press conference had been going on for hours. I was bored to tears and had started checking out the shoes of the few female reporters in the rows before me. Anything to keep me from falling asleep. I noticed her unusual shoes—pink and brown snakeskin coupled with gold studding on the heels and tip. They weren't exactly what you would call subtle, but I gave them top marks for boldness. I had no idea who she was but since she was the only other woman of my age I thought I'd go and say hello.

During the break, I went over to her and introduced myself. 'Great shoes. Definitely the best ones here. I'm Anna by the way from GNN.'

She barely looked in my direction, and instead said through gritted teeth, 'I know who you are, and I don't do small talk.'

I knew then that we were not going to be holding hands when darkness fell and scary things happened. It was only later that I learned that it would be less stressful to meet face-to-face with Khartoum's most notorious warlord than this pink nail polish-wearing beauty queen.

We were both green. I was on my second war zone assignment and Shabita had never been anywhere in the Middle East before. Despite her exotic name and looks, she was actually from Buckinghamshire and had done an internship at CNN, where she was sacked for faking a story. She then went to work for BBC and got her first war gig by 'pure chance'. Good looks got you everywhere in telly and she had long (possibly fake) eyelashes, permatan skin, and perpetually well manicured hands. Big bazookas too, although widely suspected to be paid for by an unnamed

TV executive. The world of war correspondents was a small one and everyone knew one another. If you misbehaved or fucked someone over, it came back to bite you in the arse. I longed for the day Shabita came face-to-face with her share of karma.

A few months after our first meeting, I saw her again in Sudan. After a day of chasing rebels, the crew arrived at the guesthouse thirsty, hungry, and completely worn out. Someone had made lamb stew—greasy, but filling, and my cameraman Ian had managed to procure some whiskey and cigarettes from our Sudanese fixer. We made a night out of it. We got a fire going and sat around it, swapping stories and indulging in idle gossip, while passing around the tin mug pretending as if there wasn't a war raging out there. The day had been a long one, but the evening seemed to take the bite out of the violence and misery that we had witnessed. For a fleeting moment, normalcy had returned.

It wasn't to last.

A few moments later a muddy jeep pulled up on the drive, and out stepped flawless Shabita. I heard Ian swear. He knew Shabita from his time at CNN. 'Only cockroaches come out to feast after dark,' he muttered, and nodded in her direction.

She said her hellos to a few others and then turned to me.

'Anna Sanderson! How *lovely* to see you again, what brings you here?' Shabita was all toothy smiles and air kisses, cooing like a pigeon, as if I were her long lost friend.

How the hell did she manage that perfectly smooth hair in this shithole with no electricity and rationed water? *And* dressed in crisply ironed clothes in hues of baby blue after twelve hours on bumpy roads? No one in the business understood how Shabita managed to stay on top for so long. Rumour had it that BBC's Jerusalem bureau chief, who was very much married, allegedly liked his cock sucked by an ambitious reporter during conference calls with the leaders of Hamas, might have something to do with it.

'Have you found any rebels yet hmm?' she continued to spew toxic syrup.

'Shabita darling, you know rebels' whereabouts are trade secrets,' I snapped.

I had not forgotten the shoe episode. I mean war correspondent or not, women bond over shoes. It's the unwritten code and she had spurned the hand of friendship.

'Oh you know us, always looking for trouble. Ha-haa. And there is a lot of it here. Ha-haa,' she tittered.

It was inevitable that we ended up in the same guesthouse. All news crew followed the blood trail and, in turn, one another. But little did I know that her grating laugh was going to follow me around the world's biggest trouble spots.

'Is that whiskey I spy? Where did you get that? Would love some if there was any going?'

'Sorry, there's none left,' said Ian, quickly draining the cup and licking his lips audibly.

That was very unlike the nice Northern guy who I knew. Ian would share the last coconut with you if you were stranded on an island with him. So it seemed Shabita had managed to ruffle even gentle Ian's feathers.

The sequinned dragon, of course, wasn't happy with the treatment and stormed off.

'Andreeew, please bring in my bag. I need it now!' We heard her screech, wrecking the silence of the night. We burst into a fit of laughter.

Over a decade and many encounters later, the sequinned dragon was every bit as painful as on that first day we met.

I turned to little Farid who was still standing next to us, and asked, 'Do you want us to give you a lift home?'

He nodded. It was late and we still had a lot of work to do. Tim and I made our excuses to Shabita, who looked a bit annoyed at our haste, said our thank yous to Ali and left.

In the taxi we got chatting with our brave new friend. After his initial shock had subsided, it turned out that Farid spoke good English and that too with a slight cockney accent.

'I learnt it from the soldiers, boss. Last year I worked at Camp Maria cleaning the barracks. Easy money.'

He turned out to be a little charmer.

'I was on the streets for a bit, selling stuff. But it's dirty business, for monkeys. I don't like it. Westerners are good for business, ma'am. Us Afghans like to serve you as long you are here,' he rattled on.

He told us that he was the primary breadwinner of his family of seven because his father had been injured during 'a big bang-bang'. It was the only way a little boy could describe, what I guessed, was a shoot-out.

'Some days I have enough money for a bus ride, but most of the time I walk. But now I don't have a job because the stupid terrorists have blown the building.'

I had an idea. 'Tim, we need an office boy, don't we?'

Tim nodded.

I turned to Farid. 'Why don't you come to our office tomorrow? You could help us with the cleaning and general housekeeping. And you won't have to sell anything.'

A huge smile spread across his little face. 'That would be my pleasure, ma'am.'

In a short while we arrived at Farid's neighbourhood on the outskirts of the town. The taxi's headlights threw up a row of ramshackle shacks, some of which looked like they were on the verge of collapsing. Some had tarpaulins as roofs and were fashioned out of thin boards, clearly stolen from military sites.

Farid asked us to stop outside a path leading up higher to the hill where I presumed were more slum dwellings.

He thanked us politely and stepped out into the darkness.

The taxi spluttered noisily across the empty streets. I looked out of the window. The mountains around us were like giant sentries looming ominously against the night sky. Who knew such a peaceful sleeping town could suddenly rear its ugly head and wake you up in the most brutal manner.

7

It was late when we reached the office and had to wake up the snoozing guard to let us in. Located in a quiet side street in Wazir Akbar Khan—the diplomatic area—our office was fashioned after a posh Iranian palace, topped with gold coloured exteriors and dark windows. Inside, it was just a bland block with several floors, housing many media companies—most of them local. The other companies occupied whole floors but our London bosses had been sure that the war would be soon over and had not bothered to invest in proper facilities. So here we were, well over ten years after the US invaded Afghanistan, still covering the war that seemed to have no expiry date.

We walked past the sign, 'GNN News—we bring you the latest, twenty four by seven', hung on the wall, all crooked and dusty. In the office, Tim made some tea, and we got to work. The story turned out to be quite thorough in the end, with Farid and the doctor's commentary giving it a good background. As we were getting ready to send it to London, one of my three phones rang. I didn't recognize the number.

'This is Anna.'

'Hello, Anna, this is Peter Bradshaw. Captain Pete.'

'Oh hi,' I said, caught off guard.

Tim had turned away but I could feel him listening, so I stepped out to the corridor.

'Are you busy? I can call you later.'

'No no. How are you?'

'Jolly good. I am calling you about the dinner I'd promised to take you for. How's tomorrow night?'

He sounded…so *official*. 'Sure thing. Where are you allowed to go?' There were severe restrictions in Kabul on the movement of military personnels so we had to choose a place that had been green flagged.

'Anywhere in Wazir. How's the Chinese?'

'It's edible. I've only been sick once after eating here.'

'That's as good as any other place in this town. I'll see you there at eight.'

I pressed the red button and looked at my phone, as if searching for an answer to whether I should go out with him or not. I stepped back into the edit suite.

'Who was that?' asked Tim.

'Oh, just that guy from Helmand. He's here in Kabul for some training.'

'A hot date then?'

'More like re-heated leftovers.' After all, he was married, even though his wife was too far for me to worry about. Besides, I was after harmless fun, not a family-size bungalow in the home counties with a four-by-four to boot.

Tim chuckled.

It had been a long day. We wrapped up our work and headed out when dawn was breaking.

I arrived fashionably late. We had agreed to meet up at Ching Khan's, a grubby little Chinese place inside Wazir Akbar Khan. Few people bothered to visit it because it had the strictest security system in town. A few military bosses would frequent it along with Indian guest workers, but it had none of the gossipy media types that the other places in Wazir were swarming with. It was discreet as hell and, therefore, perfect for us. Kabul was a small place and the international scene was even smaller. Everyone knew everyone else's business. And when the journos were not busy traipsing around with various armies, they revelled in making up stories about other people's love life.

I stepped inside the little cubicle, only to come face-to-face with a massive, mustachioed Afghan lady—at least I thought she was a lady—who began to grope my backside and turned me around roughly, as if I were a piece of meat. I caught a whiff of her body odour, which was enhanced by the tight nylon uniform she was wearing. She then rummaged through my bag and pulled out my cigarette box eagerly. I knew a smoker when I saw one, so I handed over a couple of smokes, and got her off my back. She laughed, revealing a set of blackened teeth and then coughed violently. As I was putting all the stuff back in my bag, I heard a familiar voice outside the cubicle.

It couldn't be!

What was he doing here anyway? I thought he had disappeared. I was about to storm out of the cubicle to give him an earful when I stopped in my tracks.

'Oh, baby, *soo* nice to see you.'

Could that be Rich? It sounded like him but what was going on? And who was he dishing all that syrup to?

I peeped through the curtain, gesturing my new friend to remain silent. Through the slit I saw Rich with a beautiful, petite, blonde woman, who not only looked glamorous but interesting too. He had an arm around her waist—ignoring local sensitivities—and she was leaning against him. Too fucking close! I watched the two disappear through the gates. Rich whispered something in her ear to which she threw her head back with a tinkling laugh.

I was furious. How could he do this to Kelly? And who the hell was that midget Venus?

The woman in the cubicle was staring at me sympathetically. She had clearly seen what I had seen.

'All man's bad. Goat is more good,' she offered.

I handed over the whole packet of ciggies to her for her wisdom and stumbled out. Poor Kelly. I wasn't sure if I should tell her. If it were me, would I have liked to know? Yes, of course. But it could just be nothing too.

Right.

I cursed myself for giving Ropey the benefit of doubt, even for a split second.

A waiter came to greet me. He led me to a booth with ragged curtains. This place couldn't have been more appropriate for a discreet tête-à-tête. I straightened my posture and ran my fingers through my hair. Dates always made me nervous. There were too many variables in the equation. What if he was a bore? What if I only fancied him because there was nothing else to keep me occupied? What if he had a case of halitosis? What if he was some freak who liked to be spanked with camouflaged whips? It was exhausting, what with all the small talk and the what-ifs. I wondered when it would stop. But would it? I stepped in through the curtains and forced a smile to greet my date.

8

He was dressed in his civvies—a golfing shirt and pleated chinos, hair neatly patted down in place. Not exactly a girl's wet dream.

'Hello, Anna. How are you?' he said gently.

He was handsome but not as dashing as I had remembered him in his uniform, with his tousled hair and muddy face. Shame. He had shaved for the dinner and looked a lot younger. On closer inspection, he was almost shiny. Had he applied face cream? I thought Kabul was a metrosexual-free zone. I sat down and ordered a beer.

After exchanging the usual pleasantries, I asked him, 'How is your training going?'

'Good. It's one of those "cultural awareness" courses that is a lot of soft bullshit, but, hey, orders are orders.' He fiddled with his wedding ring as he spoke.

I was trying hard not to get freaked out by this new and improved Pete. He sounded almost melancholic.

'I came straight from Iraq to Afghanistan you know. My life, it seems, has sort of been arranged for me as I move from one war to another. Six long years in the country and lots of dead bodies. It gets you a bit fucked up in the head but it pulls you into its fold after a while.'

'You know what these places are like—Baghdad, Mogadishu, Kabul. Bad places attract fucked-up people. Maybe we've been part of them for too long to really be able to deal with the real world,' I suggested, trying my best to make him see that I understood what he was feeling.

He nodded. 'My family insisted on an army career so I went along with it. And my wife's parents were in the army too, so she's used to it and doesn't complain about me not being around. All I have is my house back home, which is paid for by my hard work, and a small inheritance that my dad left me.'

He paused, and then started again, this time wistfully staring at a spot behind me. I turned to check if he was talking to someone else.

'I have a lovely, brand new, Alfa Romeo in the driveway. It's a classic, you know, with a V6 engine, 0-60 in 5.0. Lovely teak interiors, which I had installed,' he sighed.

Maybe it was just me but I felt a little excluded from the conversation. I tried to find common ground. After all I had no idea what V6 meant.

'I found working in Iraq harder than here in Afghanistan. The military is much more responsive to journalists now,' I ventured.

'It's not my wife's fault, it's mine. She has to raise the kids like a single parent, without any help. I send in money every month but it's not the same,' he rattled on.

Okay, we were officially having two separate conversations. As far as I could remember, it had not been like this in the camp. It was all hot, sexy and dangerous, with Taliban insurgents less than two hundred metres away. And there was definitely no talk about teak interiors. Thankfully, our bland and oily Chinese food arrived quickly, which we proceeded to wash down with cheap red wine served in teapots because the restaurant probably didn't have a liquor license.

'How was your time in Iraq?' I asked.

'It was good, the money was good. I had forty men working for me and sometimes the situations were tough but it was nothing like when I was at the Falklands. I was a young pup then—strong and ready to fight. Now I just do all the strategic stuff.' He paused to chew. 'What car do you like, Anna? Do you like Alfa Romeos?'

'I'm not sure, to be honest.'

What the fuck was the guy going on about? Most cars in Kabul were stolen and battered Toyotas and frankly it was hard for me to tell one from the other.

'Would you like to go for a drive sometime?' he asked, his gaze fixated on the spot behind me.

'Err...sure.'

The conversation didn't get any better. I was sure there were two of us at dinner but it seemed as if Pete was reading his side of the conversation from a sheet. Our frontline camp encounter had been short and furtive; there hadn't been much to chat. The adrenaline rush of being discovered had probably made that night sexier than it had actually been. Because now, under the dim lighting of Ching Khan's, sitting in front of me was a middle-aged man with a buttoned down, collared shirt, who thought the height of sophistication was taking a girl out for a drive. Gone was the sexual beast. Tonight I knew for a fact that I shouldn't even explore that. He was the wrong man in every way and sleeping with him wouldn't make me happy.

More wine appeared, this time in little flower vases.

'Do you want to go somewhere else?' he asked.

I knew I shouldn't because terrible things happen when people say 'shall we go somewhere else'. But one more drink wouldn't harm anyone, I reasoned with myself. It wasn't as if I was out of control, right? At least alcohol would liven things up a little. I gave in.

We moved on from the Chinese joint to a drinking hole called 'Lounge'. It was buzzing with people—aid workers, journos, mercenaries, or mercs, as they were known around here—all mingled in a boozy haze. The place was packed to the hilt and parts of the crowd had spilled out in to the garden. The music was loud, the lights low, and it struck me that this bar could have been anywhere in the world.

'Do you want a glass of wine?' Pete asked me.

'I'll have whiskey. With a drop of water, no more than a tea spoon.'

He raised his eyebrows but didn't say anything. Was that judgement I saw on his face? If it was, I ignored it. A girl needed her whiskey in a war zone.

We found a place to sit on a cramped sofa. The wine

from dinner combined with the whiskey was getting me a bit drunk. I looked at Pete and contemplated if he was worth it. He wasn't a bad man, nor was he that unattractive, and he had been a good fuck…once. I felt Pete's hand on my thigh and felt the old drunken longing rise in me. We began to kiss. First, no tongues, but soon it got more intense.

'Whoa…that was…nice.'

I smiled. 'Not bad at all.'

Pete tidied his hair and straightened his shirt. 'Shall we go somewhere else?' he suggested.

Here it was. The question of doom.

It must have been past 2 am when we left the bar's fortified gates, nearly falling into the open sewer and giggling drunkenly, much to the amusement of the guards standing by. I knew I shouldn't have but I was too drunk to care. And maybe a teeny bit lonely too. We ended up back at my place because Pete's base was out of the question. Pete was going to be my 'pot noodle fuck' tonight—a term Kelly had invented for nights like these—not really satisfying but you craved them anyway.

Morning came too soon. And along with it, remorse. I knew I shouldn't have but these things just happened sometimes. Pete had left without saying goodbye. After a night of lust I had to concentrate on my work. There was news to report and stories to cover and the best way to shake off a hangover was to throw myself into work. I looked at the time.

Damn, I was late!

I switched to my autopilot, threw my clothes on, jumped into a taxi and made it to the bureau just before ten. Tim was already in, fiddling with his cameras. He didn't look up.

'Tim, my angel, how long have you been here?'

'What a racket you made last night,' he said grumpily.

'Sorry, I had a few whiskies too many.'

'Where did you pick up the lucky guy this time? The usual places or did you try something more adventurous, like the local mosque?'

Ouch! Why was he being sarcastic? Our separate nocturnal adventures were something we never asked questions about before, and they weren't considered unusual or immoral in our house. Admittedly, he hadn't seen much action lately and Kelly and I had been getting increasingly worried about him; he seemed withdrawn and quiet and preferred staying back at home than coming out with us. Tim had hinted in the past that there had been a girl who had broken his heart, but he wouldn't share any details, nor would he admit that he was still upset about his loss. Kelly and I took the piss out of him relentlessly but I sensed that he was more sensitive that he let us believe. There was some inherent sadness about his character. He was such a loyal, caring friend to both of us and I hated to think someone had hurt him.

'Just someone I met before, and mind your own bloody business.'

I didn't want to share my night of lust with Tim, or with anyone for that matter and it especially didn't seem right to gloat about my shags when the man in question had meant nothing to me. I wouldn't even want to be seen in public with him, let alone invite him for dinner with us. I could just imagine him frothing about his bloody Alfa whats-its and Kelly and Tim sniggering across the table.

All the sneaking around might have sounded seedy to an outsider but it certainly wasn't my first, nor my last. My reputation among the Kabul party crowd wasn't exactly spotless. Many unsuspecting men had fallen victim to my 'carpet bombing' tactics—'anyone, anytime, anywhere' was, after all, the Anna Sanderson motto.

Pouring myself a fresh cup of coffee, I ignored the prissy cameraman and started browsing the news wires, making sure that I didn't miss any major incident or lead over the night. The wires were churning out the usual reports—ten dead in Helmand after a shoot-out; four children injured in blast in Kandahar; girls' school attacked in Logar; three soldiers dead in an IED attack.

I lit my last cigarette in the pack and tried to work out if any of the stories would be interesting to London, when there was a faint knock on the door. Tim and I both jumped up since very few visitors came by unannounced, and even fewer were meant to get past the guard.

Little Farid stood at the door, looking lost and helpless.

'Hey, little buddy, come in,' said Tim gestured.

Farid took off his shoes, carefully placed them by the door and stepped inside.

'I am at your service.' He bowed dramatically.

'Okay, Farid. No need for any fanciness around here. It's just the two of us, and sometimes a couple of others come in, so we can have a bit of rest.'

'I've come for the job.'

I smiled. 'Every job interview has a little task. And yours is to find the nearest shop that sells newspapers and cigarettes, and bring us one of each.'

He nodded and dashed off. Five minutes later he was back, clutching a packet of Marlboro Reds and the *Kabul Times*.

'You are hired!' I exclaimed.

'I won't let you down, ma'am. I will be your faithful servant. Don't beat me and I will serve you even better.'

'Don't worry, Farid, no beatings here. And no servants too,' I said.

'Thank you, ma'am. Tell me what I should do?'

'You can start by tidying that, over there,' said Tim, pointing in the direction of an ever-increasing pile of old newspapers.

'Where do they go?'

'To the trash bin, downstairs.'

'May I take them home?'

'Sure, but why?'

'They are good to cover holes in our walls.'

'You can do whatever you like with them, as long as they're gone,' said Tim.

Farid got to work immediately. And I spent the rest of the day trying to get hold of someone from the ministry, to get more information about the recent bombing. There had been no confirmation about who had been behind the attack, nor was there any information about the total casualty count. It wasn't unusual; Afghan officials were often slow to act, which meant the story dropped out of the radar and we wouldn't be covering it any more. Which was always a shame. The news machine moved too fast and in the process forgot the people whose lives had changed forever due to incidents such as these.

I got home early that evening and caught Kelly out in the garden, typing up a storm on her laptop.

'Err...Kell, you've got a minute?'

'I'm on a deadline. Will chat in ten,' she muttered, without looking up.

'Want some tea?' I asked.

'Anything stronger?' Tap, tap, tap, she continued hammering her battered MacBook.

'Hang in there.' I walked back into the house and scrounged the cupboards. There were a couple of bottles of red wine, three bottles of champagne, and some whiskey.

'I can make you a cocktail. How's whiskey sour?' I shouted.

'Yummy,' came her reply.

As I was mixing our drinks, I thought of how I was goint to tell her what I had seen last night. She would be upset, but she'd probably take him back. And I knew that Kelly would want me to tell her.

Kelly and Rich had been on and off for as long as I could remember. She was such a gorgeous girl, and made heads turn everywhere she went, yet she had eyes only for that prick. Tim and I were always telling her that she needed to flush him out of her life but she somehow always wound back in his arms. They were happy for a couple of weeks until another infidelity story would surface, sending Kelly into a fitful rage after which he would do something nice for her to quickly settle into quiet submission, as if nothing had happened. 'I can't help it,' she would say and would take him back, for the hundredth time. I called this syndrome The Drug Effect. She was addicted to the idea of Rich more than she was in love with him. Some men have that effect on women, and vice versa, when they can't get enough, and keep going back like a junkie. These relationships were never healthy and, as I'd observed, never lasted.

Or that's what I thought.

'Why do women allow themselves to be treated like dirt?' Tim would often ask.

'There are tons of decent blokes out there for both of you but you just get burnt every time—Anna by different guys and Kelly by the same lout every time.'

He was right, of course, but both of us had habits that were hard to break.

Something drastic had to happen so that she was able to finally cut the cord and run free. As for me, there would be Mr Right, or Mr D for that matter, somewhere. Wouldn't there?

I stepped out into the garden and cleared my throat. 'I've to tell you something, my dear.'

'One sec.' She typed furiously for about a minute and then looked up, smiling. 'Done. All yours, babe.'

It broke my heart to break the bad news. I handed her the drink.

'Tell me, tell me! Oooh, have you seen Mr Schlong again?'

I looked into her eyes and coughed it right up. 'It's about Rich. I saw him last night. Or rather *heard* him.'

'What do you mean *heard*?' she said, her eyebrows knit with suspicion.

'He was at Ching Khan's. With some girl.'

Kelly's eyes widened. 'What do you mean he was at Ching Khan's with some girl?'

'I was in the security booth—you know how they have these ridiculously complicated systems there—when I heard his voice. I wasn't sure if it was him at first, but I looked through the curtains and saw him. With a woman. And they looked quite close.'

'What do you mean *quite close*?' I caught the tremor in her voice.

'Oh, Kell, I'm so sorry. They looked, you know, all couply, like they were together.'

'But it can't be. He told me he's gone to Helmand.'

'I'm sure it was him. There is no mistake. I am so sorry.'

Tears welled up in her eyes. She was distraught. And I hated to be the one to make her feel like shit. I went to give her a hug but she pushed me away.

9

'WANKER! I'm going to skin him alive and feed him to the dogs when I find him. What a TOSSER!'

Kelly was shaking with rage. She stood up and started to pace around the garden.

'I'll cut his fucking cock off. That is IT! No, THIS is it. This time he has just fucking gone too far.' She was now crying and yelling at the same time.

'How can he be so fucking cruel? How many chances have I given him? That bastard.'

She was right. How many chances have we given men? Must be hundreds. Those good old, 'he can't call because he must be busy' or 'maybe he's been shot and that's why he can't reply to my text' or 'maybe he's caught some deadly disease and is dying in a field hospital somewhere, unable to reach his phone'. There was no end to the excuses we offered on their behalf. An easy let off for every bastard. But the truth is often hard, like dry bread—difficult to swallow.

Kelly now stood in the middle of the rose bushes. Her anger had dissipated, and I knew that she was trying very hard to think rationally and compose herself. Tears streaked her pretty face.

'I'm not doing this any more. It's over. I'm letting go this time.'

'You're too good for him, Kell,' I said.

She fell silent and let me hug her this time. I held her till the sobs wracking her body subsided.

'I'm not letting him off easy. I'm going to his base to confront him and finally get a straight answer out of him. I need some kind of a closure,' she said, pausing to wipe her tears. 'But I need you, Anna. I need your help.'

'What do you mean?'

'You have all the passes and know how to get into places. You know I don't cover any of the military stuff, so I need your help.'

I wasn't sure about this. After all, the military was jumpy at the best of times and using my connection in a personal vendetta didn't seem right. But on the other hand, it was Kelly—my dearest Kelly who had stood by me through thick and thin. She took me in when I got here from Iraq three years ago—raw and broken from a massive heartbreak.

It was 2006 when I met Paul. Clever and gorgeous and a long time war rat. We were both taking shelter, crouched behind a Lebanese tank, from a sudden burst of gunfire, deafened by the explosions and gunfire. There I was, caught bang in the middle of the Israel–Hezbollah war, my heart beating in my mouth and a gorgeous man right next to me. I remember thinking that I would die next to this stranger—so far away from family and friends—till he broke my thoughts.

'Whoever said tanks were dangerous things didn't know

how useful they could be when it came to saving your arse,' he yelled.

I was amazed by the fact that he could be smart at a time like that.

He ended up seeking shelter at a nearby house, and my cameraman and I got picked up by the soldiers and taken to safety inside the tank.

I looked at Kelly and realized how much I adored my dear friend. Sometimes difficult, sometimes belligerent, but most of the times the kindest person you'll ever meet.

'You wouldn't want to confront him and tell him how you felt. Remember what happened to me?'

She nodded. 'But this is different. I *know* deep down he loves me.'

'Kell, assuming someone loves you is not clever.'

Kelly sulked. 'I am not assuming anything. I just know it. Besides, Paul was just fooling around with you. This is different.'

Maybe she was right. Maybe I've had my heart broken for no one really special, just some guy who asked me to go to Iraq with him. We sat smoking our cigarettes in silence.

'I know how you feel, Kell. It was so good with him though…when it lasted,' I said quietly.

'I'm getting another drink,' she said and went in, leaving me with painful memories.

That spring in Baghdad, Paul and I spent the little spare time we had in bed. The tatty but sturdy Hotel Al Rasheed, a refuge for journos, shook every now and then from mortars. Grim as it was, it was still our love nest. Sometimes we would leave for a picnic a couple of miles out of town, where no one came anymore because of the war. There, we would fuck against hundred-year-old olive trees with the rat-tat of gunfire in the distance. It was a thrill like nothing else, living every day as if it were our last, and living only for each other in a country that was being ripped to shreds.

Later that year, Paul got posted to Palestine, while I stayed on in Baghdad until I was packed off to Somalia. During my time there, which was a couple of months, I didn't hear from him. No emails, phone calls…nothing. I thought he had been killed but despite looking for news about him, I didn't find anything. We found each other again eventually; this time in Chechnya. I was in a bar in the middle of a bombed-out hotel in Grozny. There was nothing to drink except potato vodka, which the bartender more than happily plied to weary correspondents. I was sitting there with a bunch of colleagues after a long day when I saw him stroll in, looking as sexy and confident as ever. It made me nearly choke on my vodka. That night we slept in each other's arms as though we had never been apart.

It became a pattern. Whenever we were in the same ropey country, we would bump into each other, talk and end up in bed. It was as if the constant danger that surrounded us had given us a license to love. There was never any talk of a relationship but things were so good that I didn't want to mess it up by talking about it.

One morning I woke up to see him standing in his underpants and socks in the middle of our pokey, brown room in Baghdad, struggling with his watch, looking silly but cute. It was then that I realized I had fallen for this man—utterly and hopelessly.

'Here, let me.' I kissed the inside of his wrist and said, 'I love you.'

He looked at me with his lovely eyes—a sort of icy blue with a piss yellow ring around the iris, which I loved. But that morning he had a funny look in them that I hadn't seen before.

'Anna, I have a wife. And a child. A three-year-old girl.' He pulled his hand away and fastened his watch. He then put on his clothes, picked up his backpack, and left.

Never to return.

How blind and stupid had I been. There had been signs all along, like him disappearing, never keeping in touch with me, but I had foolishly chosen to ignore them. I was devastated, and dealt with it by fucking, drinking, and fucking some more. Drunk till I was fucked. Fucked till I was drunk on it. It took me a long time but I moved on eventually, like everyone does. My work became my number one love. And along with it came many lovers. But since then I hadn't let anyone in.

Kelly came back with two drinks. I owed her big time. Without her, I would have been a mess. It was she who helped me out of my pitiful state, patiently and with a warmth I had never seen in anyone before. Kelly was my rock, and she never once gave up on listening to my story, even though I had then narrated it (Paul this and Paul that) a few hundred times a day to her. That's when I realized that there's nothing a friend cannot cure. With time, I grew to forget him, the hurt, till his memory became just a sinking sensation in my stomach on quiet nights. But that's the great thing about people—we adapt and move on.

I lit a cigarette, and turned to her. 'Okay, missy, what do you need me to do?'

'Drink up. Because we're going to be kicking some serious ass.'

10

I cursed Rich for the umpteenth time. We wouldn't have been in this position if he could keep his pants on at the sight of any girl. It felt a bit silly to be standing outside Camp Teresa, a military base for the coalition forces, dolled up in our combat trousers and little curve enhancing T-shirts, subtle make-up, and just-got-out-of-bed hair, that in reality took ages to do. You couldn't face a man you wanted to confront looking like you've just rolled out of bed, had been Kelly's reasoning. She was right of course. Exit with dignity was one of our mottos.

The plan that Kelly formulated had seemed straightforward enough. 'He works at the base when he is not posted in Helmand. If he is in Kabul, he'll be in that bloody bar. He likes to drink every night, as he calls it—"unwinding from the Russian roulette I play everyday with my life".'

More like playing the beaver circus, I thought but bit my tongue.

The plan was that we were going to walk straight in, unannounced, and catch him with his new girl. At which point Kelly was going to draw him outside and give him a piece of her mind, and if she got lucky, a kick in his groin. I had agreed on one condition—no scenes at the bar. There would be far too many witnesses.

The first gate was manned by Afghan security guards, as was the custom. They saw us approaching and began waving. 'Stop, stop.'

We stopped and one of the men walked towards us.

'I am here to see Captain David Thompson. I have a permit,' I said and pulled out my laminated pass, which all journos carried.

The guard examined it with great care and said, 'Where is her pass?'

I knew there was no going into the camp without one so I brought along with me another—an old, out-of-date one which had been easy to forge. I stuck Kelly's photo where necessary. 'Just like having a fake ID to get into a bar when you were 15!' Kelly had shrieked excitedly.

The guard wandered back into the security booth. I knew they would not bother checking with anyone, but just liked to keep us waiting…especially because we were women. From where we stood, I could see three guards inside the booth scrutinizing our passes in the light.

'Fuck, I hope that's convincing forgery, Kell.'

Kelly didn't answer. I could sense she was on the edge.

It was indeed convincing. Because eventually, he came out and let us through.

The second gate was manned by Indian security contractors who stared at us curiously, but let us through with minimum fuss. A Filipino army officer greeted Kell and me at the third gate with a much more encouraging response. 'This way through, madam.'

A small queue had formed in front of the fourth gate's metal detector by the time we got to it. There were two black armoured cars ahead of us. I couldn't see inside the car but I felt eyes on me from inside the second one. An Italian soldier stepped out of the guardhouse and began swiping my body and bag with a detector while I stared at the vehicle in front of me. He then waved us past.

My last visit to Camp Teresa had been an official one but I knew my way around. The camp's 'bar' was in fact a tent, which, during the day, operated as a canteen but at night time it became a lively bar filled with soldiers and a riotous mix of country, western, and old-school dance anthems blaring out from the large speakers. The neat rows of wooden benches and long tables gave the place a feel of a German beer festival rather than a military base.

Tonight the place was packed, and apart from us there were just two other civilians inside the air conditioned diaphanous tent with a steady stream of uniformed men stepping in and out. Tight buns and big arms everywhere. On any other night, this would have been an ideal place to look around.

Despite the seriousness of our task, Kelly and I were all smiles as we grabbed our beers and stood by our observation post in a corner of the tent. It was a good spot because we were able to survey the whole room without being seen by too many people.

'Cocktail hour is up. Cheers.' We clicked our beers.

'Every hour is a cocktail hour for you, Kelly.'

'True but now I have an excuse.'

We waited. Ordered more beer. Waited. And ordered more beer. After an hour, the crowd swelled till the tent was bursting at its seams. But there was still no sign of Rich.

'Let's have one more beer and then leave. I'm going to pop in to the loo and will then bring you a cold one,' I said.

Kelly nodded.

I made my way through the crowd when a familiar pair of brown eyes caught mine across the room.

Damn! It was Mr D.

Why the hell did this man keep appearing out of the blue, without any warning, in all the wrong places? It made me seem like I was a psycho stalker. I suddenly realized that it must have been him inside the second vehicle that made me feel strange.

I sauntered past Mr D's table, and could feel his eyes fixed on me. I looked at him and acknowledged him with a small smile and a slight nod as he was too far along the table for me to go over. Besides, what whould I say to him? Good to see you…again? What have you been up to? Does the car work? Naah. Remain mysterious and unavailable. Men love that, don't they? Act aloof and you'll get a key to their heart. Or at least to their lunchbox. Which, sometimes, was satisfying enough.

Damn beer to hell! It always gave me so much gas. I was received to be finally inside the tent toilet and be able to let rip. As I stepped out of the tent, someone grabbed my arm and pulled me between the two toilet tents. I turned around and in front of me was Mr D. I was mortified. Had he heard me in the loo?

The moon was up and his face was faintly illuminated. I ignored the pee smell that was wafting from the toilets and looked long and hard at him.

'We must stop meeting like this, in these romantic spots,' he said smiling.

I laughed, relieved that he had a sense of humour. He began laughing too. A lovely, deep laugh.

'However, this is the true Kabuli style seduction package—with toilet smells thrown in for free,' he said.

I laughed again. 'Was it you in that car at the gate?' I asked.

'Yes. I had my eyes on you before you even knew it.'

I tried not to give away the fact that my heart was pounding in my ears. 'And I thought you were a contractor, not in the army,' I said, gesturing at his uniform. Contractors rarely wore uniforms.

He dodged the question. 'Let's meet. Properly. Not like this.'

As if to convince me, he kissed me on my lips, first gently, and then deeply. It took my breath away. So it wasn't the most romantic of all places, but it made my legs turn wobbly nonetheless. I ran my fingers through his hair and took in his soapy clean smell. I could have stayed like that for hours when I remembered Kelly. Good god, Kelly! I broke away and muttered, 'I have to get back or my friend will send a search party after me.'

He nodded. 'I'll get in touch soon.'

I didn't ask him how he was going to find me. I just had a strange feeling that he would.

I got back to find a long-faced Kelly.

'What took you so long?' she asked.

'Nothing. Any signs of Ropey?' I didn't want to tell Kelly about my encounter. This wasn't the right time to gloat in my own happiness. But my heart was singing and there was a deep warm glow enveloping me.

'Let's go, I've had enough of this.' Kelly grabbed her bag.

As we stood up, I spotted a familiar little blonde girl. Midget Venus! She looked great with her sleek hair pulled back in a bun, make-up free fresh face, and was wearing a uniform that hugged her petite figure perfectly. In other words, she was every woman's nightmare. And behind her was Rich—cocky walk, cocky smile. They looked fresh and flushed. It was obvious that they had been screwing.

Kelly saw them at the same time I did. At first she just stared, but after a couple of minutes she sat down slowly and took a huge swig of her beer. In an instant, fat tears rolled down her cheeks.

'So he *is* with someone else. I should've known. I've been such a fool. But at least now I know the truth.'

I hugged her but felt my rage grow stronger. It wasn't fair. 'I'm going to get him,' I said and stood up.

'No! Don't! I don't want him to know that it affects me. I need my pride. I have a better idea. Let's get out of here and I'll tell you how we'll pay back the bastard,' she said.

We sneaked out of a side entrance so that Ropey wouldn't spot us.

Outside, more tears came.

'Let's go home, Kell, and I'll make us whiskey,' I said as we made our way towards the gate.

11

Kelly had stopped crying by the time we got home, but her face had turned hard and cold. We sat outside, in the garden, nursing our drinks. Her eyes were shining dangerously in the dark. 'I know stuff about Rich that can land him into serious trouble. I want to teach the bastard a lesson he'll never forget.'

'Ooh get even. Tell me more.'

She lowered her voice. 'Basically the guy is dodgy as hell. He's running an arms smuggling operation from the North and supplies the Taliban weapons in the South.'

I was so shocked I couldn't speak. What I knew about Rich was that he worked for a security company and had more than just a shady past. There was some report about a killing in a local restaurant a couple of years ago and rumours suggested that Rich was the baddie behind it, and his business hadn't exactly won awards for its humanitarian work. I mean, I had always known that the guy wasn't the saviour or any such thing, but this was pushing it too far. 'What! I knew he was bent but weapons to the Taliban? Where does he get them? From the Russians?'

'You guessed it. They come through Tajikistan, sealed inside fridges, cupboards, furniture, and anything that can get transported in lorries. He would have never told me, but I've been spying on him for so long because I thought he was cheating on me, that I know it all!'

'So what are we going to do?'

'What are we going to do?' she repeated and rolled her eyes. 'Anna, we're journalists! What do *you* think we'll be doing?'

'You want us to expose him?' I was aghast at the idea.

'Don't you think it's a great scoop—a British ex-army officer supplying weapons to the Taliban. It'll be a top story!'

She had a point. But it didn't sound easy. 'But how?'

'We need evidence. We need him on the scene, negotiating the deals. Otherwise it's a dead story, I mean you saw the guy tonight…all friendly with the uniforms…bastard.'

'And I'm guessing he does his deals in Helmand?'

'Right again, Sanderson.'

'You are completely insane. There's no way we'll catch him down there.'

Kelly's eyes were wide as she spoke. 'It's payback time, my dear friend. This is 'Operation Lipstick'—us single girls will finally have a chance to show what we're made of.'

'But we need proof. Files, photographs, videos, recordings.'

'Fear not.' Her burning cigarette end lit up her face and for a moment I didn't recognize this Kelly—she had a look of madness and eerie contempt.

I woke up to a text message that made me grin instantly from ear to ear.

'Meet me at Babur Gardens tonight at 6 pm.'

It was going to be a good day! And if things didn't turn out well, there was a party I had planned on going to anyway.

I read the text message again. Classy man, no extra fuss, just straight to the point. My kind of a guy. I wondered how he got my number, but I wasn't too surprised that he had traced me; maybe he knew some of my journalist friends and had asked them. I was just ecstatic to have received a text from Mr D. I waited for a bit before I replied, so as not to appear too eager. 'Okay.'

During breakfast I confided in Kelly about my date.

'Sounds like your type. Just be careful. Those mercs, you know what they're like,' she said, munching on her toast.

I frowned, adding more wrinkles to my face. 'Should I play hard to get with him?'

'Of course, my darling. You know, the way to a man's heart is not through food, sex, or a gun, but by letting him do all the chasing. Men are primitive and love a hunt!'

Hmm.

'Chasing? It's too late for me to play prim and proper, if that's what you mean.'

'Just don't start making any plans and don't demand anything from him. Keep a bit of the mystery going, love.'

Wise words. War zone or not, the rules in the dating game were still same.

'You mean not become clingy?'
'Exactly. Promise it by all means, but don't give in. Yet.'

Babur Gardens was a beautiful, spacious, crumbling mess of a garden, which used to be popular with families in the good old days before the Taliban. Many Afghan rulers had built their monuments and palaces here but they were all in ruins now. I liked it for its history and unkempt beauty. It was undeniably romantic and I was thrilled that Mr D had decided to meet at such a lovely place.

When I got there, the gardens were relatively empty, with just an odd group of men wandering around and a few young boys playing football. Local women were not allowed in.

I took a walk around the place and began fantasizing about being with him, wondering what he would be like as a boyfriend. Maybe it was too soon to think about stuff like that but I was so fed up of being alone, having all those meaningless fucks and soulless sixty-nines. I wanted love with trumpets, waltz and roses. My future plans had never included playing the happy housewife, but now, I even considered that. Perhaps we would buy a little cottage in the countryside, or have a cozy flat in London, and a couple of clever, beautiful children who would complete our fairy tale.

There were numerous happy-endings taking place in my head. My hen party would be themed Talibans and Tarts. It would begin as a grand old-world affair, which would later turn into a raucous party. And there would be no danger of explosions, unlike most Afghan weddings. On the big day, there would be a large crowd of guests, who would have flown in from all over the world, their laughter and foreign languages punctuated by the popping sound of champagne corks. I would be in a white dress and a demure veil. I had always secretly wanted a veil. But I never told anyone about it, not even Kelly. It felt a bit silly. Him—all tall and handsome, in a morning suit. I even had the music ready. Something gospely sang by deep, warm voices.

I got to the top and took in the beautiful landscape with its dramatic mountain backdrop. This was also a strategically good spot for us because we could see if anyone was approaching. Then, from the corner of my eye I saw him, standing at the far end, leaning against a pillar. My heart started beating frantically. I had to steady myself so that I didn't fall over. What if he didn't like me? What if he thought I was boring? What if I couldn't think of anything smart to say? I wanted to turn around. But it was too late because he had caught sight of me.

Walking up to me, he gave me a hug. His eyes twinkled with mischief. I felt a trickle of sweat run down my spine. The smell of flowers was overpowering, making me feel nauseous.

'Anna, so glad you could come!'

God, he was so hot. Again, why was he interested in me?

I sat down on the blanket he had brought. A man who thinks of everything! It was just perfect. He had brought a modest picnic, which consisted of a bottle of cheap red wine, some hard, tasteless cheese, and soft Afghan flat bread.

Remember, play hard to get. Play hard to get. You are a hard nut. Hard ball.

Balls. Good god, I couldn't help melting under his sparkle!

'So…how are you?' he smiled.

'Good, been busy, you know, with all the bombings.'

'This is better than our last romantic encounter I hope?'

I lit a cigarette and noticed that my hands were trembling.

'Some wine?'

'Yes please.'

'So tell me more. I want to know *everything*,' he said as he poured me a glass.

'There isn't a lot to tell. I live with a couple of other journos. I am half Danish, half English, and god only knows how I ended up here.' I realized I sounded a bit surly. Maybe that was a good thing. Men liked mysterious women, right?

'Well I'm glad that you did. A place like this needs a woman like you,' he said flirtatiously.

In any other circumstance, I would have had a witty comeback, yet here I was, tongue tied and feeling too shy to flirt back. I took a sip of my wine and asked, 'Do we have any friends in common?'

'Well he's not a friend but I think I know your friend Kelly's boyfriend—Richard.'

There was something measured about the way he said it.

'I doubt he can be called "boyfriend" any more,' I snorted.

'Oh. What happened?'

'He is just a bastard…like most men.' Now I sounded too bitter! Must get the balance right. Not bitter but not too sweet either. Like a very good bar of chocolate.

'What makes you say that?' He was a touch too quick when he replied.

'Just bad experiences.' I inwardly kicked myself for not being able to filter my thoughts and almost downed the whole glass in one gulp.

'Do you want to tell me about it or would you rather not?'

I didn't know if I was imagining it, but I got the sense that he was trying to get something out of me. 'He just screws her around but she keeps going back for more like a little puppy. I wish she could tear herself away. But maybe that night when we had our, ahem, when we met, she might have had enough. So we are looking to set him up, it seems like he is involved in something dodgy.'

Anna! I scolded myself. Giving too much away. Mystery girl. Mystery girl.

He frowned. 'He could be dangerous. Or those who he is involved with. I've a feeling that those guys aren't exactly choirboys.'

Again, the measured casualness. Was he trying to tell me something? I just couldn't figure it out. 'Do you know him well?'

'No, not really, but you know how this city is. Everyone knows each other and the bad guys leave a foul after smell.'

'And whose side are you on?'

'I think I do what is right. It may not be the most ethical choice sometimes, but generally I can sleep at night.'

Sleep at night. With. You.

He hardly drank so I ended up downing most of the bottle. Medicine for my nerves, I kept telling myself.

The evening unfolded in luxurious colours around us. We chatted about the places we loved and those we loved to hate. Mogadishu, Grozny, Beirut. Cities we knew, faces full of hope, places being torn to bits, where poverty and pain was the only life most people knew.

'Do you ever get jaded of moving from one disaster to another?' he asked, lazily stroking my arm.

No, I get jaded from moving from one bed to another. 'Not really, because every story I cover is about people and each one of them tells a different story.'

'Beautifully put.'

The last rays of sun lingered for a few minutes before dusk fell. We decided to leave as the garden gates would soon be locked.

He pulled me up. There was a half a second of hesitation when I sensed he was going to kiss me. But instead, he let go of my arm and began picking up our picnic leftovers. Why did he change his mind? I thought we were on a date. Should I have kissed him first? God, this man had me asking too many questions!

We got to the gate just in time. It was dark now and my driver was waiting outside. I didn't want it to end so soon, so I blurted out quickly, 'There's this party that's happening, we could have some fun.'

So much for playing hard to get. But I was happy drunk and wanted him...bad.

'Sure. But my clients will get a bit twitchy if I am hanging out with a journo, so I can't be seen with you. I can jump out three blocks before.'

I understood what he meant, but hated every bit of it. So many dodgy things went on in this town and very few people wanted to be seen with a journalist.

But I was just glad that he had agreed.

The party was in full swing and I greeted my friends enthusiastically. I was still reeling from our date. Why hadn't he kissed me, after all it had gone off pretty well? He was the one who had asked me out, but at the end he seemed to be more interested in Rich than me.

Since there was plenty of cheap wine on offer, I took to it with a vengeance. After all, it was my best tested coping mechanism. Cheesy Nineties Europop was blaring, filling the gaps in all the boastful 'I nearly died last week' conversations. I saw Mr D walk in a few minutes later. He was shaking hands with several merc types, this was obviously a world he occupied. I was upset that we couldn't be seen together, he had made that quite clear. And it wasn't good for my reputation either—oh here comes man missle Anna Sanderson, be careful not to be hit by her.

I stood at the doorway, vaguely listening to the brag-a-chat and feeling woozy from all the wine, when my sleepy eyes spotted someone familiar. I should have known she would be here because she was everywhere, like cheap perfume that you couldn't get off your clothes.

Shabita was wearing a collared canary yellow tight shirt and shiny cufflinks with a pair of sprayed-on jeans that hung low on her hips. And, of course, the ever present pointy boots, this time in gold. Jesus! How many pairs did this woman have? Hair sprayed on stiff, make-up so not barely there. She was now marching towards the kitchen, dangerously close to Mr D. In fact, she was now marching towards him!

I watched to my horror as she stood right in front of him and then kissed him *on his mouth*. The scene played out in slow motion. *Why was she kissing my man?* That too *on the mouth*! And now she had her arm around his waist! I wanted to scream. Mr D glanced around sheepishly. So this is why he didn't want to kiss me! He was going out with Shabita, but thought he would check out the competition first! What an asshole! I felt a wave of nausea hit me.

I wanted to go and chuck my glass of wine at him, but held myself back. Why waste it on the bastard? I finished it in one go, picked up whatever was left of my confidence, and without another word, left the party.

At home, the house was quiet, everyone was still out. I took a large glass of Indian whiskey to bed with me. Tears came as soon as I was under my duvet. Lonely and rejected, I felt my heart shatter to pieces. I downed the leathery liquid, hoping for oblivion…I could handle anything but the searing pain of rejection.

His reluctance to kiss me and to be seen with me was all too clear now. Two-timing pig! What a fool I had been. Again. I slept fretfully; the nightmares were back holding me in their suffocating and clammy grip till dawn broke.

12

Kelly was making coffee when I came downstairs. 'You look awful. Bad date?'

I told her about the sorry evening. Like everyone else, she knew Shabita.

'But there could be an explanation. Maybe they're just friends?' she suggested, while handing me a large chipped mug full of steaming coffee.

'I doubt it. You and I have had some rotten luck lately. Let's go out tonight to cheer ourselves up with some firm soldiers. There is a party at the BBC house. And I'll fill you in on my plans for nailing that bastard.' In my excitement about Mr D, I had forgotten about Kelly's revenge seeking jaunt, but now I was surer than ever that evil men like him need to be put in their place.

All day I mooched around, glancing at my phone every now and then, in case there was an apologetic text or a call from Mr D. But there was nothing. Cigarette and black coffee the whole day. At least my calorie consumption for the day would be negative. Coughing must be the equivalent of high impact aerobics in the exercise stakes.

All the convulsions and jerky moves surely must pay off. At least I'll be toned and skinny. Secretly, I was fed up of being single. But I could never let the world know about it. I would love to have a boyfriend. Someone to call when I get kidnapped by rebels. Or text, when the cops take my camera and decide to detain me for twenty-four hours just for a laugh. However, a single girl's dating carousel had to be kept spinning even if some of the wooden horses on it were rotting from inside.

When evening came, all I wanted to do was to stay in with a bottle of Italian red wine and my dog-eared *Sex and the City* boxset. But since it was my idea to go to the party, I summoned every bit of energy and dragged myself into the bathroom. I looked harassed and tired; the bags under my eyes seemed more pronounced from all the crying the night before. I put on my favourite wine-red tunic, hoping optimistically that a splash of colour would liven up my ashen complexion.

It was a hot night and a blanket of dust enveloped the city, giving it a soft brown colour at dusk. Kelly was in full steam in the taxi.

'I know his business is based in Lashkar Gah. All you need to do is arrange for us to get there. I'll take care of the rest.'

'Kelly, this is very tricky, it's not like getting on a train to Melbourne.'

'I know. But you can arrange for us to be embedded. You're the one with all the connections.'

I sighed. Me and my military connections. No good came out of it. Most journos love being embedded—a term which means us journos basically follow soldiers and report what we witness. It's one-sided and dangerous but it makes war reporting realistic.

She filled me in with more gory details and the more she revealed, the more I was convinced it had the potential of a big scoop.

We got to the gate at the BBC house where Andrew, the jovial, chubby Beeb correspondent, ushered us into an already pulsating party. Andy's parties were legendary. Despite his bald head, large tummy, and a very hairy back, he was always a big hit with the ladies. Thankfully, ours was a strictly platonic relationship—if you didn't count couple of snogs and gropes during a massive power cut once.

He handed Kelly and me tall glasses of chilled white wine.

'They're working you too hard, ladies. You guys seem to file a story almost every day.'

'Yeah, well, you know how it is with so much stuff going on,' I said.

'Are you working on anything interesting?'

Ah, that was our Andy, always checking out the competition.

'Just the routine stuff, you know how it is.'

He had a funny look on his face. 'It's just that I saw Shabita who mentioned something.'

'Mentioned what exactly?'

'She said that you had been busy with some "high ranking" officials,' he said and chuckled.

Why do guys always do that, laugh at their own jokes?

I shrugged. 'Just rumours. None of it is true.'

Bitch! So this was her game. Spreading rumours about me. It seemed the sequinned dragon was out for my blood.

Neither Shabita nor Mr D was at the party because they were probably engrossed with one another in a romantic tête-à-tête somewhere in the city.

Drinks were flowing freely and people had started to dance in little groups. Other guests were lounging around in sofas, smoking and sipping on their drinks. It was always the same—the same faces, the same talk, the same men. I suddenly couldn't stand it any more. Kelly was nowhere to be seen so the time had come for my exit.

Tim was playing solitaire on his ancient PC when I got to work the next day.

'You need some carrot juice, young lady.'

I filled him in on my latest disaster. After all, I couldn't keep secrets from my best friend and wanted a male perspective on the whole thing.

A slight smile played on his lips as he spoke. 'Just a bad egg. You get those from time to time.'

But my eggs, too, will soon be past their sell-by date, I wanted to scream.

'It was all going very well until that bitch came into picture.'

'Anna, most men, and I say this as your best male friend, do like to keep the companion of more than one lady friend. Especially when they are, ahem, playing the field,' he explained patiently.

'But you're not like that?'

'No I am not because I'm keeping my heart reserved for someone special.'

How I wish I could meet someone like him! Decent, honest, and fun to be with. I had to change the subject, for my love life was not worth talking about in any more detail.

'We need to go on an embed, next week okay?' I said.

'What? We only just came back from one! I can't take any more army food,' Tim whined. 'And it's getting dangerous down there, we're not trained soldiers, Anna.'

I looked at his face, with its numerous freckles, those lovely eyes and dimples, and thought I'd never want to make him do stuff he didn't want to, especially in this country where sometimes the wrong turn could cost you your life.

But I owed it to Kelly too.

'Come on, I promise it'll only be for a few weeks. There's nothing happening in Kabul anyway. And I think we're on to a big big story with real baddies this time.'

Tim was more than a cameraman. He had what we called journo magic—the nose for a good story. And he never let one slip from his hands, especially if it meant revealing the rot in the world.

He sighed. 'Come on then, let's hear it,' he said, as he looked at me intently with his deep, almost sad eyes. He sometimes had that unexplainable stare that seemed to follow me around but I had put it down to brotherly love.

To be honest, we were often tactile with one another and had even shared a bed on numerous occassions but he had never crossed the line, not since Kurdistan. Nor had I.

'Mates do not good mating make,' Kelly had said when I had once drunkenly considered pouncing on Tim.

She was right. It was the best way to ruin a friendship.

I told him the Rich story.

He took a moment to digest it, twirling his lighter with his long fingers.

'So what you're saying is that we risk our careers *and* our lives so that Kelly can get her revenge for some knob-end?'

'Not quite. Look at it this way—it's more like we have a good lead on a massive story, and with a bit of work, and luck, it will come together, and Kelly will get her revenge as a bonus.'

'I don't buy it, Anna. You have nothing on the geezer.'

He was right of course. I had nothing on him except that he was a Grade A bastard. But I owed it to Kelly to try my best.

So I spent the afternoon researching the meagre leads I had. Googling him threw up very little, but that was hardly a surprise since he would obviously not let the world know what he was up to. But I did find through old news clippings that, Axalon, the company Rich worked for, was a major contractor to the EU and had many political connections. They were also the main supplier of security services when bigwigs came to town. All this was useful, but I needed an inside source, someone who would tell me what went on in Helmand before we decided to go there ourselves.

My email box pinged. More messages from the dating site.

Dear Lady, I am Nigerian entrepreneur and can offer you a truly prosperous future. Before I can take our relationship any further I need to find you suitable for myself. Can you send me your bank details for ID validation?

Nigerian scammers got everywhere, even on a Dubai dating site. Delete.

Hey—I like your profile. You seem kinda of myseterious and sexy. Would you want 2 come 4 date? Jordan, from Pennsylvania, now living in Kabul.

I looked at his picture. He looked about 12. Besides, I hated text language. Delete. How depressing was this?

'He is a bit young…even for you, missy. Stay clear from under 15s. They are illegal even in this country.' said Tim, peering at my screen over my shoulder.

I hated when people did that.

His remarks about my love life had recently developed a bitter tone. Maybe he too was getting fed up of being single and wanted to get out of this dating hellhole—Kabul. Maybe.

There was also an email from Pete.

Darling Anna, Just wanted to say that I had a wonderful time the last time we met. Dinner this week?

No we didn't! You didn't talk to me, you talked at me, about your car and your wife—both of which you seemed to treat as your possessions. I had to put an end to it. But how? If I was a guy, I would just stop answering his calls

97

or not text him back. But I always found that cowardly and infuriating. If you don't want to see me, just tell me. But don't leave me hanging. So I couldn't do that to anyone, even to a man who liked talking about his Alfa Romeo more than it was necessary.

The only decent thing to do was call him. After all, he was a man who had been inside me in an armoured vehicle in the middle of the Afghan desert. He deserved a phone call.

My mind made up, I dialled Pete's number. I had to get it over with—never a nice thing to do. With business-like efficiency, if possible.

'Hi, Pete, this is Anna.'

'Hi, Anna, nice to hear from you. How're things?'

'Good good. Listen, I'll get straight to the point. It's no good for us meeting up any more. I'm not comfortable about your, umm, home situation.'

The line went silent for a while.

'But that shouldn't affect us here, we can still have a good time.'

'I agree, but it's not something I'm looking for.'

'Okay I understand. You're hunting for a husband and that's something I can't give you.' His voice was hurt. Men can be such sulky toddlers.

Well I didn't want to make it brutal, so I agreed. 'You could say that. Anyway, I enjoyed your company.'

With that he disconnected the call.

There was another email I had overlooked. It was an invitation to a formal dinner hosted by the EU. Few days ago,

I thought a bunch of corpses were more entertaining than EU-crats droning on about 'possible peace and rehabilitation co-operation framework', but I suddenly realized that I could possibly dig out some information on their security arrangements and get some leads on Rich. I immediately called the PR and confirmed my attendance.

You never know what you might find at a party in Kabul.

13

The dinner was being held at one of the EU representative's temporary residences. Strict security checks meant that we had to arrive ninety minutes before the actual dinner started.

A massive armoured vehicle came to pick me up from office. I had spruced up by wearing my emergency going-out outfit—a printed wrap dress that looked smart, but modest enough to wear in this country. I dug out a pair of high heels from under my desk, applied a spot of lippy on my cheeks for a bit of colour and was sporting my 'I'm really interested in EU-Co-operation mandate number 246–face' as I stepped in.

Inside the vehicle, the air was thick with the smell of perfume, diesel oil, and ammo. The party bus was packed with dignitaries from Europe, all fragranced and smartly dressed in flak jackets on top of their glad rags. Well-coiffed hair hidden underneath helmets. A mixture of languages filled the small space, and I was introduced to the Belgian ambassador who was sitting on my left. We made small talk about Europe's role in the war, as the vehicle rolled along the dark streets.

After passing through various gates and security checkpoints, we eventually made it to what could only be described as a shabby palace. My cheerful party group giggled as Kalashnikov-toting men searched our bags and scanned us for any security threats. We were led into a brightly lit dining hall, decorated with EU and Afghan flags.

We sat down for what seemed to be a very formal dinner arrangement. On my right was the press attaché from the Finnish embassy—a dry looking, blonde woman who looked as if she was there only because of duty. Either that, or she may have swallowed a sack of sawdust. She nodded at my direction but continued to stare ahead, as if in deep thought. On my left was the Armenian ambassador, a stocky, jolly-looking man with a thick moustache and coarse, wavy grey hair. An assortment of journos sat all across the table. No Shabita, thank god. From the corner of my eye I could see an impressive looking man in an army uniform. American. Not bad at all.

After years of practise, I can confidently judge a man by his uniform. The Nordic and German ones are very orderly and tidy, if a bit serious at times. If you gave them alcohol they'd loosen up but occasionally to the point where they got too friendly and started groping. The Italians are the peacocks of the war zone because they like their uniforms fanciful, with lots of detail and their trousers were always tight around the crotch. The Brits are more laidback, cutely scruffy, and the younger ones like to show off their heavily tattooed arms. The US military may look buff to the untrained eye and have fancier outfits and weapons, but the downside is that they take themselves very seriously. My instinct was always to stay away from American men because of this. With them, there's no humour or thinking outside the box. Their focus tends to be rigidly on 'just doing my job'. Which applies to sex too, based on the few tasters that I've had. It's hard to find anything to talk about if you're not interested in car mechanics, heavy metal, and violent computer games. Even the more senior ones seem to lack the flirting gene, which makes them awfully dull travelling companions. A lot of US army boys come from Christian backgrounds, which means that they are married by the age of twenty-two and have their wives up the duff before they hit the frontline. But I was always open to offers, especially in my current vengeful state. I was hurting and wanted something inside me to fill the void.

The American hunk smiled at the people arriving, revealing a good set of teeth.

He gets one point for those pearly gnashers in Anna's scorecard.

The food was a lavish Afghan banquet with various meat and vegetable courses. The wine was flowing generously and the many candles made the room glow romantically. It was a good setting for a bilateral dinner but like everything else in Kabul, it had a feeling of fucked-upness about it.

The official line of discussion was kept brief, with each of the dignitaries taking turns to give crisp speeches about 'capacity building' and 'holding hands in partnerships with the locals'.

Eventually, the hunk stood up, and introduced himself as Chuck Hudson, head of EU Security, Afghanistan. He began his speech with, 'Dear ladies and gentlemen, we are all gathered here with a common goal. To help Afghanistan get back on its feet.' He continued with the usual platitudes.

Yawn.

To stave off boredom, I decided to observe him closely. He was kind of attractive, in an ageing American high-school-jock kind of way. Wide chest and strong shoulders. His uniform hugged him tightly because of his bulk, smiling seemed to come naturally to him, which I liked. He had strong arms, sandy coloured ruffled hair and a boyish charm—topped with dimples. The few specks of grey in his hair spoke of a life of experiences. But most importantly...no wedding ring. Tick, tick, tick.

Nothing wrong with a bit of American beefcake after a main course. I was now imagining myself sucking his, what I hoped would be, huge cock.

'...and our co-operation with ISAF in insecure areas like Lashkar Gah. Axalon is our key partner and the only Western security company operating in the area and because we are highly specialized in conflict, we can ensure progress is being made in crucial areas along Helmand river. After all, our mission is to leave Afghanistan for the Afghans to govern independently.'

Hang on. Did he say Axalon? My oral sex fantasies came to a screeching halt.

This could be useful.

Applause. He smiled. Did he just smile at me or at the dull Finn next to me? I beamed back just in case, and took a deep gulp from my glass.

When dinner was over, we were marched in an orderly queue through various security checks to a large room down the corridor. Soft jazz and dimmed lights. Waiters weaved their way smoothly through the guests, emptying ashtrays and topping up the glasses.

I looked around the room at the staple designer labels of the diplomat crowd—Calvin Klein, Missoni, Tory Burch— that had clearly been couriered in diplomatic pouches via designer websites. Generally, the diplomats' wives favoured classics—after all they didn't want to be seen extravagant in a war-torn country. Fashion here was rarely experimental except for a few Italian ladies who were dressed in Marni, and there was another who was wearing what looked like a beautiful adaptation of a sari. I walked across the room, talking to various people when I suddenly came face-to-face with a tipsy Mr Hudson himself. We made small talk about the dinner. At some point his hand touched mine as I went to grab another glass from the passing waiter's tray. We both turned to each other and I looked at him straight in the eye. I took a deep breath. He bit his lower lip and I moved my hand ever so slightly closer to his. He responded by softly squeezing mine. I felt a jolt of excitement run through my body.

At that point the Finnish woman who was sitting next to me at dinner came over, clearly drunk and much chattier than before. She went straight for Chuck. 'Are you here all by yourself?' she slurred. 'A big teddy bear of a man like you.'

How cheesy and obvious, but I let her have her moment. More platitudes followed. I was too proud to compete for a cock and quickly excused myself to go to the ladies room. I could hear the Finn's horsey laugh echo before the door shut behind me.

When I got back to the party room, the volume of chatter had gone up by yet another decibel. Drunken diplomats are usually the worst partygoers. They spend most of their time in being in control of everything so once they have a little booze, the control goes right out of the window. Most embassies, no matter how bad the country's affairs are, have a swimming pool. And most parties end up with drunken, ageing diplomats skinny dipping in the pool. This one looked like it was well on its way to becoming one of them. And I was going to stay as far away from any naked group antics as possible.

I was just about to reach for another glass of wine from a passing waiter when a very drunk Chuck pulled me from behind and guided me to a neighbouring room.

'I thought you had left without saying goodbye,' he said looking at me intently.

'You seemed otherwise engaged.'

'Oh that crazy Finn, she was so drunk she could barely stand up. I think she passed out in one of the guestrooms after throwing up.'

Maybe I was drunk, or maybe I was just horny, or maybe it was the pent-up sadness in me that made me respond to his flirtation. Whatever it was, I stood on my tiptoe and gave him a soft kiss on his mouth. Right there, in the middle of the noisy party.

He smiled and kissed me back, much harder than I had expected. He pulled me closer, caressed my hair, the small of my back, and I could feel his cock hardening underneath his trousers. I made a quick evaluation—probably circumcized, somewhere between scary and oh-my-god-never. I pulled myself away from his eager embrace.

'I should go, the transport people must be waiting for me as my name is on the list for the next transfer out,' I said.

'Please don't leave me like this, Anna. I want you,' Chuck said hoarsely in my ear.

'Maybe we can meet soon,' I suggested innocently, although my intentions were anything but that. After all, he could be useful in so many ways.

'Okay. As you wish,' he said, throwing his hands up.

I took his number and made my way back to the transfer holding area where the drunken Finn was sitting among the others, pale-faced after her antics.

The vehicle was packed again, but this time with drunken diplomats. Most of them had started taking turns to sing their national anthems and I prayed that I got home before anyone started to take their clothes off.

When the cacophony express finally pulled outside my place, the feeling of being jilted had given way to cautious optimism. I stepped cheerfully over the open sewer. It was dark all around me but somewhere inside there was a little light, shining marvellously.

14

Powered by rage and jealously, Kelly had thrown herself into 'Operation Lipstick' and was waving a thick notebook in front of me as I was praying for a miracle to find a clean pair of jeans and underwear.

'Look, here are some transfer details. Timings, places… it's all here,' she enthused.

'Where did you find that? Come to think of it…what is it?'

'Duh. It's a log book,' she replied as if it was the most obvious thing.

I breathed in to zip up my jeans.

'Logs of what?'

'The transfers to and from Helmand. Which vehicle, what route.'

'Ooh give it to me!'

I began leafing though the log book. She was right; it was a very careful and detailed book of all the routes and timings.

'It does not actually say what is being transported or who is transporting it. Where did you get it?'

Kelly looked out of the widnow at something distant. 'Farid gave it to Tim who gave it to me,' she said quietly.

'You *what*? Are you mad? How? Why didn't you tell me?' I was shocked.

'You've been busy. Tim told me he broke in. Look, the little guy is a mini-Houdini and if he can help us, I don't see anything wrong with that.'

'Please don't take advantage my staff. I just hired him!'

'He volunteered, Anna. He told Tim that he wanted to do us a favour.'

The notes were good. But how long would it be till someone noticed that their log book was missing?

Kelly cleared her throat. 'The thing is, Anna, we need to go to Rich's house ourselves to find more evidence because Farid doesn't know what he is looking for.'

'Are you insane? There is no way we're going to do something so stupid and risky as that. But I have another idea,' I said.

'Take a look at this.' I handed my phone to Kelly.

Great to meet you last night, you free tonight for dinner?

'What does your fanny getting stuffed has got to do with "Operation Lipstick"?' Kelly asked grumpily.

I filled her in on my idea to extract information from Chucky boy.

Admittedly, I felt a twinge of guilt. The poor guy had no idea of my plans to use him for information. Okay, maybe for a bit of playtime too. But c'est la vie right. I punched in my reply as Kelly cheered on.

Sure, meet me at 8 at the UN bar in Wazir?

Chucky-chuck, we began singing out loud, we are going to gobble you up.

I was fifteen minutes late when I got to the bar. Chuck was already there, sitting on a barstool, standing out in his civvies—an American logoed T-shirt and baggy jeans. He greeted me with a kiss on my cheek and I could smell his aftershave. It was strong and almost something a teenager would wear on a date night.

The bar wasn't really a bar but more like someone's front room. It had a counter, a couple of barstools, and the walls were adorned with tired looking pictures of racing cars. I ordered a beer and talked about the previous night's party. The usual—who did what. However, I needed to make inroads and started looking for a loose thread to the ball of wool.

'So why are you here, Chuck?'

'I got divorced after I got back from Baghdad. Was out there for two years and my wife had had enough of staying all by herself. We didn't have any kids. Then, I got an offer from EU which was too good to refuse.'

'How's the work?'

'It's good and not as dangerous because we've outsourced all the fieldwork to Axalon.'

Here we go. Gently now, Anna.

'What's Axalon like?'

'They're pretty good, everything is above the board, seems to be none of the shit that went down with Blackwater in

Iraq. But it's still the early days, and I've only been here for a few months.'

I drained my beer and ordered another one. Chucky boy wasn't such bad company after all, even if a bit on the dull side. I had already thought of a few white lies to tease stuff out of him. He seemed to be one of those men who had no natural curiosity, nor the desire to ask questions to get to know his companion better.

'I may be going to Lashkar Gah to do a story about the Emergency Relief hospital. Do you know any guys down there?'

'Yes, Axalon's got two men who work pretty much full-time. And there's a third British guy, Richard, who runs the whole shebang. He's based in Kabul but spends half his time in Helmand. He's a great guy and knows the area well, been down there for something like ten years.'

I wished I could take notes. Damn.

'It's kind of rebuilding work they do out there with these teams, and they make sure no one gets killed,' Chuck continued.

I listened to him carefully, so as not to miss anything.

'And this guy Richard, what's his role?'

Chuck casually placed his hand on my leg. I ignored it, equally casually.

'Sweetie pie, you do ask a lot of questions,' he said, sipping his whiskey.

'I'm just curious because of my trip,' I feigned innocence.

'Well, I will tell you stuff as long as it doesn't come back to bite me!' he laughed.

Can't guarantee that, my dear. I smiled.

'He sort of oversees the whole project. He comes down every two weeks and goes to the villages to check if it's all running according to our rules.'

I doubt it. More like collecting his cheques.

Chuck rattled on. 'The guys are in an ideal position, because many of the villagers are used to seeing them and so they trust them. Trouble flares up every now and then, but it's usually just local warlords fighting it out.'

It seemed Chuck was blissfully unaware of his contractors' lucrative little side business of selling arms to the very people they were trying to get rid of.

'So when are you thinking of going there? I can give them a head's up,' he said.

'Oh I'm just planning it at the moment, best not to bother them because I need to get London to approve my plans.'

No point in alerting anyone about my little investigation. I excused myself and rushed to the ladies room. Once inside the cubicle, I steadied my trembling hands, dug out my notepad and wrote everything he had said. When I got back, Chuck had refreshed our drinks. He was even bigger than I remembered. In fact, he was massive.

'Enough of Axalon. Let's talk about what fun we'll have,' he drawled, putting both hands on my thighs, leaning forward, ready for a nibble.

I couldn't push my enquiries any further without arousing his suspicion. But it seemed clear that I was arousing something else as there was a bulge in his jeans. We moved on to have whiskey at some point. Chuck had heard about a party at the Red Cross compound so we decided to try our luck.

We drunkenly stumbled down to the cellar of an old Afghan style mansion where we were greeted by a roomful of revellers. It was a makeshift bar thumping with loud music. We hit the dance floor to some dreadful house mix. More drinking and haziness followed. I remember Chuck putting his arm around me as we were leaning against the bar but not an awful lot after that.

When I opened my eyes the next day, I found myself lying next to a man-mountain who was sleeping with his hand under his cheek. I tried to work out whether we had sex.

Dizzy, dehydrated, and still wondering where I was, I grabbed my mobile phone from the nightstand. Fuck—it was nearly 11!

'Shit, where are my fucking clothes?' I panicked.

Chuck stirred and turned to me lazily, pulling me close. 'Hey, babe, don't go. Last night was great but I want to do it for real, not just messing around.'

No sex then. I almost let out a sigh of relief when he said the words. God only knows what we did.

I found my clothes and jumped into them. 'I'll call you. Thanks for last night,' I said and left.

The corridor I stepped into was noisy, full of cheerful people sans hangover. At least no one was in the bathroom. Under the artificial light I stared at my sorry self, cursing my inability to say no to alcohol and sexual encounters with men who wore high waisted jeans. I splashed some water on my face and stepped out of the barracks into the blinding midday sun, ready for my walk of shame. The only difference between me and a woman on her typical morning walk of shame was that I had to negotiate my way through various security gates and answer a million questions asked by men with guns.

Tim whistled when he saw me. 'Looks like you've had a good night. A wash might have been a good idea, I can smell his Lynx aftershave from here.'

I ignored the comment.

Farid, who was sitting beside Tim, looked up from the computer screen and gave me a broad smile.

'Shut up and listen. I've been on a fact-finding mission, for a story rather than for pleasure,' I said, flipping through the pages of my notebook, trying to decipher my scrawls.

'So we have a lead. But we need something concrete. Proper evidence,' Tim said.

He was right.

But I had an idea that could just work.

15

Armed with my phone and a throbbing hangover, I dialled the number of an army press officer, Lawrence Loxman.

He picked up after one ring.

'Loxman, it's Anna Sanderson. I'm looking to do a couple of features about your boys in Helmand. Free to meet?' I said, winking conspiratorially at Tim.

'Would love to. How's lunch?' came his reply.

'Sure.'

I hung up smiling to myself. They fall for it every time. Men who don't get to fire weapons love talking about them. Still clutching the phone, I turned to Tim. 'Just hear me out. We fix the embed with the forces and treat it as a legit story. But I need you with me on this.'

'What about London?'

'Don't worry, I'll just tell them we're doing some routine stuff in Helmand. You know they don't have a clue about the ground realities.'

'So we think that Rich is using Axalon as a shield to sell weapons to the Taliban, and at the same time pretending to do security work for those fighting the Taliban. It's just too much of a fantasy story, Anna. I don't buy it,' he sighed.

'My gut tells me we're on to something big here. And if there's one thing I trust, it's my reporter gut.'

He shrugged and turned to continue the game with Farid. Farid had become a regular at the office and was jolly useful to have around—making us tea, greeting visitors, and generally tidying up. It turned out that he was a useful little entrepreneur. We would send him out for errands and he'd get a dollar as an extra bonus. Soon he was offering his services to the entire building and had subcontracted the top floor to his friend because it was the furthest and took the most time to get there. You could trust him to bring back the change, minus his bonus. But we loved him more because he livened up the place, regaling us with anecdotes, telling us precious little bits of street gossip. We adored the little fellow. He was hard working and we paid him a modest wage but it was about five times as much as he made as a teaboy in the bombed-out embassy. 'It's better here, ma'am. No one beating me with sticks,' he would say.

Tim let out a cuss when he was defeated by Farid.

'You shouldn't be a bad loser. In my country, there are no losers, just lots of dead people,' Farid said with a wink.

'Farid, for such a small boy, you are very wise. Now get out,' I mock scolded him.

'Yes, sir, ma'am.'

As he was shuffling to put his sandals on, he turned around to face us, and said matter-of-factly, 'You know your friend Kelly... the book I got for her. I know how to get into that house, the house you want to look around.'

Ah. The log book. Kelly was right after all. This was our only way to look for evidence.

'And how do you want to do that?' I asked.

'I learned a thing or two when one of my uncles used to lock me in the shed.' He winked and made a movement with his hand, which looked like he was opening a lock.

Tim shook his head vehemently. 'No no no no no,' he began.

I shushed him.

'Us Afghans are good at getting into places where we are not supposed to be,' Farid smiled as he said the words. A cheeky, disarming smile. How could anyone not love this kid?

My brain switched its gear. Farid could take me in and I could snoop around for concrete evidence. We just had to make sure Rich wasn't there and that we didn't get caught. He must at least keep schedules of the upcoming transfers. There had to be something there, and it was worth the risk.

'It can't be so easy. I'm sure there's a guard,' I said.

'Anna,' Tim tried to interrupt. He knew that once I got an idea into my head there was no stopping me.

I ignored him.

'Yes but he smokes opium every afternoon, which means he is ding-dong,' Farid twirled his finger around his head to indicate that the guy was high.

'I knew we were right to hire you. You're a genius!' I yelped excitedly at the news.

I couldn't believe that we had found Rich's little Kabuli *pied-à-terre*. Maybe that's where he entertained his ladies too. It was strange that despite all their time together, Kelly hadn't been invited to it. In a way, I was relieved that she hadn't been. That lying bastard.

'Can you take me there?' I asked.

'Anna, don't even think about it!' Tim got up.

'Tim, it's the only chance we have right now. There must be something in that house. We just have to make sure Rich is out. It's a simple in and out.'

'And how do you propose to do that? By planting a GPS in his underpants?'

'Look, it could give us a vital clue on how to nail this guy. It's a minimal risk. Farid can sneak in first, without anyone noticing, and then let me in.'

'I know it's Kabul and everything happens, but it's still illegal to break into people's houses and snoop around!'

'Maybe, but worse things go on in this town.'

Tim threw up his hands, resigned.

I wasn't going to give in. 'Anna Sanderson, you are the most difficult woman I have ever met.' He paused, and then added, 'Fine, but only on one condition. I'll come with you and wait outside. And *no funny business*.'

I hugged him with all my strength. 'You're the best! Tomorrow night. Okay?'

'Fine.'

I gave Farid a kiss on his cheek. 'We have an adventure on hand, boy wonder.'

'Okay, I'll see you there, ma'am,' he said, clearly embarrassed and rubbing the spot where I had kissed him.

To be honest, Tim's concern moved me. It was nice to feel looked after in a place like this. A single girl in a warzone had to ensure her safety and Tim was always there for me. He had never let me down, not even once.

To make it to lunch with Loxman, I had to leave early. Camp Catrina was located a few kilometres outside the city and there was no time to freshen up. I grabbed my bag and left immediately.

Loxman, with his strawberry blonde hair, toned body, deep green eyes, and a sprinkle of freckles was a perfect advert for wholesomeness. He stood outside the press tent, all tall and straight.

'Anna, good to see you. Loved your latest dispatch from the frontline. Great journalism. Not sure about your assessment on the increase in civilian casualties, but I'll let that one go.'

I kissed him on both cheeks. 'You know how it is, I have to have something to bring you boys down.'

'Allow me to take you to the fine dining room,' he smiled.

We queued up outside the canteen to wait for our turn to be served. Outside, it was hot as hell, but inside the canteen tent the air conditioning had made sure the dining room was at perfect temperature. I was half waiting for Mr D to pop up from somewhere, since he had a habit of appearing out of nowhere. But he was probably too busy feeding figs with his tongue to Shabita. We picked our plates of roast turkey, potatoes, peas, and gravy and sat down at the end of a long bench.

'You know how cost efficient the British army is. We can kill more insurgents efficiently with just a press of a button.'

'That is really interesting. What kind of technology is that?' I smiled at him.

He laughed. 'It's top secret. All I can say is that it does not have wings.'

'Oooh, you are such a tease.'

'Look who's talking.'

He continued with his mild flirting, but I felt he was only doing it to keep up a façade. I, too, thought it was time to put my most sincere face on.

'I want to do a story on real heroes, the privates who are holding fort in little known places like Lashkar Gah,' I started tentatively.

'That sounds like a good story, Anna. Tell me more.'

I flashed him an innocent smile. 'I hear Lashkar Gah doesn't get much coverage despite the heroic work you guys do down there. Maybe I could visit a reconstruction team and talk to villagers about the humanitarian side of your work. All we have are negative stories. It would be refreshing to have a positive angle for a change. People love a feel-good story.'

He nodded, and I could see he was already thinking of the positive spin he could put on the story and how he would end up looking good.

I pushed on. 'I would love to arrange a one or two-week long embed. You know, to get proper insight into the situation.'

'But two weeks on the frontline is a long time, even for someone as experienced as you.'

'Sure, but the longer we stay, the stronger the story.'

'I like the sound of it. I'll see what I can do. But I'm warning you, no funny business there. You have a reputation of being a bit of a troublemaker.'

'Do I? Ha-ha.' My laugh was so fake it made me cringe.

He stood up to get some dessert while I contemplated my blasted 'reputation'. It was starting to get to me. I wondered what rocked Loxman's boat. He clearly was one of 'the boys' but did not really fit in with all the combat chat and machismo. He had mentioned in passing that he was engaged and had plans to marry after his tour was over, but I got the sense that there was more to him than what met the eye. The good public-school-boy look and impeccable manners were unsettling, if not out of place. It seemed like some grand act.

I remember him telling me that he had been a journo at a local rag back in the Nineties but it was the military that he had always fancied. I guess guys like him ended up doing communication work because he didn't strike me as someone who was really roughing it up in the middle of nowehere.

He came back and sat down with a thud. 'Okay, you're in. Leave it to me, I'll get things fixed,' he said in between careful girly spoonfuls of custard.

'You know where to find me.'

On my way back I texted Kelly.
Things are moving fast. We have to rope in Ali Ahmad too. Come to the office at 4 pm.

16

Kelly was already there, talking animatedly to Tim, when I got back.

She joked, 'You've interrupted a moment of revelation, Anna. Tim was just about to tell me why he never goes on dates. But now I guess we'll never know. ' She was laughing but Tim looked dead serious. I noticed he was sweating.

'Oh yeah? Is it because you like a nice soldier with your eggs like I do?' I joked.

He looked at me angrily. 'Speak for yourself, Sanderson.'

'Oi, I was joking. We all know you're a fanny magnet but picky as hell.'

Kelly started humming 'Strangers in the night' and mock danced around our office.

'Who doesn't want to get married and have kids?' he cut in.

'True, but you might as well fuck as many people before you walk down the aisle, no? Because after that, it'll just be the same ol' one for the rest of your crummy life.'

'I don't think it's all that bad,' Tim said curtly.

Our light hearted banter was interrupted by Ali Ahmad, who arrived looking solemn faced as usual.

We sat around a table, all four of us smoking, while Farid busied himself with making tea.

'Do you know anything about the arms deal in Lashkar Gah? Or do you know where I could get some information on who arms the Taliban?'

'It depends.'

By that he meant how much money I was willing to pay. Typically Afghan, he never mentioned the word 'money', but would be offended if I didn't pay what was expected.

'Well, it's sensitive stuff and confidential. There are possibly two or three Western men selling arms to the Talibs, right under the nose of international forces,' I said.

Ali's face didn't betray any emotion.

'I have some information about their activities, but we need more—photographs, statements, anything. Evidence that shows what they are doing.'

He spoke measuredly. 'My cousin lives in Lashkar Gah. I will call him and let you know.'

Afghans always had cousins everywhere. But I knew I could trust Ali. He was one of those people here who wouldn't betray you, or double cross you, or sell a piece of information that he had already sold to you. To be honest, this kind of loyalty and trust was rare in a country rife with paranoia and suspicion and where every bit of information had a price tag.

He stepped out into the corridor to make a phone call and came back five minutes later. 'His name is Qais. He is a local journalist. He knows the men in question but said they are protected by a man called Shah.'

'Do you think he could tail the white men for a week or so and get me some evidence of their activities? I will pay him a thousand dollars.'

Ali Ahmad went back to the corridor while the rest of us looked at each other in silence.

He came back in a few minutes. 'He wants 1,500 dollars. It's a very dangerous job.'

I wasn't in a position to negotiate, so I agreed. 'But I need the evidence soon.'

He left without saying a word. But I had a good feeling about it because Ali Ahmad almost always delivered.

Good news arrived sooner than I had expected. Ali Ahmad called me.

'Miss Anna, I have something to share. But I can't speak on the phone,' he whispered.

We arranged to meet at my place half an hour later and he arrived punctually, as usual. He always shook my hand in a very formal way—the way Afghan men do when they greet a Western woman.

'Qais emailed me some pictures. And some notes,' he said.

He pulled out some grainy coloured photographs. They weren't the best quality, but the action in it was visible.

The photograph showed two white men about to enter a house that looked like the Taliban HQ with five turbaned and Kalashnikoved men standing outside. The next one showed the two coming out of the house. The other photographs were similar, but it wasn't hard evidence.

'And the notes?'

He settled down with his cup of tea.

The notes were more detailed.

'We know the route,' Ali Ahmad spoke. 'The weapons come in from Russia, through Turkmenistan. Most are leftovers from the Chechen war.'

'How did you find that out?'

'Money pays for information.' He crossed his legs.

'It looks as if they have a well organized transport network across the country, and pay bribes on the way to make sure their trucks are not intercepted,' he said.

We read on, our heads hunched over the notes.

Lashkar Gah was the central hub of these activities from where the weapons then got distributed to the Taliban. There was a massive weapons cache somewhere in the mountains, but Qais didn't know where it was.

After we were through, I thanked Ali Ahmad and paid him the money.

The picture was finally beginning to take some shape but there were still a lot of missing pieces. And none of this nailed Richard. We needed more. Much much more.

I had been invited to a dinner at a friend's house. It was hosted by the indomitable Ariana—fierce as a tigresss, but brimming with charm and elegance. Daughter of a French diplomat and a successful Afghan politician, Ariana was wonderfully eccentric and someone who had become a loyal friend over the years. We met a couple of years ago when I was covering a story about missing babies and she was heading the charity which had first alerted us to the story.

When I first saw her, she was sitting behind a massive desk with a mountain of papers on it.

'Ashhwaandddd,' she yelled as I stepped into her office. 'Assshwaaand! Tea! Now!'

She was nervously flicking ash from her cigarette and staring at the computer screen. Without averting her gaze from the screen she said, 'There were five of them in total. The mothers say they don't know what happened but I suspect the local mullah knows. His name is Azmanullah. You will find him in the village.'

And with that our chat was over.

In the end, we never found out what had happened to the babies. Ariana left the charity soon after, but we ran into each other at a few parties, got drunk together, and became fast friends. She was as tough as old boots, having been in the country for years and seen the worst of it. 'Annnaaa, there is nooo hooope here. Whyyy doon't youu leeave and goo and finddd a hooosband?' she used to ask me. Ariana had bags of charm and was very beautiful so she had men falling for her all the time. Yet she chose to remain single. 'I doon't like meeen. You can 'aave tem,' she would say as she laughed.

Ariana had told me that dinner would be a formal affair with diplomats and government officials, which meant dressing up was in order. In truth, all I wanted to do was bum around in my trusty tracksuit bottoms, soft jumper with a huge tub of Häagen-Dazs. But I couldn't refuse Ariana so I told her I would come.

I slipped into a pale gold tunic, cut to give me a slim silhouette—still within the acceptable modesty limits for an Islamic country, and teamed it with a pair of grey silk trousers, a scarf woven with silver and gold threads, and a necklace with lapis. Thank God for the magic foundation that I had picked up at Heathrow. Kabul wasn't really the place for make-up shopping, unless you were a fan of bright blue eyeshadow, clotted brown foundation, and soapy orangey Russian style lipstick. Final checks in the mirror made me groan, but I had done the best I could. I was hardly going to meet Mr Right over a discussion about multilateral defence policy, was I?

Ariana's house was buzzing with the sounds of a successful party in progress. She was a great host who combined Afghan generosity with French sophistication. The music was a mixture of local beats and French chansons. Her house was a typical wealthy Afghan family home—two stories high, with a spacious, manicured garden and wide wall-to-wall windows. The garden was blooming luxuriously and was looking even more beautiful with lanterns dotting it all over.

Ariana came bouncing over and kissed me excitedly like an exuberant puppy. 'Aaannnaa, hoooww the 'eelll arrre you,' she said in her unique Afghan–French accent, grabbing a glass of champagne from one of the waiter's trays and handing it to me.

'Ariana, so good to see you,' I said kissing her on both cheeks and giving her a jar of fig jam that I knew she liked.

'Coomee in, coomee in,' she enthused, 'meet zee others.'

There were many familiar faces—a couple of French and British print journalists, an American documentary filmmaker called Jack whom I vaguely recall flirting with at a party, diplomats, and a couple of Afghan ministers, a painter, and a few others.

'We are still waaiiting for a few more people to get here so pleez jus relax and enjoy yourself,' she said, tucking a wisp of shiny black hair behind her ears and downing the champagne.

I spotted Martine, a French journalist, who I had worked with on a couple of stories in the past. She was perched on the arm of a sofa, smoking short fat cigarillos, waving her little feet about, and narrating something exciting to a group of people who were listening intently. I always envied women with dainty size 3 feet. Mine were huge, long, and wide. Whenever I went shoe shopping, the assistants always looked genuinely sorry, but at the same time visibly relieved that they didn't have my freakishly large and ugly feet. Thank god for high-end designers' foresight when it came to women with boat-like feet because most of my favourite designers made large sizes. I wish the same could be said about their clothes.

Martine was an excellent journalist and gained notoriety when it came to light that she had paid 50,000 dollars to meet a few members of the Taliban. The paper she worked for had been desperate for the story and they coughed up the cash. There were times when all of us ended up paying a few hundreds here and there to keep someone happy— policemen, prison officials, or to get to a source. However, it was only occasionally that it came to light and rarer still to dish out that much for a story. Even though some admittedly paid with their lives.

Martine took a lot of risks when she went to meet the Taliban. She had no security details, no back-up plan. She had a photographer with her from France who had been assigned by the paper, someone who did not even know the country. Martine's arrangement raised eyebrows because there was such a large sum of money involved, and many doubted whether she was meeting the real Talibs at all or a rogue group of criminals wanting to make a pile of money. She did get her story in the end, and it was big news in France. No story in this country is without a risk and I couldn't help admire her for getting the scoop of a lifetime.

I went and said hello to her and she greeted me warmly. We talked a bit about this and that, when she finally said something that caught my attention.

'You know what I am chasing now, Anna?' she leaned over drunkenly and whisperd, 'Taliban weapons. I want to know where they are coming from, who supplies them... everything,' she said, taking a swig of her champagne.

I couldn't believe my luck. Poker face on, I said, 'Interesting. Tell me more.'

'Well I know of these Chechen fighters that have some connection with the Taliban. And there are rumours about a couple of Americans that have switched sides.'

I nodded. 'Reliable sources, that's what we need.'

Martine flicked the ash from her cigarette. 'It wouldn't be impossible, but to make matters—how should I say— tricky, I've heard that Shabita is planning a major scoop on this and she has some top notch Intel bloke feeding her information. Merde.'

Merde indeed.

Of course Shabita had to be involved; how could she not be chasing the most wanted story in all of Afghanistan? I wondered if the Intel guy was Mr D. But it couldn't have been; he was muscle, not a strategist. I brushed my wandering thoughts aside and decided to enjoy myself.

The doorbell rang several times, letting in another trickle of people. Our little group grew to take in more people and the chatter became noisier. As time went on, a steady stream of guests slowly filled the house. As I was getting my third refill of champagne, I saw a tall man who nearly hit his head on the doorframe while entering the room. Giggling, I looked to see who the newcomer was and nearly dropped my glass.

Double Merde!

17

What was it with this guy? Why did he always appear wherever I went, like some wind-up merchant? This town clearly wasn't big enough for the two of us.

I checked if he had the sequinned devil with him. But she wasn't hanging off his arm like a shiny orangutan. I swallowed hard and tried to continue my conversation with someone…anyone…in the vicinity.

'Ha-ha! That is funny!' I heard myself saying. I grabbed another drink to calm my nerves. Had he seen me yet? Part of me wanted to run away, and the other part was curious to see what his reaction would be if he saw me. Don't be stupid, I told myself, remember he really is a GAA—Grade A Arsehole. But why did I still feel nervous and silly when he was in the same room? I shot a sideways glance in his direction. He had shaved his beard, revealing a strong jaw line. It made him look much younger. His eyes were serious as always, as if he was trying to solve a riddle that was puzzling him.

'Your last trip, did you have any contact with the Taliban?' Martine asked. 'We're trying to work out what's going on down in Helmand, and typically, the military is not giving us anything. You are the only one who has been out there lately.'

'Um, yes it was rough, contact was daily, but we moved our base twice and managed to escape a couple of near-hits too. It was pretty rough.' I realized how lame I sounded and this seasoned group would think I was ditzy for my tepid analysis on the war. But my head was in turmoil.

'Dinner is reaaaaddddyy, laaadies and geeentlemeen, if you could please come this way,' our exuberant host yelled out.

Thank god for that.

The dinner table was beautifully illuminated with dozens of candles. I watched Mark's tall back as he walked just a few metres ahead of me. I was hoping he hadn't seen me yet. As I turned to pull out my chair, I looked up and saw him looking at me. His brown eyes were expressionless. I smiled as graciously as I could. Sweat was now trickling down my back. Stay calm, stay calm, he is just a man, I kept telling myself, but couldn't stop the room from spinning.

'Sit down, sit down, Mark daaarling,' Ariana hurried him along.

I half collapsed onto my seat and somehow managed to control my breathing. To my left was a friendly, bearded NGO worker, Michael, and to my right was another television journalist from Al Jazeera, Zina.

And across the table on the far right was the man who I had thought was the 'one'.

'Everrrryyyone,' bellowed Ariana, clapping her hands, 'I want you to go roond and introduce yourself because you don't know each oteeer.'

The man seated next to Mark went first. 'Hi everyone. I am Jack Patterson from Newcastle and I'm a contractor.'

Then, Mark.

'Hello everyone, I am Mark Trevor, also a contractor, but from Devon, UK.'

Hah! Mark Trevor. A contractor from Devon. Almost like a silly little bullshit poem. At least I learnt what his last name was. To be honest, it was quite usual for me not to know a guy's last name. I usually paid attention to such details only post-coitally. Soon it was my turn, and I turned bright red and felt a stutter coming on. I took a huge swig of wine and said, 'Um, I'm Anna Sanderson, journalist with GNN.' I didn't dare look Mark's way.

Once the introductions were over, wine began to flow, and chatter started to fill the room. The usual war stories were being swapped. We were served a starter called boulani—a delicious local pancake stuffed with greens. Zina, a beautiful Lebanese girl, who was in Afghanistan for the first time, was gushing with debutante excitement about her plans here. Despite the fact that she had just stepped off the plane, she was firing on all cylinders.

'I can't wait to cover the country; it has been my dream for so long.'

I was talking like a robot because inside I was desperate to see if Mr D was looking at me. 'It's intoxicating, almost addictive, but you can easily get lost with all the smoky mirrors. It's very hard to trust anyone, or work out who is telling the truth and who is not.'

Try to look interested and engaging, I reminded myself. I stole a glance across the table, to where Mark was sitting—talking to the animated French blonde sitting next to him. I felt a twinge of jealously. What is wrong with me? I don't even know the guy. Get a grip, Anna. But I couldn't help myself. While Zina enthused about Afghan politics, all I could think of was how lovely he looked and how much I wanted him.

'At the end of the day, the fundamentalist ideology in the Islamic world is not the beast everyone in the West seems to believe it is,' Zina carried on.

I was unable to follow her thread but tried to be polite and asked her questions about her work at Al Jazeera.

The main course came—a delectable local mutton stew served with pilau and naan.

'So I've heard that you've had quite a few good scoops from the frontline recently,' said Zina, spotting my lack of engagement in her high brow analysis.

This girl sure had done her research.

'Umm, yes, I guess so. But I do spend a lot of time down there, more than any other television journo I guess, so it's not so hard to get the stories.'

The conversation with Zina petered out when dessert was served. Tarte Tatin. I overheard Ariana explaining to someone how long it had taken her to teach her cook to make this sweet pastry. My head was reeling with all the champagne I had drunk. But Ariana had brought out the French dessert wine and I was more than happy to be an obliging guest.

'So are you single?' Zina asked much too loudly for my liking.

'Yes. I guess everyone is when they are in Kabul,' I said, trying to hide the apparent bitterness in my voice.

'How's the dating scene here?'

'Honestly, dating is difficult here. But it depends on what you like. You can have your pick with the security lot but it's hard to find a decent man.' I half hoped Mark had heard that. 'When people arrive in Kabul and stay for longer than just a few weeks, they very quickly forget their other halves back home. Maybe because life is relatively restricted for many of us here, or maybe because tomorrow you might just drive into an IED, so we make sure that at least we don't die sex starved. But what goes on in Kabul stays in Kabul.'

I wanted to scream that I didn't want to be single any more. What I wanted was to find a decent man who was honest and who loved me for who I was. Someone I could call after a day of dodging bullets. Someone who would tell me every now and then that the world was an okay place after all. No more games, no more fooling around, no more nonsense.

I was drunk like most people. The slutty looking blonde sitting next to Mr Contractor was beginning to irritate me. She was purring at Mark and sticking out her chest a bit more than was appropriate. She was probably stroking him under the table too. Or maybe my imagination was running wild like a pack of wolves. But he seemed to be hanging on to her every word. What about Shabita? He clearly was a total bastard. They deserved one another.

Why did I care anyway?

Fuck him. I didn't care about blondes with visible dark roots stroking a hot man's arm like she fucking owned him. No, not one bit. I suddenly needed to get out. The dinner was suffocating me. I managed to steady myself and escaped to the bathroom. There, staring back at me in the mirror was an ageing correspondent with bewildered eyes, smudged mascara, and red cheeks. No wonder he preferred artificial young blondes. I splashed some cold water on my face and fixed my make-up and hair. Straightening out my clothes, I stepped out holding my head high, even though it took a lot of effort to do so.

The dining room had cleared out; everyone had retired to the lounge. I sat down on a chair, and downed a glass of Arak, a potent Lebanese aniseed drink. The bitter liquid burnt my throat. Music was booming through the walls. I felt alone and vulnerable even in this lovely gathering of people. My sight clouded up with tears; first a small drop in the corner of my eye and then finally, a stream running down my cheeks. I held my head in my hands and let it all out. I was drunk and miserable and didn't even know why I was crying in the first place.

'Can I talk to you for a sec?' said a voice next to me.

I looked up to see Mark. I quickly brushed the tears away, not wanting him to see me like that. I tried to get up but my head was spinning way too much. Not a good sign. He took me by my hand and walked me out to the garden. The fresh air was like a slap on the face. Focus, Anna, focus. I tried but failed. Where was my drink?

'Anna, please don't say anything, just let me speak.'

I nodded, grateful for getting a moment to try silencing the rants in my head and not giving away my wine breath.

'We are being watched so I have to keep this brief. I have been trying to track you down since we last spoke, but there were…there are some people who are trying to put a stop to it.'

He spoke quickly and it took me a while to process everything he was saying.

'There are things that I cannot tell you about. It's to do with my work and your friend Kelly. But you have to trust me when I say I am not messing around with you, Anna. I want to be with you.'

'What about Shabita?' I couldn't stop the slur in my voice.

'She means nothing to me, silly.'

Nothing he said made sense. What was that about people tracking him again?

'What are you doing here?' I finally managed to speak.

'I came here to see you. I knew you'd be here. But things are difficult…complicated. I hate it for it to be like this but it's all too well…complicated. I just want you to be careful, okay, and not do anything stupid.'

With that he left. What was that about? What the fuck was his game? I was so enraged I nearly walked after him.

But even in my drunken state, I knew that would be a stupid thing to do. I hated scenes, so I stood, rooted to the spot, watching him go.

'Trust me,' he had said. I wanted to trust him so badly but he was so darn difficult to make sense of. And so unavailable. I stood there for a while, in the darkness, focusing on staying upright and wondering if this surreal conversation had actually taken place. It was all too much for one night.

I sought Ariana out, and thanked her for the lovely dinner and said my goodbyes to whoever was around. Mark was nowhere to be seen by the time I staggered into my waiting car. It had been an exhausting evening and I, for one, was glad it was over.

18

I woke up with my head weighing a ton. My flash cure for a hangover was sex. But in the absence of a man, DIY had to suffice. Images from the previous night raced through my mind. And I remembered Mark. Good God! I hoped I had behaved myself and not said anything stupid. What had he said? I want you? I wanted him so bad that it ached.

I touched myself with urgency. After the two-minute finger emergency relief was over, the longing for Mark still remained, gnawing my insides.

I was pulling up my jeans and trying to find a bra when it came to me like a flash. Mark was somehow involved in the Rich mess. It suddenly made a bit of sense. His interest in Rich on our date in Babur Gardens. 'It's to do with my work. And your friend Kelly.' He had said. It's all a happy merry-go-round. But what the heck was the connection? Why should Mark care what Rich was up to? Why did he say that there were people trying to put a stop to us seeing each other? How did I matter in all this?

No matter how hard I tried, the pieces did not fit.

I jumped into a taxi to get to work. It wasn't always the safest way to travel around here, but I didn't have time to wait for the car to come back after it had dropped off Tim. As the taxi rattled on, I stared out at the bustling Kabuli streets and thought of my recent escapades. Why did I always fancy the wrong guy? I realized, much to my horror, that in the last week, I had let two men—neither of whom I saw any kind of future with—fuck me. And one I used for information. Momentary pangs of guilt swamped me. My eyes followed a man pulling a heavily loaded cart. This was a country where human life was worth less than an animal's and if I could—even in a small way—help save lives, I would try my best. With renewed determination, I focused on the plan.

I dialled a number.

'Well hello, Chuck. How's it going?' I said sweetly.

'Anna, my flower. How the 'ell are you?'

'Good good. Fancy a spot of lunch?'

'With you—always.'

We arranged to meet at a local Lebanese joint. But before any fun and games, I had some work to do.

Tim was out, and I was relieved. Lately, he had been behaving like a sulky teenager one minute, and a sarky man in need of a good seeing to the next. Our happy little commune had been a tense place recently, what with Kelly suffering a mother of all PMSes and Tim acting all weird. I secretly hoped we would all be close again when we got closer to the action. After all, it was what we loved doing more than anything else. For the time being, I couldn't work out what the matter was with Tim. Maybe it would sort itself out.

In the office, Farid was busying himself with tidying up the place, but I could sense that he was desperate for an outing. He was a fidgety little monkey. The kid needed excitement all the time!

'Farid, let's go to the Axalon house.'

'Now? I thought we were going tonight?'

'No. Let's go now.'

There was a twinkle in his eye. 'What are you waiting for then, ma'am?'

Outside, the merciless afternoon sun blinded us momentarily. So often Kabuli days were like this, with its silent piercing blue skies and livid heat. Farid led me around another part of the town. He picked up a snaking back alley, a shortcut, he said. It was a narrow lane, surrounded by tall fences and latched doors. The stench of urine mixed with rotting garbage filled the air. Although there were fewer chances of us being seen here, news around these quarters travelled quickly, and the last thing I wanted was some overly curious guard signalling ahead that there was a foreigner in the neighbourhood. The only good thing was that it was late in the afternoon, the sleepy hour in Kabul when everything grinds to a halt. Most people here take the term 'winding down' literally, and dope themselves with opium or alcohol. And who could judge them? Misery, death and even everyday hardships create a need for escape, however temporary.

In no time we arrived in front of a metal gate with barbed wires around the top. This wasn't unusual. Most Kabuli houses had these to keep away unwelcome visitors.

'This is it, ma'am,' he said, pointing at the gate.

'Are you absolutely sure? Could this be someone else's house?'

'No, ma'am, this is the Axalon man's house. He has a jacket and cap with the logo. The guard is probably drugged out by now,' Farid went on, and made a funny snoring sound as he produced something that looked like a blade from his pocket.

'What's that?' I was intrigued by what seemed to be a homemade pen knife with a very sharp blade and a wooden handle.

'A Kabuli key!' he said, proudly showing off his lethal looking device.

I watched with a mixture of admiration and astonishment as he expertly slid the blade in to a small gap in the lock, shook it around a bit until it clicked open. Farid cautiously pushed the door. We were in!

'What if there is a dog?' I whispered, pulling Farid's hand.

He shook his head and whispered. 'No dog. We have at least half an hour before he wakes up. I stay here. Two whistles if I see anyone coming, okay?'

The courtyard was empty, except for two languid cats that were enjoying the afternoon sunshine. They lifted their heads lazily to look at me and went right back to sleep. The silence was broken only by the rhythmic snoring emanating from the little chowkidar hut. That must be the guard, I thought. Farid had thought this through, smart little fellow.

I creeped into the house, trying to walk on the balls of my heels to make minimal sound. My heart hammered in my ribcage. Us journos get up to dodgy situations and often end up in places where we shouldn't be. But I had never blatantly broken into someone's house like this before, that too in broad daylight. But it had to be done so I steeled myself.

The main door opened into a large living-cum-games room. It was straight from an 'Afghan Guesthouse' catalogue, with cushions on the floor, plush carpets strewn everywhere and intricate rugs hanging from the walls. A massive wooden dining table with rustic chairs dominated the room. There was nothing personal in it, so my instinct told me I would find more clues upstairs.

I wasn't sure what I was looking for, but knew that when I saw it, I would instantly recognize it. It could be just a small piece of information—a gun catalogue with a price next to it and a post-it with 'sold to Taliban written on it.' Hah, as if! The stairs were to the left of the main door. If someone were to come in, I would not be able to escape unnoticed. I climbed up anyway. My heartbeat in the silent house seemed magnified. I creeped upstairs. The trick to not making a wooden staircase creak is to step on the middle. Or so, I had read in detetective novels. And it actually worked.

Upstairs, I was faced with four doors. I went for the one on the extreme left. A gentle push and it creaked loudly. Shit Shit Shit.

I quickly slipped into the room and found myself in an empty space with a massive bed in the middle. There was a macabre hook hung on the ceiling directly above the bed. A hook? What kind of person has a hook above their bed, and what for? On second thought, it didn't really surprise me too much. He was, after all, Ropey. Kinky or not, I didn't have the time to ponder over Rich's weird life. Plus, apart from the carefully made bed, there was nothing else in the room, so I decided to move on.

The next room was a spacious and surprisingly clean bathroom with tons of girly products! Hair spray? Self-tan lotion? Crème de la Mer? Who has face cream worth over a hundred quid in a bathroom in Kabul? Huge boxes of condoms too, but that was hardly a discovery. The bathroom didn't throw up anything of note. The next door opened into a sort of spacious walk-in closet that had neatly folded bed linen and clothes. It looked as if someone had colour coordinated all the items and lined them up with a ruler—a woman perhaps. This house was turning out to be very odd.

I tried to push the handle down of the last door several times, but it didn't give in. Locked doors either meant there were things of importance inside, or even better, secrets. I needed Farid's magic key.

I went to the window that overlooked the courtyard. I had to get Farid's attention and ask him to quickly come up and help me with the door. I looked out and saw him sitting in front of the gate, looking alert.

'Farid,' I called out in a loud whisper. The boy looked up.

I waved him to come up, and mimed that I needed his key. Farid made the 'are you crazy' sign, twirling a finger around his temple. But I frantically gestured, then made a pleading face, folding my hands as if I were praying.

He rolled his eyes and gestured for me to wait where I was.

In a few mintues, I heard him come up the stairs. He hadn't bothered with the kind of caution I had shown. He got to work and soon the door opened without any sign of a forced entry. He sneaked back downstairs to his post. The child was a genius!

There had to be something in this room. It smelled like a boy's room—stale and sweaty, with a lived-in feel about it. I was sure this was Ropey's room. I took quick mental notes.

Windows on both sides with hastily draped sheets. Unmade bed, or more like a thick mattress with clothes strewn all over the floor. Two wooden nightstands on each side. Boxes of condoms on them. I picked up one of the dirty mugs from the floor—it wasn't mouldy, which meant someone had stayed in this room quite recently. A pile of porn magazines were kept next to the bed. Teenage sluts and anal fisting. Getting anal fisting annuals past the world's strictest moral police must have been child's play for a seasoned arms smuggler. I looked around. A wooden desk stood by one of the windows, but there was no computer. Instead, there were piles of note books. Aha!

I began leafing through the well-thumbed books but the information made little sense to me. Column after column of what looked like rudimentary accountancy but nothing that could serve as evidence of illegal transactions. I took photos of them anyway because they just might make sense at some point. Disappointed, I began looking for further clues.

A large Ikea-style clothes rack-cum-wardrobe covered with a tie-dye cloth was propped next to the wall. I lifted the curtain and whistled. Guns, all sorts of guns, were neatly piled up in rows. There were at least a couple of AK47s, a few hand guns, several hand grenades, and three RPGs. I pulled out my camera and took a couple of photos. Maybe it was his sample collection! Still, it wasn't illegal to have weapons in your house; almost everyone slept with a gun in this city because you never knew who was going to pay you a visit.

Two sharp whistles broke my train of thought. It was time to get out.

As I was about to leave the room, something on the nightstand caught my eye. It was a boarding pass. For a military flight to Camp Bastion, scheduled for next week. And next to it was something that looked liked an itinerary. I quickly photographed them and left, closing the door carefully behind me.

Just then I heard two more whistles screech through the air. There was urgency in them. I ran down the stairs, nearly tripping over, and straight out into the courtyard to find Farid bang in the middle of it, franctically pointing at the hut.

There was someone moving inside it. The guard was up!

Deep breath, nothing to worry here, I kept telling myself, as I quickly walked across the compound. The cats sat up and stared at me with their green eyes.

The gate was a few metres away and the guard could easily step out of his hut and stop me. My heart was pounding in my throat and sweat trickled down my back.

Shit. Fuck. Shit.

This never happened to the clever detectives in my books. All I could think of was making it to the gate. The gate. The gate. Farid was holding it open for me.

The guard had just opened the door to his hut when I reached. Farid quickly shut the gate behind me and then yelled, 'Run!'

I bolted straight out, and didn't stop to look back. Farid was already ahead of me, running down the alley. I could hear someone shouting behind me, but I didn't dare to look back. I wondered if I should hide or carry on running...if he had a gun, I would be an easy target. But there was nowhere to hide because the alley was too narrow and all the houses that flanked it were locked. I ran faster than I had ever run in my life. I wasn't sure if I heard footsteps behind me, but I was too petrified to look.

'Left,' Farid shouted.

We took the corner, Farid was well ahead of me. The narrow alley now veered slightly to the right. No people, just goats in front of us. We kept running despite the fact that I was now wheezing. I followed Farid blindly as he expertly navigated through the serpentine alleys. I could see the end of the alley and the main road up ahead. No more than fifty metres and we would be able to blend in with the crowd. I pulled up my headscarf. Few more metres. The road got wider and wider and in another moment we were out in a busy roadside market. Finally, we slowed down. No one was following us. We walked normally in the crowd, trying to seem like casual shoppers. The crowds enveloped us in their safety. I hailed a taxi and we got in.

Inside, we high-fived.

Farid beamed at me. 'Did you find what you were looking for?' he asked.

I smiled. 'I think I did, Farid.'

'We did it! We are supermen!'

I smiled. 'Indeed Farid-jan—superman and superwoman.'

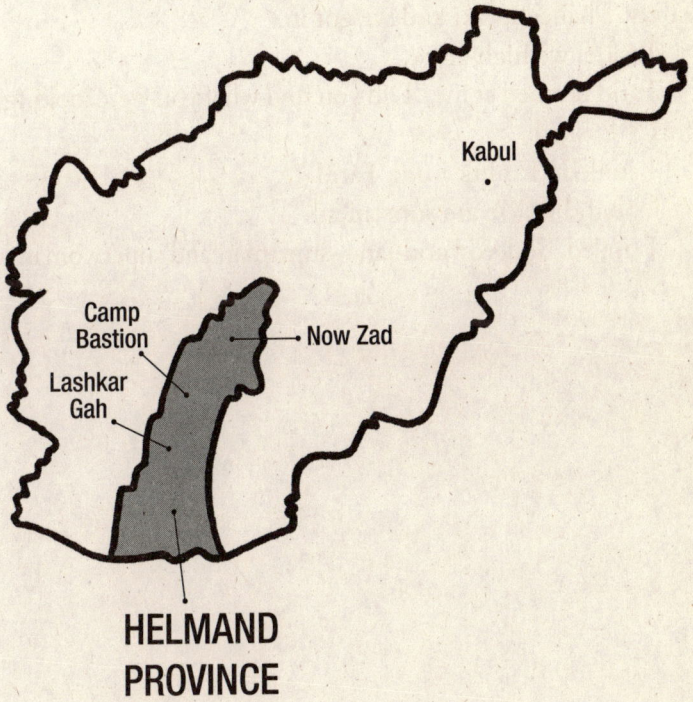

Kabul

Camp
Bastion

Lashkar
Gah

Now Zad

**HELMAND
PROVINCE**

19

It wasn't even 5 am and the airbase was bustling like a beehive. As if it was completely normal for people to be cheery and functional with their coffee at this time. The holding area had hundreds of soldiers waiting to board the plane. Some were going back home to the UK, some to fight another war against another enemy. I loved waiting to get on a military plane. The thrill of an unknown adventure! But my situation was, in truth, very different to the hundreds of uniformed men around me, who were queuing up for the battle zone. We could always get out if things got too hairy, we always knew that the awful conditions we had to endure were only for a few days, not months on end. But most importantly, we knew that we wouldn't have to kill anyone. Here, like everywhere in the military areas, there are strict rules. If you don't obey them, you get kicked out. We waited in a slow snaking line that ended at the plane.

Tim, Kelly, and I wore our flak jackets. Our blue flaks stood out amid the sea of khaki and camouflage. It felt good to be back in my body armour, similar to a heavy waistcoat with the exception that this could save your life. It had a massive ceramic plate stitched into the front, designed to protect your heart from an impact. It was embossed with my blood group, A+, should I need a blood transfusion after being hit. And my name—A. Sanderson. I don't wear the ones that have 'PRESS' written on them, it makes no difference because insurgents can't read. The flak weighs nearly ten kilos and takes some time getting used to. But when I take take it off, I feel naked, vulnerable. You learn to love it, a bit like your favourite designer jacket, but for a very different reason.

On board, we sat on thin benches next to the wall. Seatbelts were hanging from the walls and our luggage was piled up in the middle of the plane, among other military paraphernalia, water tanks, and mail bags. The lights were switched off and in a few moments, the flight took off. The soldiers had blank expressions and stared solemnly into space. We were flying first to the Kandahar airbase and then to Camp Bastion where we would be put on a convoy going north. It's a drill I had done hundreds of times before and knew it well.

'I'm scared,' Kelly whispered in my ear. 'I've only been to one embed before.'

I understood what she was going through because I remember how terrified I had been on my first trip as an emebedded journalist. It meant living like a soldier, even though you have had no formal training in frontline combat.

My first time was in Iraq, with the Americans. In the end, very little had happened but I developed the taste for it. There was an adrenaline rush to it, which I loved. I squeezed Kelly's hand and whispered back, 'Don't worry, they won't let us die.'

But even as I consoled her, I was half-wrecked with guilt.

152

I was taking the people I loved the most to the frontline. I know it had started off as an idea to nail Ropey, but suddenly it had become bigger than life. Taking the decision to go on the trip had been the only easy part. I remembered telling them about my findings.

Tim, Kelly, and I had been hanging out in our favourite spot at L'Atmosphere restaurant, with the afternoon sun on our faces, sipping cold beer, and watching the stream of people wandering in and out.

'Shall we play "I shagged him/her" again?' Kelly asked.

'No because you know you'll lose. Plus we have work to do,' I replied.

I showed them the text Loxman sent me about the embed to Helmand being approved. Our plan was to go down to Camp Bastion, and from there, take a lift with a convoy to Lashkar Gah. I showed them the photos I had taken at Rich's house and the itinerary I had found.

Wednesday CP. Thur LG. Fri NZ Camp. CP for Camp Bastion, LG for Lashkar Gah, and NZ had to be a name of another frontline camp.

Kelly had been excited. 'We can just try to follow him and then, ta-da, surprise him when he is about to seal the deal,' she had said.

'I don't think it'll be as simple as that. Remember it's a military zone and they'll be watching us like hawks,' I had explained patiently.

'You always manage to sneak out for extra curricular activities,' Tim had said, his voice dripping with sarcasm.

'Sex is a powerful weapon. It gets you to places,' I retaliated.

'So I don't see why can't we use it now?' said Tim.

'What? Shag our way to the Taliban?' I snorted.

'Well, not exactly, but we could send our lovely Kelly there to seduce enough high ranking buggers who will then open all the important doors for us incase she'll kiss and tell. Gentle blackmail, dear!'

I had wondered why he didn't say that I should do the seduction bit but maybe he was just trying to be nice after his acidic comment about me shagging my way around military bases. I had let it pass.

It was dawn when Camp Bastion's lights sparkled below us. It was a mini town bang in the middle of the Afghan desert. One day I hoped it would be gone because that would mean the end of the war.

After landing, we were transferred into a minibus that trundled away to the main base.

Rows and rows of tents billowed in the gentle breeze. Signs to 'showers', 'toilets', 'gym'—all spoke of an orderly, disciplined life, but at the same time it felt freakish to be in this desert mini-town. The bus dropped us off outside a tent that was identical to the hundreds around us. We dumped our bags inside and stepped out to have a look about. The sunlight was spreading through the sky and the ghost tent city was slowly waking up to a new day.

We settled into the main camp bar with our coffees and cigarettes. A feeling of restlessness gripped me and I couldn't quite work out whether I was nervous about this trip or whether I thought coming here was a big mistake. It was stupid to put our lives at risk. I watched the non-stop stream of soldiers go past us on their morning jog and convinced myself that it was all for a good cause. But there was one eventuality I wasn't prepared for. As my eyes wandered past the uniforms, I saw a flash of colour in the sea of camouflage.

It was a pink flash. And it only meant one thing in this part of the world.

I checked again to make sure I wasn't mistaken. Nope. There she was, amid all the hunky soldiers, polished and shiny, despite all the dust. Was she immune to dust? Maybe she used a glossing spray to cover herself with. Her head was turned towards the runners so I was able to observe her without her seeing me. She looked as if she had just stepped out of a fashion glossy. Even her handbag was OTT designery with big glitzy padlocks and dangly things. Dior I think. Not very war zone like. She did, however, have her blue flak jacket casually hanging from her arm. I bet none of the soldiers dared to tell her to put it on. Fashion faux pas aside, there was one question I wanted an answer to—why was she here?

We finished our cigarettes and strolled into the press tent for our briefing with the A Company—a name usually given to a group of soldiers who were going to be our host. There were two tents, one for the press bodies to live in and the other was a makeshift office where they held the briefings in. It was all set up to look like an ordinary corporate office, complete with whiteboards and projectors, which was a bit freaky because we were, after all, in the middle of a desert.

There were lots of important looking men, all standing very upright, eyeing Kelly and I hungrily. Name tags. These men loved name tags. It gave them a sense of identity.

'Look at Major Donald and Sergeant Duck,' Kelly whispered, reading my thoughts.

They were standing next to Loxman along with a couple of other press types. Loxman had flown here a day before to host us. They did look comical and it made me snigger.

Tim nudged me to stop playing the fool.

The plan was for us to travel north with a supply convoy. Loxman had already warned us several times that the trip was risky, but our cheery trio knew the drill.

The briefing began with Loxman introducing everyone. 'This is Major Donald, head of strategy, and he will fill you in about the trip and answer any question that you have. 'I wouldn't mind him filling me with something,' Kelly whispered in my ear and I had to surpress my snigger.

'Always bring the bar just a bit lower, Kell,' I whispered.

Loxman looked at us and cleared his throat.

'The road is littered with bombs, so the sooner we get to Lashkar Gah, the better,' said Loxman. 'We will only stop en route if necessary, and then push on north.'

'If necessary' meant if there was an attack and there were casualties. We were only allowed to travel in the vehicle at the back of the convoy, since that would be the one which would take the least hit, should we get hit by a bomb.

Major Donald, a man in his fifties, spoke, 'Once you get to the town of Lashkar Gah, you can go on a foot patrol to meet the villagers. They are holding a shura—a meeting of village elders—which you can attend. You need to follow our rules at *all* times. You know this better than anyone else, Anna. Kidnapping two journos might be a good idea for the locals, so you are at your own risk. Is that clear?'

We nodded in unison.

Loxman interrupted. 'The entire trip is about a week-long, depending, of course, on the circumstances. We should be able to Chinook you back from Lashkar Gah. But all the plans may change at a moment's notice as you may already know.' Chinooking back was military talk for a copter ride. We were lucky to get that because journos were not a priority, but fighting was.

'We are unable to give you a time schedule yet, but we should be able to get on the road in the next few days. Any questions?' Major Donald asked.

We shook our heads. Our lesson was over.

'Are you thinking what I am thinking?' Kelly asked as soon as we stepped out of the tent.

'We get to Lashkar Gah. Work the shura for clues and then get on the road to this NZ place.'

'Exactamundo, my dear. That indeed makes a good plan, you're a step ahead.'

'But will the bastards let us talk to the villagers?' Tim asked.

'Sure they will, we'll just give them some bullshit about needing to talk to the villagers without the army being there.'

'And if they don't, we can always get Kelly to distract them.' Tim and I laughed.

20

Back in our tent, the three of us were trying to catch up on some much-deserved sleep. We had arrived early, and were tired from the journey. However, my ringing cell phone did not give me that luxury and woke me up from my deep sleep. Disorientated, I turned over on my bunk bed to reach for it.

It was 11 am local time, quite early in London, too early for anyone to be in the newsroom, but still the familiar number of the GNN newsdesk flashed up on the screen of my new, MOD—Ministry of Defence—provided phone. They gave us phones here because they liked to keep a track of us. Little did they know that we had, a couple of other phones. The reason for tracking us was that a couple of journos had been caught red handed trying to sneak into Camp Bastion's detention centre where the so-called war criminals were held. Something that did not delight the defence ministry. War criminal is an ugly tag and conjures up all kinds of ghastly images. Not that Camp Bastion was a cuddly place. It was the key to all logistics involving the killing of people. After the incident, they installed twenty-four-hour surveillance on all hacks. I still managed to sneak in and out of a few places where I shouldn't have been at Camp Bastion, well, mainly in and out from various bunk beds.

'Anna Sanderson,'

'Sorry to wake you, Anna.' It was Phil. And it wasn't a courtesy call.

'That's okay, you know me, dreaming of news twenty four by seven.'

'Well done for getting there so fast,' he said and took a deep breath.

There was more to come. People like Phil didn't do niceties.

'Um. I know you've had no preparation, but we've just discovered that the Prime Minister is going to be at Camp Bastion the day after tomorrow. You know how Number 10 works—they never tell you anything about his schedule. I want you to focus on that and leave the other stuff—for now.'

Fuck. The plan was crumbling right before my eyes. London doesn't waste any time. We had only just got here. So they couldn't get anyone else here on time for the PM's visit but it seemed a bit brutal. Then again, TV channels are not known for being huggy-feely work places.

'Okay, Phil. But on one condition. You get these guys to take us north after the PM's visit.'

'What is so important up there?'

'I can't say much right now but we are onto a biggie.'

'Well I can't authorize it unless I know more.'

I was getting irritated by his bureaucracy.

'Phil, how long have you known me?'

'What's that got to do with this?

'Because when I say trust me, you should. You know I always deliver.' I tried to convince him.

'Anna, you know what the permits are like these days, the military has gone hysterical about who it wants to take on embeds. Luckily, it seems you are their number one pet right now, so I guess I'll just leave it to you.'

Number one pet? Where did he get that from?

'Wow, that's what I always wanted in life,' I yawned. 'I just have to clear it here first. Can you email me a permission request?'

'Okay. But please bring me a tough one with the PM, no softly-softly there.' He rang off.

I was jumping from one story to another endelessly and there was no end in sight. Life at the moment felt like the surrounding desert sand between my fingers, rapidly slipping away. But maybe it was good for me. After all, I wasn't very good at doing nothing and I had no one to go to home to. I wanted to continue doing what I did best—uncovering and reporting news. The PM's visit would mean that our trip out to the wild west of Talibania was likely to be delayed because of massive security ops. Then it struck me.

That explains the pink dragon's presence. Never one to miss out on a big story. So maybe she wasn't after our story. Or maybe she was. Who the hell knew what Shabita was after anyway? Did she know something I didn't? Was Mark feeding her information? I pushed the last thought aside and concentrated on the work that was ahead of me.

It was going to be a busy couple of days. We had satellites to book, research to do, questions to write, filming spots to scout. The first press conference was scheduled for tomorrow. Then there would be meet and greets and after that, departure.

Later in the morning, Tim and I sat eating cold scrambled eggs with soggy toast discussing our work for the next few days. Kelly rarely ate anything you couldn't have a beer with, so breakfast wasn't her thing. Oh the glamour of war reporting!

All this time I could sense that Tim had been increasingly getting uncomfortable in my presence, but I couldn't tell the reason behind his prissy behaviour. Something was bugging him, so I decided to bite the bullet.

'Tim, may I ask you something?'

He barely nodded.

'Have I done something to upset you? You have been acting weird recently, ever since I got back from my last embed.'

He chewed his mouthful carefully, and then looked at me, straight in the eye, with an intensity that was unsettling.

'Anna, I've been meaning…' he started, as if measuring every word. 'It's just that…'

Suddenly a bouncy Kelly came over and sat down all excited. 'What a great place, a bit like a spa holiday with hot men but without the spa.'

'Do you two never talk about anything else except finding a man?' Tim said. The bitterness was back.

'What else is there?' Kelly laughed.

He stood up, muttering something about going to sort out filming spots and satellite co-ordinates, and left.

'What's up with him?' Kelly asked.

'I've no idea. Maybe it's all the testosterone around here that's making him behave like a jealous old queen.'

I hoped Kelly was right.

It was a hot, slow afternoon. Camp Bastion seemed quiet for once. I decided to take a walk to think things through. The madness of the past few weeks was beginning to take shape behind the safe walls of this place; Rich was surely involved in the arms trade with two other guys. I had a foreboding that something was going to happen in the next few days.

I looked around at all the men going past, busy with their duties. Why couldn't I just find a nice man to date? Why did things with me and Mark have to go off the boil? Mark, lovely Mark, a man who I could not shake off, no matter how hard I tried. I had to force myself to repeat the single girl's mantra of 'plenty more fish in the sea' in my head. I reminded myself that this was the ideal place to enjoy some eye candy. Pretty much the only perk of this miserable job. I recalled seeing a gym a couple of tents back, so I decided to cheer myself up—not by working out, but with some good ogling.

Dance music was thumping out from the tent as I approached. The gym was divided into two separate areas—one section for weights and another for cardio training. It was a bustling hive of toned and bronzed male bodies. I was wearing sweatpants and trainers, so I could easily pass off as an innocent gym-goer, rather than a horny spy. I climbed onto one of the exercise bikes and began pedalling, not something I do very often. Exercise was not my thing, and I felt silly pedalling in one place. But the view that I had from this bike was priceless.

In the far left corner of the tent were two late twenty-something males, both blessed with what I would call 'ideal muscle tone'. Both men were taking turns to lift weights, and their hard torsos provoked a feeling of warmth inside me, which I knew was not related to my token efforts at cycling. I began to fantasize about what it would be like with these two hunks together.

I imagined them caressing me very gently, their hot breath on my neck, their hands running over my breasts and arse. My nipples hardened at the thought. One of them would pull down my pants and slip his finger inside my knickers while the other would push down my bra and kiss my nipples.

I was beginning to feel hot and wet between my legs.

We would undress one another and I would lie in between them, allowing both men to suck and lick my erect nipples while their hands caressed every part of my body. Their hands would travel down my stomach and caress my thigh. One of them would move down and run his tongue along my pussy, slowly, while the other would bend over my mouth and make me suck his hard cock.

My breath was now coming short and fast. I kept my eyes on the two men who had now started to work on their abs.

Soon they would both be playing with my pussy while I pleasured them both at the same time—their hard cocks pulsating in my hands. When we were done with foreplay, one of them would fuck me from behind while the other would feed his firm cock into me from the front.

I pushed my throbbing clit hard against the saddle but couldn't contain my urges. I felt tight and tense and decided I had had enough of this kind of exercise. I hurried back to my tent, hoping there would be no one there. I was in luck, Tim and Kelly were out.

I stood in the doorway of my tent, pushed my hand down my trousers and rubbed my swollen clitoris. After just a few strokes with my finger, I felt weak at the knees and gasped as I felt the sweet, orgasmic waves overtake me.

21

The press tent was a beehive of activity. Journos were drifting in and out and about twenty MOD flunkies were handing out our name badges and briefing packs. Womanizing war-hacks and diva correspondents, all happily pretended to be friends with one another. But only until the curtains went up. Then there would be tantrums over who would get the exclusive with the PM. Most journos at this level were prissy. They all wore a look of self-importance, with notepads and laminated passes hanging around their neck. For this briefing, UK's finest political hacks were in town and they were all smiles, flak jackets, and desert scarfs. Their chatter rung through the tent.

'You know me, tough as old boots. We've been through worse. Remember that time in Lebanon?'

Air kisses.

'Have you just got back from Syria?'

Hand shakes.

'Weren't you in Libya last month?'

There was no end to it.

And yours truly was no exception. You weren't in this business for over ten years without knowing who you were in the pecking order. Okay, so I wasn't particular about my hair or my 'good side' on TV, but I did not want to be told off for looking like a wreck after doing a decent job. Which has happened to me a couple of times. I was once on a particularly tough assignment in Liberia for five weeks, only to be told by some Diane Von Fursterberg-wearing newsroom boss to 'comb out my nest'.

I was just about to grab one of the press officers to ask about the day's running order, when I saw the sequinned dragon at the back of the tent.

Fucking hell.

I just couldn't deal with her right now. Her shiny, black hair was neatly in place and her make-up was flawless. She was wearing very tight jeans and heeled boots with gold studs on them. Her pink v-neck top was generously cut and she was wearing what seemed like large diamond studs in her ears. She caught me looking at her.

'Hey, Annaa my daaaarling, fancy seeing you here,' she cooed.

Why was she speaking in that weird fake accent? What was it now? Pashtun?

I muttered my hello and turned my back to her. But she wouldn't leave me.

'Have you come here for the PM, or do you have bigger fish to fry…hmm?'

My face fell. Bigger fish to fry? She wasn't meant to know anything. I wanted to punch the shine out of her. All of Afghanistan was like a playground for journos with its own bullies. I didn't let out anything, and decided to ignore her. She was sizing up my appearance but I pretended not to notice. There was nothing wrong with my well fitting combat trousers and simple white vest top. My hair was in a ponytail and I had my trusted desert boots on. I was ready to run if something happened. The way I was dressed was far more appropriate than looking like an ageing Spice Girl sans dog/children/arm candy, ready for a photo shoot.

'You know the *Mail* does make-over stories—they could do a story on you and get rid of that "war-zone" chic,' she sneered.

'Thanks for your concern, Shabita, but really, no thanks. I feel pretty good like this,' I tried to contain my irritation.

'Think about it, Anna, you might even get a double spread. And I'm sure you have plenty other heroic military tales up your sleeve,' she continued sarcastically. 'A little birdie told me about your special relationships,' she said looking past me.

Special relationships? What did she mean?

I already knew she had no morals when it came to furthering her career, but what on earth gave her the impression that I might be interested in talking to the likes of her? I turned my head slowly towards her but did not respond, just looked over her shoulder.

'If you're not prepared to share what you know, I may have to resort to other means.'

I loved the way she called it 'sharing'. In my circle, this would be branded as outright blackmail.

'What do you want?' I finally said.

She spoke very slowly, in a measured tone, this time without the fake accent. 'Anna, I know all about your men and your desperate attempts to pull any man in a uniform, you sad cow. There is more than enough in it for me to write a pretty nice piece for the gossip mags. "A desperate single girl's sexploits in a war zone". Frontline fuckfest,' she spat out the words, and smiled.

I couldn't believe what I was hearing. Bitch.

'It's a *Daily Mail* dream—the promiscuous career woman. Not that you would have much of a career after the piece!' she continued venomously.

I had no idea what she had on me—how did she know about my penchant for uniformed men? Had I left a trail of too many broken hearts? Panic started to rise up in me. I had lost count of how many officers, majors, and lieutenant generals I had slept with over the years.

'I have no idea what you're on about,' I said coolly, trying not to show my fear.

She smiled slowly. Like a serial killer.

'I know why you are really here. We want the same story but I want you to drop it. Go home instead, or back to Kabul,' she said sweetly, inspecting her nails.

That horsey snort. Those horsey teeth. Glistening in the sun like a bad advert for tooth whitener.

'Aww, don't look so crestfallen. Okay, how about I cut you a deal. I'll let this juicy *Mail* story lie, but in return you give me all the names of the guys down in Lashkar Gah and your notes in exchange for my silence.'

'Why should I give you anything at all? I have nothing to hide,' I was seething.

She scoffed. 'Oh honey, I have a list of names as long as my arm. Let's just say your life hasn't exactly been, how should I put it…discreet.'

Something snapped in me. 'I'll keep an eye out for your piece. Good luck.' I stood up with my back straight, and turned away from her.

Tears were streaming down my face as I walked towards Tim. He saw my face and grabbed me by the arm.

Once outside, he took one look at my face and handed me a ciggie. I told him, in between sobs, about Shabita's threat.

'She's full of shit, you know that. There's no way any of those guys would have told her anything. They'll be risking their reputation. But you have been very discreet. Right?' he asked.

Neither Tim, nor anyone else, knew the full extent of my adventures. Christ, I lost count past 100 but I think he had a pretty good idea, and still never judged me. He took my hand. 'Just try to ignore her. If she goes to the *Mail*, she will have to give you a right to reply. It's the best you can do because I know you, Anna, you would rather die of shame than give away this Lashkar Gah story.'

'My worry is that she'll follow us and try to snoop around. There is nothing worse than spotting a bit of leopard print in the undergrowth in Helmand.'

'Stop worrying, she has no idea. It's just all talk, you know how she operates.'

His words offered little comfort to me. Despite the hot day, I felt a chill run down my spine. Just then, we got a call from the press tent—the conference was about to start.

The PM, who was followed by ten well-armed and beefy bodyguards, looked more haggard than when I saw him last. And his morale-boosting speech hardly revealed anything new. It was simply a lot of clichés put together—'victory', 'sacrifice', and 'world peace'.

Shabita had perched her perfect bottom right in the front row, and as soon as the floor was open for questions, her hand shot right up.

'Mr Prime Minister, is there an exit plan in sight?'

What a stupid question, I thought. He had clearly said that there would be a review in two years. Hadn't she listened to what he had said in his speech?

The PM who had enough experience dealing with journalists patiently answered her question. She tried to get in more questions but someone took away the microphone and she sat there sulking for the rest of the press conference.

The conference was over in just an hour. We were ushered to the officers' mess where the PM would be served lunch, just like 'one of the boys'. It looked as staged as it was in reality. The PM kept flashing a toothy smile for the cameras but nothing could rescue him from the artificialness of the situation. He sat down eating mass-produced, poor quality English food, and tried to keep up a polite chatter while wrestling with a tough cut of roast beef with a plastic knife. Tim kept himself busy, trying to get some good shots. After one last mouthful of roast beef, some firm handshakes, and a statesman-like wave, the PM was gone, and the base returned to normalcy.

Tim and I headed out to look for a good spot to do our live link to the London studio. It was still early in the day, but the heat was already weighing heavily in the air. We got lucky and found a nice, shadowy corner with a good backdrop of a row of armoured cars.

If there was time, I always preferred to practice my live reports before going on air. However easy they looked for people at home, I still got butterflies even after several years of doing them. Sometimes I worried if I would start laughing or swear uncontrollably in front of the camera. Reporter's Tourettes, it was called in the trade. I've fucked up a few times, got figures and names wrong, but I take a lot of pride in my work and even with a heavy hangover, I can usually deliver a couple of minutes of chat in fluent 'journalese'.

As we started to test out our equipment, the queen bee herself marched over, yelling at her cameraman. Her fake accent was gone again.

'You idiot, why didn't you set up here before like everyone else?' she yelled. 'We've missed all the best spots now. Let's go next to the GNN guys, at least someone here seems to know what they're doing.'

They pitched up their camera just a few metres from us. Tim wasn't happy.

'Guys, if you set up there you'll be interfering with our sound. Do you mind moving a bit further?' Tim asked politely.

'Sorry, but as accredited media, we have the same right

to be here as you,' Shabita hissed. Her hair shimmered in the sun as she tossed it back in annoyance.

This was TV bitchiness at its finest. If only I could have recorded it.

'I know that, and sorry to point out the obvious, but your voice will come through to our broadcast, so please, can you move? There's miles of space around us,' he replied, standing his ground.

Shabita's cameraman looked sheepish and apologized when Shabita's back was turned. I thought I had seen him before in Kabul. He seemed like a nice guy but had sadly ended up working with the sequinned dragon herself. Shabita and her cameraman shunted their kit closer to the tent which, in my humble opinion, wasn't such a great backdrop. She then busied herself with a pocket mirror and a make-up palette. More lip-gloss and hairspray, and a comical pouting rehearsal followed. She really was in love with herself.

We finally got a line to London, albeit a bad one, and off I went with my well-rehearsed routine. Before I realized, our time was up and I got a 'Cheers, Anna' in my ear before the line went dead. Hours of hard work over in just 2.5 minutes.

As we were packing up, I looked around one last time. I wondered how things would be here in five years' time. Would the foreign soldiers be gone and the guns have fallen silent? How nice it would be if the Afghans could wake up to the sounds of normalcy—cooking in the kitchen, the bleat of goats, bird's song, and the happy chatter of children—instead of news about their country being torn to pieces.

22

It must have been half past twelve when I woke up with the urge to pee. I groaned and heaved myself but of bed. The day had worn me out and I don't remember at which point I had fallen asleep. I cursed myself for being lazy. The women's toilets were two blocks away so I had been using the boys' cubicles instead. Just as I was about to leave, I heard someone else come in. The last thing I wanted was being admonished by the staff for breaking the rules and that too for using the wrong toilet.

The person seemed to tiptoe in and didn't seem to notice that one of the cubicles was occupied. Thankfully, I hadn't turned on the lights. After a couple of minutes, I heard a second voice. They were both whispering, but all I could make out was 'it's all clear, come in'.

A sound suggested that one of them had gone into a cubicle. It was followed by more whispers, some shuffling, and then what sounded like kissing. Suddenly a familiar voice cut into the still night air. The tone was commanding. 'Stand on the seat.'

I couldn't believe it. It was Loxman, who, it seemed was

having some forbidden fun with a colleague in the middle of the night. I stifled my giggle.

So his macho act made sense now, it was all a front.

One of the men was now breathing heavily and I assumed he was either giving or getting a blow job. They stopped every now and then to make sure no one came in but I could recognize familiar slurping sounds and occasional sighs.

It didn't last long and the men clearly took turns in pleasuring each other. I didn't dare move and focused on keeping my breathing as inaudible as possible. I just hoped the two would finish their playtime quickly.

I wondered how often these two men met, and whether it was a proper love affair or just a bit of fun to pass the time. Loxman didn't get to take part in frontline fighting, his role was to chaperone journalists around and act as a mediator in discussions. Maybe he was bored of being stuck with his non-combatant role.

Or, given what I was hearing, maybe not.

Either way, the MOD would not be happy if they got a wind of this. It would be a scandal. The military PR machine always tries to cultivate an image of soldiers as courageous, muscular, uber-hetero men who are monogamous and dedicated to their families. Or, if they are single, as sports-loving, straight men.

This is, of course, all bullshit. Like in the real world, the army has men of different sexual orientations, which some may find hard to stomach. It's this macho image that helps the army recruit young men. If I were to report my nocturnal discovery, it would cause a real scandal and no doubt lead to an internal enquiry. A media blackout would be imposed and, if word got out, denials would be issued and a marketing campaign would be put in place to ensure the army's reputation as a place for 'real men' remained untarnished.

Loxman's secret would be safe with me. In a way, I felt sorry for him—we all need a bit of closeness, one way or the other. Their affair may not have been the love story of the century but who was to judge that a quick blowjob in a portaloo in the middle of the desert was meaningless?

Maybe the story of his so-called fiancé was just a front.

It sounded as if Loxman and his partner had nearly finished their illicit fun. One of them was very close to a climax. 'Faster, harder,' he whispered.

'That's good, oh god, oh yes.'

The heavy breathing gradually came to an end and I could hear the two men cleaning themselves up and zipping up. They left the cubicle one after the other. 'Same time, Thursday?' whispered the other guy.

'Sure thing, sexy,' came Loxman's breathless reply.

The door closed behind them and silence followed. After waiting for a minute or so, I sneaked out.

Back in the tent, Tim and Kelly lay sleeping, blissfully unaware of the twilight shenanigans. This wasn't the first time I had come across gay sex in the military. When I was in Baghdad in the Green Zone, there were plenty of clandestine liaisons going on behind the scenes—in empty rooms, cars, and, of course, in the gents' toilets. I heard stories about wild orgies taking place because people who were stuck inside the Zone had so very little to do to entertain themselves.

Many military men are sex-starved, having left their wives behind and being bound by strict rules. As usual the male-to-female ratio here was about 1:100, so if no women were available it was kind of inevitable that some guys looked to their male counterparts for sexual gratification, and even a relationship.

It was upto Loxman how he got his rocks off. Portaloo maybe seedy for many, but for him there was no other alternative.

Heart FM was blaring out from the next tent. It was a smooth jazzy Sunday for the listeners of the station that liked to think Cher was still the epitome of cool. Kelly, Tim, and I huddled over the mobile, trying to block out the music. Ali Ahmad was on the speaker phone.

Ali Ahmad had been hard at work in Kabul and brought us some much needed good news.

'You need to meet someone at Camp Bastion's Afghan workers' quarters tonight. No one must see you,' the phone crackled. 'This man, his name is Omid, knows the contact you need in Lashkar Gah.'

'I know where the workers' quarters are. What's the lead?' I said.

'Omid's cousin is part of the chain and he knows the

details about the next transfer. It's not easy to keep things secret in Lashkar Gah. He can also tail the Westerners if you can't.'

It all sounded pretty straightforward, like all good plans, but experience had taught me that this was rarely the case. Still, I usually went along foolishly, hoping for the best. Besides, we didn't have anything else to follow up on.

'Tonight at 8 pm. Be there.'

'Roger that,' I said as he hung up.

The darkness shielded us as we sneaked out of our air conditioned tent. Earlier in the evening, I had casually strolled around the camp to work out where the entrance to the Afghan workers' quarters was, and to map out escape routes, which is always an important factor. A fence ran along the perimeter of the quarter. And I had spotted something—a tiny break in the fence, enough to get me in and out.

There were thousands of locals working at the base, helping out with cleaning, cooking, and often just carrying things around. It was cheaper to hire a few hundred Afghans to transport things manually than send a great big lorry out into the desert. The workers were housed in modest tents, very different from ours. Just a basic piece of tarpaulin, shielded them from the sun and dust. No air conditioners or showers, they had to get by with an outdoor tap and some buckets.

'"Shaft" is going to be your indicator to get the hell out if it looks like trouble,' Tim had told me earlier.

The three of us were almost back in the good old days. He had played the song on his mobile as we danced to it, sang along and laughed.

You're damn right!
Who is the man that would risk his neck for his brother, man?
(Shaft!)
Can ya dig it?

Who's the cat that won't cop out
when there's danger all about?
(Then we can dig it.)

He's a complicated man,
but no one understands him but his woman.

We were hysterical by the time the song was over and I felt like Tim, my friend, had come back from the dark place he had been.

I slipped into the area through the opening while Kelly and Tim kept vigil. I had told Ali Ahmad to inform Omid to meet me near the break.

If we were caught in here, we would be thrown out of the camp and it would put an end to our careers—at least in Afghanistan. What we were doing was not illegal, but accessing unauthorized areas was strictly forbidden. But we weren't the first journos to break the rules, and surely weren't going to be the last.

Omid was waiting for me in the shadow of a tent. He was a kind-looking man, maybe in his forties, with a wrinkled face and tired eyes. Maybe he, too, had seen too much and had had enough of the war. He gestured me to sit down on the tattered carpet. I took off my shoes and sat next to him. He handed me a notepad with Pashto writing on it.

'My cousin was pretending to be a cleaner who didn't speak English. He was spying on these two Westerners who are in Lashkar Gah. He got to their guesthouse by bribing the guards. One takes care of all the money matters, while the other oversees the transfers,' he spoke quickly.

I looked at the notes as he translated the text.

'They deal with anything you can think of, mainly arms, but raw opium too. And occasionally they sell humans too—children, to rich Arabs,' he said. 'It is rumoured that the group has some Pakistani nuclear heads stashed away somewhere,' he continued in a steady voice.

They were good notes, but wouldn't stand up in court, because they were merely story leads.

Omid said there were about twenty people involved in the operation and that everyone took a cut. The highest earners were the white guys. The one who arranged the deal made about USD 50,000 per sale, depending upon the number of stolen weapons he sold, but a little-used RPG could fetch upto USD 7,000. He showed me more notes from phone calls to various sources. Now, this was good evidence.

'The transaction does not happen in Lashkar Gah but in Now Zad—an empty town further up north,' he said.

Ah. NZ.

He looked at me and said, 'Now Zad is not a good place, Miss Anna.'

'Why not?'

'There are many things that are wrong up there.'

I asked him to continue.

He told me that the weapons were often stored in Now Zad because it was essentially a ghost town with just a few insignificant villages around that were loosely supported by the Taliban, but not in any strategic way. No one suspected anyone to be there and the two sides could make their deals away from prying eyes. There were more details, and I was writing it all down as fast as I could.

'Who is protecting the men there?' I asked.

Omid took a deep breath. He got a wild look in his eyes, as if he was frightened that someone was listening. 'There is one guy...'

'What's his name?'

'Shah. Shah Jayan.'

'Where do I find him?'

Omid shook his head. 'You can't. He is more likely to find you.'

Suddenly I heard a familiar tune.

Who's the black private
dick that's a sex machine to all the chicks?
(Shaft!)
You're damn right.

I got up, handed him two hundred dollars, and thanked him.

'Be careful out there, ma'am,' he said, as he carefully folded the money and slipped it inside his salwar kameez.

I had to nail these guys. I was so close now.

Still holding my shoes, I started to hurry towards the opening in the fence. The night was silent, as if it was holding its breath. Twenty metres and I was through.

Ten.

I could see the break in the fence right in front of me. I took a deep breath, and just as I was about to step through, I felt a hand on my shoulder. I froze. And then suddenly another hand grabbed my waist. I suppressed a scream and turned around.

23

Even though it was pitch dark, I could still make out Mark's familiar outline.

'What the hell?' I hissed.

'That's what I want to ask you. I followed you, you idiot. You know you are trespassing a military zone.'

'How did you even know I was here?'

'Anna, you have to listen to me. What you are about to do is not only extremely dangerous but also very foolish.'

'Do tell me more. You seem to know my plans better than I do. And why don't you broadcast it to your journo friends while you're at it.'

He ignored my spite. 'I know about Rich and his henchmen. You have to believe me when I say stay away from them.'

'I have no idea what you're talking about. And who are you to tell me what to do?' I huffed angrily.

Who *did* this guy think he was, ordering me around like I was his kid sister?

Suddenly it came to me. He was sent after me by that sequinned devil herself! She knew my weakness was six-foot-something mysterious types, and this was possibly the worst plot she could hatch.

Before I had a chance to pour my anger on him, he grabbed my wrist and pulled me to a narrow gap between the fence and a large container.

Just in time. I saw three soldiers approaching the area on what seemed like a routine patrol. We waited quietly for them to pass. The desert night stood silently, listening to our urgent heartbeats.

Whose side was he on?

He could have easily grassed me up and had me kicked out. That would really give Shabita a kick.

He held me tightly in his grip. I felt like a pathetic little girl, not the strong, independent woman I told myself I was.

'Anna. You have to trust me,' he said looking into my eyes.

'Why should I?'

'Because…because I care about you.'

Oh yeah. Because Shabita gave you good head after you've been a good boy.

'Leave me alone. You know nothing about me. Nor should you care about my business. You're one of those egotistical men who think they can have every woman eating from their hand. Well, you're wrong. I am not one of those women.'

'It isn't like that,' he said quietly.

'Then how is it?' I mocked him.

'There is simply too much at stake. This isn't some Nancy Drew plot where you and your sidekicks go unearth a mystery, it's simply too big. Anna, please, let it go, this is no longer just a story.'

I was slowly shaking with rage. How dare he come after me, undermine our investigations, and call my friends 'sidekicks'! And asking me to give up? Doesn't he know Anna Sanderson never gives up on a good story!

It was hard to stay angry because his brown eyes shone in the dark and his body was warm and inviting. I wanted to bury myself in his arms, and believe in everything he said, but somewhere flashes of alarm in the colour of glittery pink kept surfacing.

'I don't have to listen to this bullshit,' I tore my hand off his grip and started to run.

I was desperate because he was hurting me. Not physically, but by just standing there, all lovely. I've had boyfriends before, but with Mark, things were so complicated. It was as if my normal, rational brain was somehow replaced by a huge bleeding heart. Something I didn't know I had before.

Tears were streaming down my face as I ran across the yard.

Suddenly a powerful light focused on me and I heard a shout.

'Stop running. You are a suspect. Drop your weapons.'

Bollocks! I knew that lark wasn't a little birdie. I just hoped Kelly and Tim hadn't been busted.

Three soldiers came towards me. 'This way,' one of them said, and I had no choice but to follow them. I looked behind me, but Mark had disappeared. Where was my hero when I needed him?

The room was lit with a single bulb, and had nothing but a table and four chairs. It looked like an interrogation room and it creeped me out. One of the soldiers gestured for me to sit on a chair that was facing the three others.

'What is this about?'

'Sit.'

I pulled the chair forward, my knees trembling.

The three guys sat in front of me and the eldest one spoke first.

'You were trespassing a military zone. The maximum prison sentence for that is three years.'

I stayed silent. I had been in trouble before but had never been interrogated in this manner.

'What were you doing there?'

I could make that from his striped uniform, the man who was asking the questions was a sergeant. He was unpleasant, almost snake-like with unnaturally pale complexion and flaky skin. British, in his mid-thirties. Not enough frontline activity, I thought, so he had to put his energy into bullying behind the scenes.

Even then, I was scared. My heartbeat was racing through the roof and my hands were trembling.

'I couldn't sleep so I went for a walk,' I said, trying to keep a straight face.

The bulb flickered as he spoke.

'And where did you go Miss Saaa-anderson?' he asked.

Stay calm, I told myself. He is only trying to scare you.

'I have no idea.'

'Didn't you see the signs that said—"For authorized personnel only"?'

'It was dark Mr…?'

'No need for names.'

Just then his walkie-talkie cracked to life.

He stood up, followed by his two henchmen.

What was going on? Was I off the hook?

'You will hear about our disciplinary procedures in the morning. For the moment, you will be escorted back to your tent immediately. Do not leave it till we will come and get you.'

My heart sank. They were going to take this seriously. I blamed Mark. If I had gone when Tim had played the song, I would have been safe. My career that I loved so much was now in danger. What else could I do apart from being a frontline reporter?

I wanted to kill the idiot. On second thoughts, that would land me in even more trouble than I already was. But who cared? I had to blame someone, and who better than the man who plays ping-pong with my emotions.

Kelly and Tim were waiting outside the tent, their faces grave.

'What the hell happened?' Kelly hugged me.

Tim too took my hands. 'Are you okay? Did you get…?'

Kelly was about to say something when she saw the soldier tailing behind me, so she stopped.

Once inside our tent, I put my finger to my lips, indicating them to keep quiet and took a piece of paper and began to write.

I scribbled—I'm sure the tent is bugged. I got caught and they are not going to let this one lie. We may all have to leave. Let's talk about our strategy tomorrow, after we know more.

'Fuck,' said Tim.

'Double fuck,' said Kelly.

At around 6 am, a young corporal came to our tent and stood awkwardly at the door as the three of us, bleary eyed, scrambled for our clothes.

'We will not take any further action about last night's incident. It has been recorded as a nocturnal walk. Your trip to the north will commence within a day. Any questions?' he said.

I was speechless. I stared at the man and thought I was still dreaming. What did he mean by 'no further action'? They were not going to call my bosses in London and tell them that I fucked up? They were not going to dispatch me back to Kabul? They were not going to make a fuss about it? This was incredible! In my time in journalism and experience with the military, something like this had *never* happened.

'No further questions,' came my stunned reply.

He walked out. The three of us looked at each other, surprised. We pulled out our cigarettes and went outside. It was still early, the air was fresh and dust free, with the first rays creeping across the mountain range. We walked towards the canteen area.

'What was that all about? I thought we would be thrown out in less than a nano-second,' Kelly said as she took a deep drag of her ciggie.

'Anna, someone high up must have put in a word for you. Bailed you out, otherwise something like this has major repercussions. This is unbelievable,' Tim said before getting up to order some coffee.

'I have no idea what happened, but boy am I glad they dropped it. I agree with you guys, it's pretty incredible. But maybe they didn't have enough evidence to pin me.'

'But they don't have to have anything, it's enough that you left your tent at night to get you kicked out,' said Tim.

There was something deeply unsettling about the whole episode. Almost as if there were higher powers who were controlling our journey and we were merely the puppets. I mean I've had too many scrapes with death to believe in afterlife but this was just a bit creepy. The army did not let journos wander about in the night without getting into a hissy fit about it.

'Anyway, let's move on, we have a lot of work to do.'

I pulled out my notebook and filled the two in on my chat with Omid. We went through the notes in detail.

'Where does Rich fit into all this?' Kelly was quick to remind us why we were here.

'He is sort of a chief operations officer who sorts out contracts, employs local staff, and does away with any evidence.'

'He really is a piece of work. I'll never ever shag a man like that again.'

Tim and I exchanged 'been there' glances.

I flicked through my notes to check if I had missed anything. 'One more thing. All the dealing is controlled by one guy—Shah. His staff protects the transfers and he's in both the Taliban and the army's pockets, simply because of his ability to charm the pants off a tribal soldier.'

Tim nodded. 'I've heard of him. He is sort of a legend in Helmand. Apparently he is a true womaniser and has a legendary dick. He is quite educated, and having lived abroad for years he got the taste for "white pussy".'

'How do you know all this?'

'Everyone knows about Shah. He is said to be the third most important guy in Afghanistan, after Karzai and Mullah Omar,' he said.

'Why don't people talk about this guy?'

'Because he doesn't want to be talked about. Apparently he used to enjoy the company of high class hookers on his visits to London, and particularly liked tall European blondes. Anna, you've got to be careful,' Tim said, taking a drag of his ciggie. 'He has two wives living in Dubai. Both are said to be very beautiful. To top it, he has seventeen or so children with various women. He travels out of the country once a month and spends a few days with each wife, and then he is off sleeping with hookers,' he continued.

What a creep.

'Where is his money stashed?' I asked.

'Most of his bank accounts are abroad and he has properties in the Gulf. He launders some of the drug and arms money in the gold bazaars of Dubai and then resells it for a slightly lower price to Indian buyers.'

We googled Shah and used a couple of other databases for more information.

Nothing.

We tried different combinations but it was clear that he had either managed to stay off the radar of any Western journalist, or had simply managed to keep mouths shut. Even the local Pashtun papers threw up nothing. Who was this guy really?

'So what's next?' I asked.

'We wait till we get our lift to Now Zad,' replied Tim.

My phone rang suddenly and it made us jump. The whole incident had left us a bit on the edge.

'Anna, this is Chuck. How are you? Didn't realize you were in Camp Bastion. Why didn't you tell me, you naughty minx?'

Argh. I hadn't seen the All American Jock since we last got horribly drunk. How did *he* know I was here? And what was *he* doing here? My conspiracy antenna began to beep.

'Umm, our trip was unplanned. How are you?'

'All great, thanks. I'm here for a bit of business actually. Fancy meeting up later?'

The thought of him pounding me in a miniscule tent, in this heat wasn't terribly attractive. But he could be useful.

'Where are you?'

'I'm at the shooting range behind the running track. Come over.'

I winked at Kelly and Tim conspiratorially.

'I've got to see a hunk about a lead.'

Tim looked away.

A steady stream of rat-tat-tat greeted me as I approached the shooting range. I spotted Chuck poised to take a shot.

'What brings you down here?' I stood next to him as he aimed.

'Don't distract me, missy, or I might blow someone's head off.' He put down his gun. 'I haven't seen our boys down in Lashkar Gah in ages, and since Major Pullman invited me, I thought I should come. What about you, nutkin?' he smiled.

'Erm, you know, the usual routine embeds.'

Think of something clever. You need him.

'In fact we've been invited to cover a very special shura, which is an honour, since these events are rare.'

'Be careful with those bearded blokes. They may not be able to control themselves with a fox like you,' he grinned.

'Very funny. You know it will be military-led and we're just going along for the ride.'

Chuck had moved to an automatic pistol now and was firing fast. Lowering his voice, he asked with a wink, 'Do you have a special trip in mind?'

Lord, really?

But I had to go along with it. 'Ha-ha, you naughty man.' Out came my fake laugh, but my eyes were glued to his face, trying to trace any signs of recognition, anything.

'In fact we were hoping to push further north after the shura in Lashkar Gah, to Now Zad. Do you know the area?' I asked cautiously.

Not a flicker in his eyes, which could only mean he didn't know anything about his staff's activities. Or if he did, he was a bloody good liar. 'There's nothing there, it's the final frontier before Taliban. You be careful out there, nutkin, I want you back alive.'

'What about your two guys in Lashkar Gah, could they take us somewhere?'

'Anna, there are no whiskey bars in Lashkar Gah, only men in mean turbans, if you know what I mean.'

'I was thinking more like a sightseeing trip.'

He fired and missed his target. I could see he was getting annoyed. 'There is nothing to see there, Anna, it's a war-torn town where foreigners are not welcome.'

I was pushing my luck now. 'But your guys seem to manage?'

He put his gun down. 'What is it that exactly you're after, Anna? Every time we meet you keep pumping me for information, which, frankly, is irritating. You think I haven't noticed but it's obvious you are after something.'

I had been a cocky fool to think I could get away with looking all-so-innocent and fishing for stuff.

Chuck shifted his position and took aim. Bullseye.

'Honestly, Anna, just leave it. You will find nothing but trouble if you keep asking all these questions.'

Was he warning me off?

'Sorry. You know us journos, just need all the facts.' Then I threw all caution to the winds. He already knew I was after him for information. 'There is one more thing I was hoping you could help me with. There is a guy named Shah who is famous in Lashkar Gah, and I would really like an interview with him. Do you think your guys could help?'

He missed his shot so badly it bounced off the nearby container wall, back to the training racks. Narrow slits of eyes now stared at me.

'Look at what you did, I could have killed someone. If you like your life, Anna, stay away from Shah because he will take a great deal of pleasure in killing a pretty thing like you.'

24

When I came back to the tent, I found Loxman there, talking to Tim and Kelly.

He was looking neat and polished...like a choir boy. I smiled at the thought.

He greeted me, and then said, 'We are ready to leave early tomorrow if everything goes as planned. We will stop at Camp Aberdeen where you can take some shots and then push on north to where the shura is taking place.'

As Loxman's lips curled into a smile, I couldn't help wondering how many men he had sucked off in this camp.

Our last night at Camp Bastion. It was time to party. That night, the army bosses had arranged another high profile visit—a gaggle of page 3 girls had been flow in from the UK to boost the morale of the boys. These moral boosting trips were quite common. Frankly, parading large-chested, semi-naked women in front of sex starved men was not my idea of boosting anything but their nether regions, but it wasn't my call.

A wet T-shirt contest, along with some heroes of the months was part of the programme. There was a band too—

some unknown act from the UK along with a comedian. The tent was in high spirits despite the fact that not a drop of alcohol was allowed in the premises. Amid a lot of clapping and cheering, we sat down on the wooden benches outside the main coffee shop with our two Fantas. I was dying for a real drink. Tim stepped out for a ciggie.

Two silicone enhanced ladies sashayed past our table, wearing teeny shorts and loose tops.

'Helllooo Camp Bastion,' the shorter one grabbed a microphone.

The tent erupted with cheers.

'I'm not quite Ross Kemp, but I'm here to lift your spirits all the same.'

'Show us how!' someone shouted from the audience.

A third silicone enhanced Barbie came into my line of vision. I got a headache the minute I saw her. It was a Burberry affair tonight with tight pink jeans studded with diamantes. Sweet Jesus. Shabita came straight over—no hellos, nothing—and sat down next to me on the bench, straightening an imaginary wrinkle in her blouse. Yes, this woman wore blouses in Helmand.

The noise soon became overpowering as the girls on stage did a dance routine to Rihanna's 'Umbrella', wearing nothing but bikini tops and teeny shorts. They moved up and down the stage like animated dolls and pretended to sing with the mikes but couldn't even do a proper job of lip-syncing.

The crowd was now in a frenzy of whistles and cheers, and I saw one of the girls running past our table but only half registered that she was topless, because despite the noise, I was expecting an opener from Shabita.

'I am coming with you to Lashkar Gah,' she said without looking at me. 'Your game is up, Anna.'

I nearly choked on my Fanta.

It was just after 7 am in the morning when we arrived at the departure area. The armoured vehicles, or mastiffs, were neatly lined up, ready for the trip. People were buzzing around them, making final checks and loading supplies. Half an hour later, we were on the move.

It took us three hours, two pints of sweat, and zero smiles to travel just a mile out of Camp Bastion. We were part of a convoy of seventeen mastiffs, known as 'coffins on wheels', because of their inability to sustain a serious attack. The convoy was well stocked with water, food, ammo, and other essential kits for Operating Base Aberdeen, where we would have our first stopover.

The convoy had to stop just after a mile because of a security alert five miles ahead. I sat near the door because at least some sort of breeze came through it. It was excruciatingly hot, with daytime temperatures hitting over 40. I could feel sweat oozing from every pore, even my eyelids became heavy with sweat—thank God for waterproof mascara! The dusty desert road stretched out ahead of us. There were mountains in the horizon but nothing except arid land could be seen. I seemed to have spent a lifetime travelling along quiet roads, wondering what was around the corner—the story of a lifetime, or the end to my life.

We continued our painfully slow journey to Camp Aberdeen. Our trip to further up north was scheduled after a few days.

A man with a little boy approached the convoy, gesturing for us to stop. We couldn't because he could have been a suicide bomber so we kept crawling slowly ahead. I saw his scarred face through the grill, looking sad and weary, much older than his years.

We had made good progress over five hours. The privates, drivers, and their superiors were all weary and silent. The bomb disposal team, travelling ahead of us, had located a cluster of seven homemade bombs. Each one of them could have been a disaster to our convoy. The commander told us to wait—there was no point in moving before nightfall because of the possibility of a rocket attack in the valley ahead. So we passed the time by sitting around and smoking outside the vehicle.

Most of the soldiers were dozing in the shade, except Dave, a young lad who sat across me. I struck up a conversation.

'Why did you join the army, Dave?' I started.

'Dunno, there wasn't a great deal to do in Barnsley. I would like to get promoted to a rifleman, but it's difficult. You have to do three tours, pretty much back-to-back.'

I probed on. 'Are you afraid of dying in the frontline?'

'No, not really. If it happens, it happens. We'll all die one day anyway, and my family will at least know that I died protecting my country, and not being stabbed by some wanker in a chippy fight.'

This was the answer I got from most people I spoke with, but especially from the young soldiers. Dave looked like he was fresh out of high school; he should have been in college, getting drunk with his mates, chasing girls and playing pool—not making split second decisions that could lead to a premature death. But he seemed happy with his lot.

'My mum and dad are very proud. They think it's important I serve the Queen and the country. Me granddad was in the war and me dad always regretted not signing up. So I thought I would make them both proud. It's better than staying in Barnsley. It's shit up there.'

I guess he was right. Maybe his hometown wasn't able to offer him employment and the excitement that he craved. Maybe fighting for a war far away meant more to him that any of us could understand.

'I want to be part of making British history,' he said, stubbing his cigarette out with his boot.

They were making history of sorts. By the summer of 2010, there had already been three hundred deaths among the British forces. It made big news back in England. Looking back, I remember thinking there would be many other equally grim milestones long before this war was over. Newsrooms around the world were obsessed with the Afghan story and the 'number game' was a popular one. 'One hundred deaths!' screamed the headlines. 'First female casualty', 'Father of three killed'. All sad stories of brave individuals, but for us journos they were just neat numbers that made good breaking news. Often we were just waiting for the numbers to tally up. Honestly, we were always prepared for the broadcast and just needed to fill in the blanks—the name and age of the 300th, 400th, 500th soldier. Sometimes the profession made me sick to my bones. Working with news about a conflict was a bit like trying to guess the lottery numbers…you never knew what was coming and people rarely got a second chance with lady luck.

We finally got back on the road at sunset, but again at a snail's pace. There was still a chance of hidden explosives along the road. On the upside, there was no sign of the glossy dragon that morning. But it was only a matter of time before she caught up with us. We drove through a sleepy, deserted village where no one seemed to be at home, although we could see little flickering lights through the walls of the mud houses. I saw a little girl peeping through a window, holding her little hand out—as if she wanted to reach up to touch our vehicle. Our huge mastiff dwarfed her tiny frame. I often wondered how much more pain the Afghans could take. The earth is red with their own blood, yet the spirit of kindness is almost tangible. Strangers will be helped without question, hardships would be shared, and hospitality offered. The country has been the playground of world powers for so long, and millions of people have died, or escaped. Yet, the war rages on, continuous like a wave.

Above us, an Apache helicopter, or, the 'angel of the sky' as they are known, kept a watchful eye, ready to shoot down anything suspicious. The convoy crawled slowly past more deserted villages. The night was quiet except for the reassuring hum of the Apache above us.

Suddenly the convoy came to an abrupt halt and a loud explosion shook the night. You could cut the tension inside the mastiff with a knife. My heart was beating in my ears.

'Fuck,' said Tim.

The radio crackled and we heard a broken sound: 'It's all clear, Dexter (one of the dogs) got hit, an IED.'

'God bless, Dexter, he was a good boy,' said one of the privates.

They would normally try to recover the dog's body to give him a funeral but today it was too risky, there was the possibility of more hidden explosives which might just take one of our guys with it. Our convoy gathered speed so as to get to Camp Aberdeen before dawn. Driving on pitch black roads wasn't the easiest of tasks since the road was non-existent and littered with deadly bombs.

The familiar man-made hesco wall—a type of thick wired fake wall made of sand, gravel, and stones that missiles couldn't penetrate—eventually came to sight ahead of us. Its job done, the Apache turned away and the mastiffs crept in through the gates.

25

The previous occupants of the room had kindly left me pictures cut out from men's magazines and an assortment of swear words scrawled on the muddy walls. Cozy was not the word I would have used for the room Kelly and I were assigned. Plus, the room was too hot to sleep in. So I decided to sleep out in the yard, until I realized that the burning Helmand sun made sure that there was not a chance in hell that you could sleep past sunrise or anytime during the day. Not that you would ever be able to do it even if it wasn't this hot, what with the intermittent explosions that kept you awake.

Tim had his patch about twenty metres away from our hut. He had a bunk bed and an open sky. He also got a mosquito net, which, by Helmand standards, meant that he was getting five star services.

I freshened up—if you could call it that—and got my notepad and pen. At least I did not have to wear a helmet, so I ran a brush through my hair, pulled it up in a ponytail, slapped on some sunscreen and swished a mouthful of toothpaste. Lippy and mascara, and that was it. War zone grooming at its finest.

Kelly was checking her face in a tiny mirror. 'I hope this is all worth it. That bastard better get his comeuppance "cause Hotel Hilton this ain't".'

It was just past 6 am when we headed out to the communal area where the smell of coffee and grease filled the air. I grabbed a mug of hot black coffee and went out to meet the company commanders. A group of riflemen were getting ready to go out to what looked like a patrol, while the remaining privates were sitting around the tables, eating a bad imitation of breakfast. I spotted Loxman and he got up to introduce us to a very important looking man.

'Welcome to Forward Operating Base Aberdeen. This will be your home for the next two weeks or so. If there is anything I can do to help, please let me know. Did someone show you your bunk?'

'Yes, thank you very much for letting us stay,' I said shaking his hand.

The greetings were delivered by Lieutenant Colonel Roger Toynbee. I was too exhausted to even think about naked men. I sized him up, not because I was up for some cocking, but because it was helpful to have the top dog on your side. We also had to predict the kind of trouble he might cause us. He looked tough, like a man who would not give up easily. I guess that's why he was in charge.

Silence had swept through the chatty groups of men and everyone stared at us. Typical. They'll soon get used to us hanging around.

'You are an old hand at this, Anna, so I suspect you know the rules. We'll have a briefing at 8 o'clock sharp,' Loxman said as he got up to leave, followed by a dozen of his flunkeys.

After breakfast we decided to take a walk around the camp with Loxman leading us. The camp was spread over an area of about four miles and was built where an old town hall used to be. The hall itself was now a sad, bare building, functioning as the Central Command Room, a place we had access to.

Our tour took us past the toilets, where someone had scribbled 'Ladies—Diahorrea Dave' on the door. A fetid stench emanated from the makeshift cubicles. We continued past the shower area. Kelly and I got our own cubicle—three bits of plywood, with an old sack hung up as a door. There was also a sign—'spa'—on it. There was seemingly no end to the bad jokes at Camp Aberdeen.

A young soldier, who looked no older than eighteen, took us up to a manned post in a type of watchtower where he told us that a private would spend his day watching the enemy and guarding the camp from all possible attacks. It was done the old fashioned way, with binoculars, and if he saw something suspicious he would raise an alarm. We got a view of the village, but nothing much seemed to be happening, only a few shepherds tending to their sheep and children running along the narrow dusty roads. All seemed quiet.

'The lull before the storm,' Loxman said with a wry smile.

'What do you mean?' I asked.

'Our main efforts now are just to try and keep everyone in this town happy, but at the same time try to halt the Taliban's arms supply route.'

Hah! Funny that your own guys are bleeding the weapons to them.

'And how are you planning to do that?'

He tapped his nose like some irritating know-it-all freckly frigging schoolboy.

Might help if you screened your auxiliary staff a little better, I thought vehemently.

I tried to streer the conversation to Now Zad but Loxman was vague about it.

'All in good time. All I can say is that the camp in Now Zad is kind of basic—a bit like sleeping in a cave,' he said.

Meaning it would be as rough as hell.

Back in the communal area, a group of senior soldiers were already waiting for us. A briefing—mostly full of don'ts—followed, and our schedule for the next few days was laid out. Among others, we were first supposed to follow the company attending the shura. This was something I was looking forward to because we would get a chance to meet local heads and probably get some leads. We might even get them to talk on camera, I thought optimistically.

My head was a little fuzzy with all the war talk and lack of sleep, so I headed back to the bunk. Exhausted, I fell into a deep sleep.

It was a whizzing sound that woke me up. I knew that sound only too well and jumped up with a jolt. It was an incoming RPG, which meant we had only a few minutes to take cover. The sound at first was quiet and innocent, but when it hit its target, the whole place shook, along with our insides, followed by a massive cloud of dust. We were being attacked!

There was pandemonium. Everyone around me was running for cover. The next one could have my name on it. Fear gripped me. A deep, terrifying fear.

I scrambled to pick up my body armour and helmet from the floor and tried to get out as fast as I could.

Kelly came running towards me, screaming, 'Come on, Anna, come to the shelter NOW!' Her face was ashen. She grabbed my hand but our escape was interrupted by a massive explosion that rocked the entire camp. In the cloud of smoke and dust, I lost her hand, but carried on running.

For a second, I thought how my charred body would be transported back to Britain if an RPG got us.

'We've had contact again,' someone shouted through the dust.

No shit.

I ran towards the tiny makeshift shelter that was basically a shipping container—a large metallic box with some sandbags around it. It was the third time the base had been attacked, but this time from close quarters. Kelly got in after me.

'The Taliban fighters got two of the boys earlier with an IED outside the FOB,' someone inside the container said.

'There will be more,' said another soldier.

'Where is Tim?' I looked around but couldn't see him.

'I think he's in the other container,' Kelly said.

'I need to find him. I can't bear to think he's not safe.'

'Anna, stay here. He is in the other container.' Kelly's voice had a quiver in it.

'I have to check.'

Another explosion, and our little makeshift shelter shook violently. One missile could easily pierce the container. All I could think of was how to find Tim. I counted to ten. No more missiles. I moved closer to the door and opened it.

A voice behind me shouted, 'Hey, what the hell do you think you are doing?'

I didn't bother to respond. The dust hit my lungs and I ran. I vaguely knew where the other container was—across the yard—although I couldn't see anything clearly. Suddenly, there was a hissing sound. I had seven seconds.

I had to find Tim. There was a door in front of me. I pulled it open and closed my eyes. My ten seconds were up.

A massive bang and my ears rang.

'Tiiiim,' I managed to shout.

'I'm here, Anna.'

Someone pulled me in. There was noise and light on Tim's face. I hugged him tight. And he cradled me like a baby.

There were a few more missiles, but they didn't hit too close. We sat in the shelter for an hour, waiting it out. When it was finally quiet, we emerged cautiously. The bright daylight was like a slap on our faces. I found Loxman amid the rubble.

'The FOB is not secure enough. We are worried about prolonged attacks and an increased number of IEDs,' he spat out his rehearsed lines. I could see he was frightened.

In plain words, the Talibs were on the move and the camp was under attack. I gave Loxman the usual spiel about our responsibility and how we needed accurate information about the situation. Tim nodded enthusiastically next to me. The bottom line was that we needed pictures and I would not give in until I got what I wanted. Attacks made news and cost lives. They also made the war a reality. It's no good doing a story about soldiers cleaning their boots. Our industry thrives on competition, and if you're not the first on the scene, you may lose out on that important exclusive. Sometimes it's a matter of seconds. I remember when we arrived at a market place in Iraq after a bomb had gone off, we were told to wait in case there was a second explosion before we could enter the area. When we finally made it to the area, our arch rival, NNI, News Network International, was already there and had got the best pictures. I was furious.

NNI then offered me a job a couple of years back as the Chief Correspondent in the Middle East. It was a well-paid, senior level job, which meant that after a few years in the region, a cushy retirement job as a rotating news anchor—reading news from different locations around the world—would await me. I turned down the offer.

Someone said I was mad to do so. Instead of dusty lungs, it would have meant footsie under the anchor's desk with my male news reading partner, and long glances at the studio manager's fit body over the autocue. It would have meant hello to carb-free sashimi lunches with fresh ginger dressing, and goodbye to powdered eggs from Meals Ready to Eat and fried rice cooked in oil full of dead insects.

But I would rather eat a bowlful of dead insects than work for NNI. Why?

Because Shabita worked for them, and there was no way in hell that I was going to share a sofa with that self-obsessed, war-zone pin-up. I suspected she would eventually become the face of NNI's 'News Day Around the Globe'—a flagship show, which did a mix of serious news, political analysis, and banter, as the channel called it. It would be more like a mix of botox, tantrums, and shiny helmet hair if Shabita were to present the show. In any case, she must be nearing the TV's graveyard age of forty. Passing the dreaded four zero in TV land essentially meant an end to running around with the lads and dodging the Taliban. Planning your outfit for the next day was the most daring thing you would ever do.

My thoughts were interrupted by Loxman, who had now calmed down and had even managed to comb his hair.

'Are you all okay? Can you come for a meeting in an hour? We need to decide about our trip to town,' he said.

I smiled graciously. Finally.

26

The room reeked of body odour, cigarettes, and unwashed clothes. Sweet Afghan tea was being passed around, along with almonds and dried fruit. Forty pairs of eyes were fixed on Kelly and me. Some of the eyes were rimmed with kohl—a local custom among men—which made their burning eyes look even fiercer. I had never felt so uncomfortable in my life. We had covered our hair with a hijab—a simple scarf, that we both wore under our army helmets, and long tunics under our flak jacket so that our clothes wouldn't offend anyone. But despite my modest outfit I felt naked in front of all those eyes that were burning through my sinful Western woman's body. To them, we could have as well been dressed in a bikini.

All of a sudden, the room was full of sharp sounding words in Pashto. It looked as if Kelly and I were the subject of debate. Loxman, who was in charge of the morning's operation, turned to his translator, Hassan, and asked him to explain to the men what we were doing there.

The grand mullah in the corner tapped his walking stick on the floor and said something gruffly. Hassan looked at me. 'They are upset because women are in a public arena,' he said.

'Please tell them we're here just to observe things and will not disturb them in any way,' I said, my voice rasping from the heat and thirst.

An old man sitting next to the mullah raised his right hand and said something which sounded like an approval. His gnarled face looked like a map of numerous stories.

'You can stay, but only if you stand behind the pillar over there so that you don't distract the meeting,' said Hassan.

There was nothing unusual about this; any woman would have been subjected to similar treatment. Afghan men just weren't used to seeing women, especially Western women, in public places. Kelly and I took our position behind the pillar so the meeting could start. The grand mullah cleared his throat.

Earlier in the morning, a meeting had been called where Loxman and the rest were gathered around a table littered with maps, secrets, and phones. They discussed the identification of the insurgents responsible for the attack and the damage that had been caused. They also ran over what we were going to be discussing at the shura and what we were to do there. We could film the proceedings and I could speak to the villagers. It was a good deal for both of us—the army could prove to the viewing public that they were not just engaged in a military mission but also that the so called 'Hearts and Minds' efforts were also taking shape in Helmand and we could get the information we wanted.

After that, we drove down to the town of Nadi Ali, a bustling market town where Afghans sold their goods from roadside shops made out of shipping containers. The women, dressed in blue burkhas, hurried across the market, and the children ran barefoot in the morning heat.

'It is my utmost pleasure to have my foreign visitors here with us today. The mighty Allah has been kind to us to let us have such a meeting and I thank you all again for coming together on this splendid day,' Hassan went on translating the mullah's elaborate sentences.

Loxman responded with a similar litany of meaningless compliments and greetings. It made me smile. I doubted that the grand mullah wanted these men in his village. In fact, I wouldn't be surprised if he was fully aware of what went on with the Taliban, but both sides had no other choice but to agree to this farce.

Today's discussion was about a special operation called Zewertia—which meant courage in Pastho—that would soon take place in the town of Now Zad. My ears pricked up.

Loxman's voice echoed in the room. 'The arms supply route runs through the wadi (dried up river and the lush forest area next to the valley). Our aim is to try and block this route in the coming days, but we need information about possible civilians in the area.'

So they thought that the arms were coming through the wadi.

'There are few civilians and the word will travel—our tribal communication system is faster than your Western mobile phones,' the grand mullah responded, his grin exposing a row of rotting teeth.

The meeting went on and on. Negotiating with Afghan elders was never easy, and I admired Loxman's negotiating skills. I looked at Tim from the corner of my eye and caught him yawning. The room was getting stuffy, my legs starting to ache, and the flak jacket felt heavy. Talk about Now Zad was now over and I had drifted off into a world of my own after staring at Loxman's steely buns for half an hour in an attempt to stay awake.

The shura eventually finished with elaborate thank yous from both sides. We were ushered into a small room adjacent to the gathering hall that was lit with a single bulb hanging from the ceiling. Red cushions adorned the bare floors, but the smell of boiled cabbage gave it a touch of homeliness. Two solemn-faced bearded men trooped in. One was in his seventies, while the other slightly younger but with a stoop. They didn't want to shake my hand (I was a woman after all, and touching me would be inappropriate) but instead gestured for us to sit.

Loxman stood by the door and said, 'These are two of the most well informed village elders. They will be able to give you an overview of the situation. You've got ten minutes. Hassan will stay and translate.'

'And you have to stay behind,' he told Kelly, 'they want only one reporter at a time.'

Kelly pulled a face behind Loxman's back and marched out.

Tim had his camera ready. He looked at me and then at Hassan. We knew that with the army translator doing the job, we wouldn't get anything. Both men had sat down on the floor.

'Salaam. I want to talk to you about the Taliban,' I began. The older one nodded.

'Do you think Lashkar Gah and the north are growing in numbers?'

Hassan translated for us. 'We are afraid for our lives every day, oh Allah the Merciful. But what can we do? There is no one here to help.'

'Where are the weapons coming in from?' I tried.

'Oh Allah the Merciful, these terrorists, their ways are unknown. What can we do? There is nothing we can do, for we are just innocent villagers.'

The interview went on in similar fashion for the next seven minutes, giving no headway whatsoever, and I could see that Tim was starting to look worried.

I pressed on. 'There are stories that the weapons are coming in from the north. Is it true?'

Both shook their heads, almost in unison.

'Lord most Merciful, we have no knowledge of any weapons.' There was a pause after which Hassan spoke. Then the younger man started to speak slowly, in a guttural voice—a language so familiar yet so alien to me.

Hassan flinched and then said, 'He says you foreigners shouldn't poke your nose into our business.'

Tim shuffled.

I had just one more idea left up my sleeve. One that could easily backfire.

I pulled out a fistful of dollars.

'I need the information and I can pay,' I said in a steady voice.

The older man took the roll from my hands and slowly studied the bills carefully. All I could see were his blackened teeth and his pink tongue as he let out a bellowing laughter.

'You foreigners are so stupid. You think everyone here is up for sale. But you forget one thing—our tribe is stronger than your stupid dollars. We protect each other,' he spat out the words.

Hassan looked at me as if I had lost my mind.

The man then stood up, put the dollars in his salwar kameez pockets, and smacked his lips. As he turned around, he said something to Hassan.

'Watch your back. Shah knows everything in this place and he doesn't like foreign women poking their nose into our business. May this be a lesson—you offer us money, you'll lose it. An old Pashtun proverb,' Hassan translated wide-eyed.

The pair shuffled out.

'Fuck. Fuck. Fuck. That went tits up,' I said, pacing around the tiny room.

Tim started to pack his camera. 'What a waste of time. We hung around the whole day playing along to their charade.'

There was a knock on the door. 'Has to be Loxman hurrying us along. I'll tell him we're coming,' I said.

On the other side of the door stood the younger of the two men, the one who hadn't taken our money.

'What do you want?' I asked tersely.

He gestured for me to let him in.

'I have five minutes,' he said in clear English.

'What the…' I wasn't expecting this.

Tim stopped his clearing up and pulled out his camera.

'No filming!' he said gruffly.

'Okay but you must tell us what you want.'

'I want justice. The white men, the Axalon men—one of them took my daughter and used her.'

Here we go. Slowly, Anna.

'We can help you, but first you must tell us everything you know,' I said.

'I don't know much. My lips are sealed because people here get protection from the army. I could lose my life over this. But I want revenge for my daughter's suffering.'

Another bloody Pashtun thing, I thought.

'Go on,' I said.

'All I know is that the next transfer is due to take place in Lashkar Gah in two weeks. It will come from the same route—the north. Via Now Zad. There are three white men, and they work for Axalon security. They know a lot of locals and people trust them. They operate together with Shah. They go to his house in Lashkar Gah. That's where you will find them,' he said hurriedly.

'We can't just walk in there, we'll get killed,' I said.

He nodded. 'I can't help you with that. All I know is that when they are in Lashkar Gah, they stay as Shah's guests.

Everything happens there. But there is a large depot in Now Zad, you can get there from the base. Take the first street left, opposite the post office. Grey door.'

'How can I trust that. That you're telling me the truth?' I needed to know.

He shrugged. 'I'm all you've got.'

He was right. We had nothing else.

He stopped by the door and turned to me with a nervous look. 'You mustn't tell anyone it was me who told you all of this.'

'You have my word.'

27

September had brought with it a nip in the air but the days were good to sit out. The air was filled with the promise of an impending winter.

After our meeting at the shura, the three of us waited patiently for the convoy to move up north. If we wanted to bust the arms deal we had to move fast but instead there was no sign of leaving. We couldn't just walk out of the camp looking for Shah. It would be a breach of security. Plus, we had other problems to sort out. How could we be absolutely sure that we would find this arms depot? And if we did, it had to be guarded. How were we supposed to get past the security? If we got caught, we would definitely be killed by the Taliban. I was growing more and more anxious and restless with each passing day.

Life in a war zone consisted of moments of extreme terror and boredom. We spent our days waiting around, playing cards, and smoking. We had managed to smuggle a little flask of Indian whiskey for emergency. If Camp Aberdeen wasn't an emergency, then I don't know what was.

My inability to hold down a proper relationship bothered me in these quiet moments. Occasionally, I would feel a twinge of pain when I thought of Mark. But it would pass when I thought of our bigger problems.

Loxman faithfully followed us like a little guard dog. His careful mannerisms had begun to grate on my nerves. He was desperate to be a proper soldier, but his guns were just for show, they had not been fired in ages, if ever.

Tim and I tried to patch our fragile relationship, but sometimes it seemed he was slipping further away from me. Every time I tried to bring up the unfinished conversation, he clammed up.

One morning an announcement came in the shape of Loxman who, with his puppy dog enthusiasm, told us that we would be taking the chopper up north. We had half an hour to pack and were shifting to Camp ANA, named after the Afghan National Army, who had held their HQ there before the town fell to the Taliban. It was a place solely dedicated to fighting and was built like an early Nineteenth century hiding hole with deep tunnels dug into the mountain. I was told that the Russians used it when they had tried to occupy Afghanistan back in the Eighties.

A short ride from the base took us to the helipad, which really was a bit of an open space in the valley. We grabbed our bags and ran into the open back of the chopper.

The valley below us was breathtaking. Ringed by lush mountains and crystal clear lakes, it was set against a sky so blue that it blinded you. Rich sylvan belts dotted the area.

It was a wild and perfect heaven, one that was slowly being bombed into submission.

Nestled deep in the mountains, Now Zad must have once been a beautiful place, before the fighting began. As we went up its streets, I thought how Omid had described the place to me, and couldn't agree more. It truly was a ghost town. There were telltale signs that life had once existed here—an odd piece of furniture lying wastefully, an open door to a darkened house, a child's toy in a garden. However, the bullet casings quickly reminded you that that was all in the past.

We made a short journey through deserted streets into the camp, and up the mountainside and through the familiar Hesco-reinforced gates.

Camp ANA was more than intriguing. When we reached, Loxman gave us a quick tour of the base. The place was meant for nothing but fighting a war. It felt weary and heavy with history. I couldn't help thinking, how these walls and tunnels must have seen thousands of soldiers sitting in the very same bunkers, with carvings on the walls and posters of pin-ups. Through the turbulent years, so many different flags had been raised on this pole, and hundreds of commands had been given in various languages.

Loxman led us through a network of tunnels. We walked straight for the first few metres but as the tunnel got narrower, we had to drop on all fours. Towards the end, the tunnel became so narrow that only one person could crawl forward at a time. We got to the sleeping area. These were also the troops' living quarters. There were little bunk beds that had been welded into the mountainside and we had to share the tiny space with four other men. They had tiny openings to shoot through, in case the enemy got too close.

There were two mortar positions—places where giant mortars were launched at the enemy—and an observation tower with specially designed binoculars that calculated the distance between you and the enemy, and then fed the co-ordinates directly to the mortar positions. I was given a sleeping bag and was told to be up at 6 am for the morning routine. A pinprick of light came in through the tiny opening.

We continued to crawl and got to a broader space, which we found out was the eating space. It was an area of five by four metres, with benches made of mud. The table was an old aeroplane wing.

'They say the wing was from a Russian Tupolev that had crashed in the mountains back in the Seventies,' Loxman explained.

The crawling continued, and we came to a little alcove carved into the mountainside, shielded from the world outside. It was breathtaking.

'The showers are a barrel of water, the toilets are another barrel, but with a wooden lid for comfort, and a shower curtain for modesty. But it's not all that grim,' Loxman chuckled, 'it has the best view in the world—overlooking the mountain range.'

'Taking a shit has to be the only luxury here,' Kelly whispered in my ear.

We got back to the main gate and climbed up the steep steps to the observation deck that had been disguised cleverly.

Once there, Loxman began briefing us on Camp ANA's rules. 'As you have seen, the camp is pretty secure, so there is no need for any extra measures. I should however mention that we may get a visit from an Intelligence unit tonight, but just ignore them. They're coming up here to check on an operation they're working on,' he told us.

Now that sounded more interesting than a toilet with a view.

I wondered what operation this was. The lads from Intelligence always made good stories, if you could only get hold of the buggers. They were the world's best soldiers, top of their careers, both physically and mentally. They were intelligent and highly educated, but very very secretive. In my years as a war correspondent, I had only met a few of them, and each time, I was totally captivated by them.

'Why are they coming here?' I asked.

Loxman sighed wearily. 'Anna, you of all people should know that everything they do is top secret. So I don't know anything.'

'What time are they coming? Can we interview them?' I carried on regardless.

Loxman clearly regretted giving us this bit of information. But it would have been worse if they had just shown up and we had rumbled them. 'I'm afraid that won't be possible. Best just to ignore them.'

Ignore them? And miss what could possibly be the biggest scoop of my life? Okay, second biggest—if this arms smuggling story worked out. I made a mental note to listen in on their briefings. Rules could be bent if it meant a good story was at stake.

The sun was going down and silence had fallen over the mountains. Loxman had told us that here one would rarely even hear the call for prayer because there were no functioning mosques nearby. Darkness came and we were given something to fill our stomachs. We washed the food down with an overly sweet orange squash, which, thankfully, disguised the taste. After our meal, Kelly, Tim, and I crawled back to our caves.

'This must be your most idiotic plan so far,' said Tim, blowing smoke out of the tiny opening.

Kelly giggled tiredly, half asleep.

'Sorry, darling, I'll make it up to you,' I stretched out my hand to stroke his arm.

'You better. This place is really the shit pits.'

Despite the discomfort, I was ready to stay up till dawn, only so that I could sneak out of my cave to spy and the Intel boys. In no time, Tim was snoring in his bunk and Kelly was curled in a ball on hers. The place had a magical quality, unmatched in the world. But life must have been pretty darn shitty for the Russian soldiers here, holed up during the biting winter months, surviving on potatoes and tinned meat.

A shuffling sound woke me up. So much for trying to keep awake. I tried to sit up and listen. There were people crawling in the corridors!

I sneaked out of my cave and followed the sound, which seemed to move towards the central point of the mountain. In no time my knees and hands turned raw from moving around on all fours. Even from far away I could sense that the observation point was a beehive of activity despite the fact that it must have been only about 3 am. I got to the stairs that led up to the deck and stopped, there seemed to be a heated conversation in progress. I crouched and took my position at the bottom of the steps, calculating that if anyone were to appear, I would have enough time to hide.

'This is not where we go in. Intel says the Taliban base is half a mile further north,' said a voice.

'Wrong. They'll spot us from miles away if we go any further,' said another voice tensely.

'The area around the post office is secure. Our calculations show there are only two guards there at the time.'

I tried my best to hold in my surprise. It was a voice I knew very well.

28

What the hell was he doing here? And what was Mark doing with the oh-so-secret Intel guys? I thought he was the bodyguard type, zipping around Kabul in flashy armoured cars, protecting hapless diplomats. It was all too confusing.

The argument went on for quite some time and my legs started getting stiff from crouching. Thanks to Intel jargon, which I was not familiar with, I couldn't understand much of the conversation. However, the words 'post-office' and 'civilians' had alerted me, and I tried to get closer, to listen more carefully. As I stood up, I realized that I had a bout of pins and needles and as I tried to pull my leg forward, I lost my balance and fell face down on the ground. The converstion in the tower came to an abrupt halt.

Fuck. Shit. Piss.

The earth smelled of rotten life and tasted sour. Before I could get up, there were torches on me. 'What the fuck is going on down there?'

More shouting.

'Who's there?'

'It's that journalist woman!'

'Are you okay?' someone asked.

'What are you doing here?'

There must have been about dozen or so people around me, and somewhere out there in the darkness was Mark who had just witnessed me spying on his colleagues. Someone helped me up and pulled me inside the control room. There were ten pairs of eyes looking at me.

'Are you hurt?' someone asked.

'No, no, I'm fine, I just fell over in the dark, I came looking for the toilet and must have taken a wrong turn, nothing to worry about. You get on with your business, I just need to sit down for a sec.'

My eyes were getting used to the dim light of the control room. I looked around, narrowing my eyes, but couldn't find what I was looking for. There was no way I was leaving before I had seen Mark. I was starting to regret this attempted rendezvous. With the light on, I realized I was wearing a pair of not so flattering leggings that had a hole in one bum cheek and a stained vest top that had seen better days. No bra either, which made my tits flop around unflatteringly. The whole get up was topped by my a crow's nest. Lord. Why do I always turn into Miss Clumsy when this guy's around? And why does he keep showing up where ever I am? I couldn't help thinking that all of this was too much of a coincidence.

My welcome reception seemed to be over, and I stood up to leave.

'Here, let me help you back.' Someone grabbed my arm.

I turned around to find Mark holding my arm. He looked furious.

We started our slow, silent descent down the steps. I could feel his breath on my skin. Once we were down in the caves, we both got on all fours and began to crawl.

'What on earth are you doing here?' he whispered angrily behind me.

'I'm working on a story. I should ask you the same thing. I thought you worked in security, not on some secret operation in Helmand,' I spat out.

'Don't try to fool me, Anna. What are you working on that you've ended up in Now Zad?'

There was no way I was going to volunteer my information. I had seen enough back in Kabul—him with a certain pink-loving correspondent.

'I'm here to help Kelly find her boyfriend who has disappeared. Happy?'

'Rich? You two are planning to rescue him? That is the most idiotic thing I've ever heard in all my life. He doesn't need rescuing, he is probably screwing some aid worker in Kabul as we speak. Plus, I thought he wasn't her boyfriend any more,' Mark snorted.

I turned around ready to give him an earful.

'Keep moving,' he hissed.

I was fuming. How dare he speak to me like that? No one has ever bossed me around like this before. I mean who does the guy think he is?

We crawled on. My hands and knees were burning with pain, but it was nothing in comparison to how much my ego was hurting.

'Look, Anna, I'm only going to say this once and for the last time. I know what you're upto. What you are trying to do is both dangerous and stupid. Just drop it, will you?'

I snapped, 'Don't you dare tell me what to do! In any case what is it to you, what I get up to?'

He suddenly grabbed me by my waist and pulled me in a sitting position in the widest part of the tunnel against the trench wall. I took a deep breath—that familiar smell—and realized how every cell in my body yearned to be with him. He held me close, planting little kisses on my neck and forehead, soothing me like a baby.

Then, we kissed. It was soft, intense, filled with anticipation and hunger.

It probably was the most romantic encounter I had ever had—there, down in the goddamned damp tunnels that smelt of earth and filth. He pulled away and looked at me with his deep dark eyes, and then kissed me again. I responded to his every touch. The movement of our bodies was instantly familiar, like a dance we had once learnt long ago.

'I have wanted to kiss you for such a long time,' he whispered.

His tenderness melted away my hard corners. He was the first man I had met who didn't want to pull my trousers down or start groping me.

And after that, there was no longer any need for words. My hard corners melted away like ice cubes in a glass left out for too long. I didn't say anything. There was no need to talk. We sat there for a few minutes, catching our breath until he said he had to get back. We kissed tenderly, for a long time, and then he turned around and began crawling back through the tunnel.

I lay down in my narrow, hard bed, my body and soul aching. I began to cry quietly. He was so close, yet I couldn't have him. What I needed was alcohol and a good old moan with Kelly back in our house in Kabul. Instead, I was stuck in this fucked up underground ghost town where I had no idea what I was doing. I so wanted to wake up Kelly to tell her everything, but didn't want to disturb her.

The quietness of the camp lasted for only what seemed like a fleeting moment, as a powerful explosion rocked the place. I thought my ear drum had burst. I was groggy and half asleep but I instinctively putting on my flak jacket and helmet. Tim, Kelly, and I crawled out of our hole and as swiftly as we could we made our way along the trenches and reached the main observation area.

'We have just located an enemy position and have launched a mortar attack,' came the matter-of-fact explanation from Loxman. He was whispering excitedly like a little boy who had found his long lost toy soldeirs.

The noise was unbearable. It was made worse by the

echoes booming across the valley. We stood there, looking at the mortars being launched and exploding at targets. And then it stopped as suddenly as it had begun. Morning would be here soon enough.

'We are getting our positions ready and also preparing to respond with frontline fire if necessary,' Loxman explained.

'Remind me why we're in this shithole again?' said Kelly, coming out of her bunk.

'It's all your doing. You and your bloody Rich.' I couldn't help myself.

'He's not mine, he never was,' she retorted.

We climbed up to the observation post. Tim handed me a pair of binoculars and pointed out in the direction of the forest. There was some movement among the trees but I couldn't tell whether it was just a group of frightened shepherds or Taliban fighters armed with RPGs.

The next minute all hell broke lose. The noise was overpowering and the whole mountain shook as the RPGs kept coming in thick and fast. Our outgoing mortars were equally fierce, but the chaos that ensued was incalculable.

More bombing.

The Talibs were unlucky because they couldn't get a close enough a hit. Most of the missiles were coming from the green zone. The bombing lasted for about 45 minutes, and afterwards we had a quick on-camera briefing from Loxman.

'We must have hit at least five to six targets, which was a great result for us,' he said, beaming like a man who had just gotten laid.

'Any casualties?' I asked.

'There will be many on their side for sure,' he said cockily.

I climbed up on top of the pile of sandbags and spoke to the camera, 'As you can see from the smoke rising behind me, the fighting here in Now Zad has intensified in the last few days and both sides are now fortifying their positions. This is Anna Sanderson for GNN in Now Zad, Helmand, Afghanistan.'

It was going to be a piece full of action shots, which the TV bosses loved. We were now done for the day and it was only 7 am. Luckily, everyone was still feeling the post-battle europhoria and analyzing the strategy, which meant I could quietly sneak away to explore further. I found a little cave where two Afghan translators were working and even though I was strictly told by Loxman to stay away because it was prohibited to speak to translators, I crept that way. Plus, I had never really followed any rules in my life.

The two young Afghan men invited me in, probably out of sheer boredom, and no doubt intrigued by a foreign blonde woman. I crouched in their little cave. There was barely enough room to cross my legs on the floor and the heat was unbearable. Their job was to intercept any radio conversations they overheard in Pashto that might be relevant.

'So are we the only visitors here?' I asked.

'Naah, there are a bunch of other guys here. They've been up here for two days now.'

'Apart from the regular guys?'

'Yup. These dudes are part of some special operation. But you know those bosses, they won't tell us anything.'

'How many of them?' I probed.

'I dunno. Maybe about five or six guys, top guns like.'

'Soldiers?' I asked.

'Yup or some agent types—the ones you never see or hear of. You know like James Bond. Hahaha.' He made a pistol out of his hand and pointed it at the door. In one swift movement he had turned around in the tiny space and was pointing his finger at me. 'Ay, I think they are on their way north, covering the transit point near the main Lashkar Gah road, like.' He sounded Liverpudlian.

It was hard not to laugh at the mock Scouse playing an agent.

'Do you know what will happen?'

'Ay, ay, there are at least a dozen special soldiers. And there are some tactical experts too. But they can't stay in the area for more than forty-eight hours or so 'cause it's too deadly, like,' he said.

It wasn't much, but any nugget of information was useful. And it confirmed what Loxman had already told me. At least he wasn't lying. Not that I could act on it, as last night's shoddy stumbling episode proved I was no good, not even under supervision.

'Where did you learn your English by the way? It sort of sounds Liverpudlian, you know the town in North England.'

'Yer not wrong, love. Me first job was like with a group of soldiers from Liverpool few years ago. Me English was okay back then, but not great. 'Cause it was a quiet summer they took their time to teach me,' he said.

'It sounds almost native. How's that possible?'

231

'The lads told me Scouce was a bit similar to Pashtun, and it sounded beautiful with its singing style, so I decided to copy it. I was made up when they told me I could speak it like.'

I thanked the wannabe Scouse and his mate, and crawled out of their cave without anyone spotting me.

A lovers tiff in the tunnels, a Scouse interpreter, and toilets with the best view in the world—this place seemed to grow more eccentric by the minute.

Early mornings in Afghanistan were always startlingly serene and beautiful. The desert landscape that morning, outside the gates, looked like an advert for an adventure holiday—endless, dusty roads, snaking through mountain valleys, dotted with occasional orchards.

Loxman had promised us a tour of the village, and we could even take part in a foot patrol once we got there, which bode well since we could try to get nearer the arms cache. With pictures and couple of testimonies and research from Omid, we would have a strory of sorts. But still nothing that nailed Richard.

There were eight of us inside the tank, including Tim, Kelly, and I. Loxman was in one of the middle tanks, which gave us a breather from our tail wagging guide dog. We were off, travelling in a convoy of seven battle tanks. My place was in the front part of the vehicle, so I could see through the tiny hole of a window.

We had been travelling for about ten minutes when we reached the mouth of a valley, and our convoy came to a sudden halt. No one asked why. Kelly's eyes were filled with fear. The driver's radio was crackling with commands that I couldn't understand. Everyone was awake now and I noticed that the soldiers were clutching their guns tightly with sweaty hands. It was becoming hotter inside the vehicle, and I was desperate for some air. We waited for another half an hour until the tank began moving again. This time at a snail's pace, almost like an animal silently stalking its prey. Inch by inch, we crawled along.

'Situation over,' I heard from the radio.

The soldiers seemed visibly relieved and loosened the grip on their guns. I took a deep breath and the driver increased our speed in a bid to keep up with the rest of the convoy. We had been on the move for just a few minutes when suddenly a deafening bang shattered the morning air and rocked the tank. It seemed to come from the front of the convoy.

'Holy fuck!' the driver screamed.

'Stop, stop for fuck's sake,' screamed another.

I looked across at Tim, my heart pounding. He was sweating, but trying his best to stay calm. Kelly was taking deep breaths and counting silently with her eyes closed.

Tim's face didn't betray any emotion when he turned to me and said, 'Anna, I love you. If we die now, I just want you to know that.'

I looked at him speechless, trying to comprehend what he had just said.

I held him tightly.

We sat there in silence, our breathing getting heavier and more pronounced. I couldn't swallow. A whizzing sound rang out, this time closer. The driver hastily started to turn the tank around. I suspected we had driven into an ambush replete with IEDs and a gang of Taliban fighters lying in, waiting on the other side of the narrow passage.

That was my last thought.

In an instant, our tank came under fire. A rocket-propelled grenade pierced through the protective layer of our armoured shell, sending a wave of burning heat searing through the vehicle.

'Everybody OUT,' yelled someone.

The front of the vehicle had burst into flames and we had seconds to get out, to avoid being burnt alive in an inferno.

I scrambled for safety and then everything blacked out.

29

When I came around, I found myself in a ditch—an ominous silence around me. I looked around but couldn't see much. About ten yards from me, a young soldier lay with a gaping, bloody wound on the side of his neck. He was bleeding to death. Vultures circled nearby, waiting patiently. His body had already given up, and the rest of him was ready to follow. Further ahead, I could see the tank we were in—in flames. I had to move fast before it exploded completely.

My arms and legs and parts of my torso were screaming in pain. I began crawling in the ditch, away from the tank, remembering what all those ex-SAS boys used to tell us in hostile environment training courses. This was the kind of hostile situation we were told about. I crawled across the stones and weeds that rubbed harshly on my already broken skin. The ditch opened out into a ridge that seemed to slope downwards into a barren shrub land. If I could somehow roll down on it, the shrubs would be able to offer shelter from the fire, in case the Taliban was still lurking somewhere. I slowly pushed myself over the ridge, and pulled my hands together, ready to roll down the hill. I counted to three and then launched into a steep tumble.

By the time I came to a stop, my mouth was full of dust and my clothes caked in dirt. Every inch of my body was hurting now, but I crawled ahead until I reached some undergrowth, tall enough to hide under.

My throat was parched, and I suddenly remembered that I had a bottle of water tucked into my flak. I took a deep gulp from the bottle, which had miraculously survived my plunge down the hill.

Suddenly the familiar rat-tat-tat of machine gunfire filled the air. It was close, so I pulled a bunch of parched ferns tighter over my body to provide better camouflage. My heart was pounding, and I felt a warm trickle of pee between my legs. 'This is it, the end to my story,' I thought, and closed my eyes and held my breath. Think of all the love you've had, all the friends and laughter. Dying alone in the middle of Talibania was not part of my plan, but shit happened sometimes!

The gunfire continued. I could hear people running, but it was hard to guess how far they were. More shooting followed, this time what seemed like from a greater distance. By now, I had no idea how long I had been lying there on the filthy ground, with the sunlight beating down on my leafy hideout. I lay still, with my eyes shut, waiting for it to pass, and praying that I wouldn't be discovered.

After what seemed like hours, everything around me went quiet, except for the distant bark of a dog and an oddly serene birdsong. My ribcage loosened up and my breathing settled.

I thought of Kelly…and Tim. We had gone from confessions of love to death in less than ten minutes. I prayed that they were okay. And what about Loxman, Dave, and the other boys? I was living my worst nightmare.

The adrenaline slowly drained from my body and I suddenly felt exhausted and couldn't keep my eyes open any longer.

I must have dozed off because when I woke up, the sun had already climbed behind the mountain range and the oppressive heat had subdued a little. I fumbled around for my phone in the front pocket of my vest, but the screen had been smashed into pieces.

Shit.

I fiddled with it, and it turned out that the camera was still working. Bloody mobile phones, no good for saving my life but hey, don't worry, it can still take scenic pictures en route! The voice recorder was also in good condition—good to record my will, I guess.

With the phone being of no help, I realized I had to try and move myself so that I didn't get caught. I started my desperate slow crawl again, ignoring the ever growing pain in my body, and eventually managed to reach a forest area and slowly stood up with shaky legs.

Dusk had descended and I could no longer see the terrain in front of me, but there was no way I could risk going back to the sight of the explosion. Using my torch would not be a smart idea either because it would attract attention and make me an easy target. So I started taking tiny, baby steps in the pitch dark forest, fully aware that every step I took could be my last. Landmines were a common danger in Afghanistan and every step meant dancing with death.

Eventually I came across a kind of path, which felt safe to walk on. I could see some flickering lights in the distance and, with a gladdened heart, headed purposefully towards them. I was exhausted, in pain, and freezing. The evening temperature often dropped to minus five and my clothes were still soaked because of crawl. This was not a good situation to be in.

The only good news was that I had enough resources for some immediate relief. Nutri-bars in my flak pocket, water for another twenty-four hours, plenty of water purification tablets, a first-aid kit, British military rations for about two days, a head torch, matches, a Leatherman pocket knife, and hallelujah, clean socks. Not bad for a situation like this. Not bad at all.

What I needed the most, however, was a detailed military map with every booby trap marked on it!

I must have been walking for well over three hours but the little lights in the distance did not seem to get any closer. I walked another hundred metres and suddenly came upon the silhouette of a shed. It was a small, mud-walled hut, which must have been used for storage by the farmers. Feeling brave, I pulled the door and flashed my torch to inspect it. It smelled of stale hay, but more importantly, it was dry inside.

Elated, I sat down, and took off my armoured vest and jacket, which were both soaked through and through. I managed to gather enough dry hay and wood from the shed to make a small fire to try and dry my clothes and warm my hands. I took off my boots and socks, and had some water and a plate of reconstituted Chicken Tikka and dried apricots for pudding.

Small things, but god, they felt good.

Where was Tim? Kelly? Were they okay? I was worried sick again. Everything around me was beginning to blur as tears started rolling down my face. Why couldn't I just have a normal life, a nice desk in London and a nice boyfriend who worked in a bank? Instead, I was stuck in the middle of an Afghan desert, most likely to die alone.

I didn't realize when I fell asleep, but the first rays of the sun woke me up. Disoriented, my brain tried to work out what had happened. The hopelessness of my situation hit me within seconds. I wanted to cry but suppressed the urge, realizing it wouldn't be of much help.

Stay calm. You have been in worse shit than this. Actually you haven't. But keep telling yourself that.

So I did.

I was unable to move my stiff and battered body, but thank the lord I had heavy duty painkillers in my first aid kit, which I sometimes used recreationally. Nothing like a bit of ibuprofen for breakfast. But this time it wasn't to cure my hangover, or get high, but to get me moving. The fire had gone out during the night, but luckily both my jacket and flak jacket were just damp, and no longer soaking.

I had to get out of the shed quickly, in case anyone came in and found me. My body still ached from the heavy weight of the body armour. Lacing my boots, I mentally prepared myself for another twenty-mile walk with no real direction. If I made it out of this alive, I would reward myself with a five-star spa in an exclusive resort along with a lovely strappy pair of Jimmy Choos. I didn't feel guilty for being girly, and planning a shopping spree in a country where people survived on less than a dollar a day. I worked in a man's world, covering other people's miseries every day, so my little pleasures every now and then felt justified. Besides, what else is there for a single girl like me? The lack of sex was simply too much to bear without my favourite shoe fantasy.

Back to reality, Anna. I snapped out of it. Now wasn't the time.

Bright sunlight hit me when I opened the shed door and fields of, what I guessed to be, autumnal poppy sprawled out in front of me.

A sure sign that indicated the presence of the Taliban.

There seemed to be no one around. My phone wasn't working and I had no idea what time it was. I took a gamble and started off in a direction that I thought was south.

The uneven and muddy path under my feet seemed to be well defined and I optimistically told myself this was probably because it had been regularly used by humans. The landscape stretching out before me was barren and arid, with the odd splash of greenery. A valley loomed ahead and I was struck by the untouched beauty of my surroundings. I wondered if I was the first foreigner to see this remote part of the country.

As I walked on, I weighed my options, limited as they were. On one hand, I could seek help from the nearest village. On the other, I still needed to be mindful of the Taliban. I had no idea where I was, or how far I was from Lashkar Gah or Now Zad. Either way was not safe.

Despite each step being agonizing, I kept walking. As the hours slipped by, my body became accustomed to pain. Soon, the sun rose over me, and beat down mercilessly with its scorching heat. I sat down on a jagged piece of rock and sipped some water from my well-worn plastic bottle to wash down a small chunk of a muesli bar. My supplies were getting low. This was good for weight loss—I humoured myself—skinny jeans, here I come. Tired, my eyes became heavy and I gave in.

A small Afghan boy stood above me, staring at me with his big round eyes. He was dressed in loose white traditional clothing which contrasted sharply with his tanned skin and a Pasthoon style embroidered skullcap. Two little dimples appeared on his face.

We stared at each other.

A herd of scrawny looking goats nibbled the sparse patches of grass around us.

'What is your name?' It was probably the only sentence he knew in English because he didn't respond when I answered, 'My name is Anna.'

I tried again. 'Where am I, my friend?' I asked in my elementary Pastho.

'Jervendz,' he replied.

I guessed that was the name of the village.

'Mother, family…?' I continued.

He signalled with his small dirt-stained hand to follow, and I nodded gently.

This boy could be my saviour.

We started walking. Me, the little boy, whose name I gathered was Mohammazi, and fifteen skinny goats marching in an orderly line. We must have been a sight. The boy was quick over jagged rocks and avoided deep crevices deftly, as if he had done it many times before. It took me all my strength to keep up with him. But he clearly knew the terrain well and that made me feel safe.

After about an hour, we arrived at a village, nestled in the valley. About a dozen mud huts were huddled together in a circle, and herds of goats and flocks of chickens wandered about at will. There seemed to be no one around. Perhaps it was tea or prayer time.

Or maybe they were all polishing their AK47s.

Little Mohammazi approached one of the huts, forcing a stubborn black nanny goat out of his path. My heart began to pound as I had no idea what awaited me inside the modest hut. It could be home to a group of Taliban fighters who may realize that a lost foreigner could be exchanged for a lot of dollars. It was too late to turn back now.

30

Mohammazi knocked on the wooden door and a woman about my age, opened it, wiping her hands on her tattered dress. I saw the alarm in her expressive, jade coloured eyes when she saw me. The next minute she started to scream in panic.

I gestured for her to calm down, gently touching her shoulder and trying to explain in my bad Pashto that I was a journalist, and that our vehicle had been attacked, but she didn't understand. After some desperate and animated gestures to show her what had happened to me, she finally seemed to realize that I was not dangerous.

'Fauzija,' she suddenly said with a shy smile, and touched her heart.

We stood there, looking at each other, not knowing what to do next. Her deeply lined face told a sad tale of a hard life. She probably looked older than she was. She gestured for me to come in. Her trust touched me because in my current state, I would have looked scary to anyone, let alone to an Afghan lady living far away from the world of foreigners.

I stooped and stepped inside her tiny home, immediately relishing the coolness of the dark place. The hut had two small rooms with two miniscule holes for windows. The smell of freshly fried onions, lamb fat, and damp clothes wafted through the place. Fauzija gestured for me to sit on a rug on the floor and ordered Mohammazi to prepare tea. Two toddlers playfully waddled into the room and sat in her lap, gurgling with delight. They seemed shy, but well looked after—hair neatly brushed, faces clean, and their little eyes carefully lined with black kohl.

Mohammazi brought us the tea and Fauzija continued to stare at me as we sat in silence, sipping from our cups. When I smiled, she smiled back, but I couldn't help wondering if she was just imitating me.

The first thing I tried to ask her was if she had a phone. I pretended to make a call on my mobile and then showed it to her that it was smashed to pieces. She smiled, but shook her head, draining all my optimism. At the back of my mind, I was worried that she had a husband fighting for the Taliban and that, at the end of the day, he would return and find his wife drinking tea with an infidel. But I tried not to show it.

The silence deepened and I wondered what her life was really like. Living under the Taliban, who liked to say that 'the only two places for an Afghan woman are in her husband's house and the graveyard,' must have not be easy. With no education, legal rights, or voice of her own, her life, through a Western woman's eye, seemed to have very little

pleasures. She must have given birth to her children here in her house, alone, with no one to help. But somehow, looking at her fussing over her children, taking pride in her humble surroundings, and going about her daily tasks—Fauzija looked happy.

After a while, she gently lifted the toddlers from her lap and went outside. I sat there, wondering what to do, and watched patiently as she began preparing a fire outside the house and chopping what looked like lamb's intestines. Clumsily, I offered my help, but she turned me down.

I tentatively asked Mohammazi about his father, and in response, he gestured towards the mountains, which, I meant that he was either out herding goats or killing Western soldiers.

I hoped it was the former.

After some time, Fauzija brought a metal pot full of steaming stew of lamb intestines. I noticed she had put the lamb's heart to the side, on a plank of wood, next to the pot. Mohammazi then went outside and brought in a fresh plate of naan. I realized giving me meat was a special treat. I was touched by her kindness.

Fauzija asked Mohammazi something while gesturing in my direction.

'Tomorrow,' is what I understood from his gestures. They must have been talking about getting me out.

I was hungry and the stew tasted good with the tenderly cooked intestines. We ate in silence and I gestured several times to indicate my appreciation of the food, cursing myself for not learning Pashto.

After we had finished eating, I tried talking to Fauzija again, to determine my exact location. Instead, she insisted that I stay the night. She gestured towards the mattresses. It was a tempting offer, after all it was getting dark outside and I really didn't like the idea of scrambling alone at night with the fear of getting kidnapped or being shot at.

Fauzija's warmth seemed genuine, but I had to stay alert in case anyone came in. Not that I could do anything to protect myself. I was completely at her mercy.

Mohammazi cleaned the dishes and Fauzija put the babies down to sleep in the living area. They slept on the hard floor with just a thin rug to shield them from the damp and cold. Watching this little family going about their nightly routine, I vowed that if I made it to safety, I would try and help them in any way I could. The simplicity of their life was humbling and their love for each other admirable.

But something was bothering me. I was still unclear about what the husband did.

Night had fallen and the small room was illuminated by candlelight. Fauzija had settled on the floor and was sewing a patch over a hole on a small child's T-shirt. I offered to help despite the fact that I had not sewn anything since primary school. But she turned me down again.

Looking around, I started making mental calculations. What I knew now was that I was in a village somewhere in Northern Helmand, possibly a donkey ride away from Lashkar Gah. Damn the GPS for not working! My journey must have taken me across several miles, and it was a miracle that no Talibs had crossed my path. There was a military base in Lahskar Gah from where I could get help…if I could find it that is. My mind was racing with a million questions to which I had no answers.

Fauzija roused me from my thoughts and led me to the mattress that had been prepared in the furthest corner of the dark room. I sank into the makeshift bed, and in the darkness, watched her silhouette as she lay down on the rags and pulled a piece of cloth over her. Little Mohammazi curled up next to her and the two were soon fast asleep.

Other than the lone hoot of an owl and the distant howls of wolves, it was dead quiet. A flickering lantern threw shadows on the dark walls but eventually its light dwindled and the room faded to darkness. What a stupid fool I had been to think that I could nab Rich. Mark's words came back to me, before I fell into a deep slumber, and part of me wished that I had listened to him.

The call to prayer was loud and clear. Morning had arrived. The young man's pitch perfect recitation indicated a local imam in progress.

I lay still on the bed, wondering if I should just get up and leave in the darkness. It was tempting, but I decided it would be rude and disrespectful, after she had shown me such kindness. And anyway, if the plan was to kill me, she could have easily done so by now.

Fauzija too was awake, and was already busy with the her household chores. She gave me tea, a kind of broth made with lamb fat and root vegetables, and bread. Afterwards we sat down on a patch of earth outside her little home, enjoying the new day. Clasping a twig, I knelt down and sketched a line on the dusty terrain, positioning a pebble at one end and slowly said 'Lashkar Gah' pointing at myself. She nodded, and said something to Mohammazi who ran off for a few minutes, only to return with two donkeys.

He was beaming when he said, 'Your vehicle is ready for fighting.'

Mohammazi must have learned his odd phrases from the radio, I thought, since it was odd to hear such words from someone who spoke very little English.

He had made a makeshift saddle from old carpets on the donkey to make my journey more comfortable.

I realized Fauzija was offering to lend me her donkeys to make the journey with Mohammazi, who would then drop me to safety and bring the donkeys back. Her act of kindness moved me to tears. Not only had they shared the little they had, this kind family was now willing to make sure I got to safety. The two toddlers came out to the yard, looking at both of us with curiosity, gurgling and laughing, unaware that they lived in one of the most dangerous places of the world.

It was time to say our goodbyes. I knew I had been an unexpected drain on the family's limited food resources, so I offered Fauzija some money, about 60 dollars, which was all I had on me. She refused with a gentle shake of the hand,

but kept on repeating the name Shahrokh Jalabadi. I finally understood this to be the person who would be waiting for me in Lashkar Gah and who, I was hoping, would arrange my lift back to the base.

As I hugged her goodbye, she smiled and said something I couldn't understand. I guessed it was something similar to a message of solidarity, about one woman helping another. But then she handed me one of her blue burkhas, hanging near the door. Touched by her concern, I dutifully pulled it over my head. Once fully covered, I could only see through the grid-like gauze and, since it sat tightly on my head, my vision was severely limited. My movement too was limited because it was so long and cumbersome, and I ended up dragging the hem after me, like a veil. Oddly, I felt safe in it. Fauzija pointed at my chunky desert boots, which would be a dead giveaway to my real identity. Afghan women always wore heeled slippers or shoes, regardless of the weather. She went into the hut and came back with a pair of black plastic slippers. They were a size too small and felt uncomfortable, but I was in no position to choose otherwise. At least my combat trousers were hidden under the burkha. In return, I gave Fauzija my boots, which Mohammazi accepted, grinning from ear to ear. It was easy to forget that shoes were only such a luxury in this part of the world even though they were only an old pair of boots.

In a final act of kindness, Fauzija prepared us both a packed lunch of fresh bread and sliced lamb heart that she had saved from the evening meal. I accepted the package gratefully, and stuck it inside the top of my backpack.

With her watching us thoughtfully, we slowly melted away into the distance, and started our journey along the shadow of the mountains.

Mohammazi had explained that it would take about two hours to reach the first village, called Zahidan, and eventually we would reach Lashkar Gah, hopefully, before nightfall. The donkey was well behaved and despite my burkha, I managed to balance myself, perched side-saddle, without falling off.

The path climbed higher up to the mountains and the landscape became drier. There were a few shrubs here and there, but no other vegetation to speak of, which made me sick with worry—there was nowhere to hide in case someone discovered who was really under the burkha.

But so far so good, I kept telling myself, and relaxed into the seesawing rhythm of the animal.

The path kept on narrowing, but the brave donkey managed to skillfully navigate through the terrain. After a couple of hours of sandy nothingness and several blisters on my bum, we reached a sleepy village. Mohammazi turned around to face me and silently made a gesture of decapitation, which I understood to mean that there were Taliban soldiers in the vicinity. I was grateful for my burkha, and pulled it down even more securely.

We approached a hut that was overflowing with arms. RPGs, AK-47s, and grenades lay strewn on the floor outside—like some kind of ramshackle war zone car boot sale. I had never seen so many weapons in one place. Maybe they were doing some spring cleaning, I thought cheerfully. Two bearded men dressed in black turbans came outside.

'Here we go,' I said to myself, holding my breath, calming my rising heartbeat.

'Salaam alaikum,' Mohammazi shouted.

'Wa alaikum assalam, Mohammazi,' one of the men greeted my little guide.

The other man kept looking at me. He then asked something about Fauzija. Mohammazi replied with something that must have been a lie because I understood he said something about his mother being ill while gesturing in my direction. Clever little boy!

We rode past the weapons cache very slowly with my donkey swaying from side-to-side. My heart was pounding so heavily that I was sure the two men would either hear or see me through the burkha. This is it, this is it—I thought—you've had your nine lives, Miss S, someone will soon realize you're a scam and put a bullet through your head.

Keep calm, keep calm, I told myself. But I couldn't stop shaking.

I clung so tightly to the donkey that my hands began to hurt. Sweat slid down my back and my whole body was filled with terror. I kept looking at the men through the netting, their eyes following us intently.

At the back of my head there was a part of me desperately wanting to take pictures of the arms cache, but for once I had to put my life ahead of the story.

Ten metres away, one of the men shouted something but Mohammazi just waved back.

Twenty.

Thirty.

Forty.

Fifty.

Phew.

Mohammazi must have been the coolest kid in town. Being caught with a foreigner would almost certainly mean a death sentence. My pulse started to slow down as we passed the village and Mohammazi turned around and smiled. 'Some people good weapons, some people bad weapons,' he said in his broken English, grinning.

'What is the name of that place?'

'River name Malakas.'

I made a mental note of that.

We continued on our journey. The steep path started to climb higher and my backside began to feel numb. I was hot and thirsty. I wondered how Fauzija would make such a journey if she was sick or expecting a baby.

As the sun reached its midday peak, we dismounted and found a spot to eat our lunch. We sat together in silence, admiring the lush valley and the majestic mountains stretched out in front of us. It was deserted and peaceful, and all we could hear was the sporadic drone of flies and wasps, the tumbling steps of an odd stray goat, and our two donkeys who were guzzling down a well deserved drink of water. I removed my burkha and closed my eyes, absorbing the fresh air and the baking sun's rays.

From a distance it looked like a small market town, consisting mainly of low-rise mud coloured buildings and rows of shops converted from old shipping containers—a common sight in Afghanistan.

'Lashkar Gah,' Mohammazi said with his voice full of pride for having navigated us to safety.

The afternoon light cast a golden light on the town, giving it an ethereal feel, but as our donkeys carried us closer, I saw the ugly signs of war everywhere. Bombed out buildings, abandoned tanks, and pock-marked concrete walls. Mohammazi tapped my shoulder and pointed to my left, making explosive noises and gestures.

'Landmines,' I guessed, and grasped the coarse hair of the donkey a bit tighter. This could be the end for both of us.

The road towards the town continued to weave up around a steep mountainous pass. At the entrance to the town, a rusty, bullet-holed road sign welcomed us, in Pashto and English, to the 'Town of Flowers'. And above the sign was the picture of Mullah Omar, the spiritual leader of the Taliban. Not a single Western soldier could be seen anywhere.

This meant we were entering unknown territory. I cursed Ropey Rich again.

My arse was stiff and bruised, and I was keen to get off the donkey but I had no idea how far we were from the house of Shahrokh Jalabadi and safety.

We rode along a busy road and turned off the main street to a narrower passage and soon approached what could only be described as a palace—an opulent, elegant mansion, guarded by a gold plated iron gate.

An armed guard opened the gates and gestured for us to leave our donkeys outside. Facing us was a large, several stories high building which looked more like an imposing prison rather than a home. In front of the house was a large tiled courtyard. The yard itself looked as if it was straight from the latest edition of the Afghan *House & Garden* magazine with well tended rose bushes and creepers of all varieties. Perhaps it was trying to cover up the place's prison-like feel.

Scattered on the terraced ground were red coloured handmade rugs and pillows where a group of men were gathered in the shade, drinking tea. On a closer look, the numerous AK47s carefully placed next to their owners, the heavy duty metallic door and bolted windows gave the place a more sinister aura. I shivered in the bright sunlight—the place gave me the creeps.

One of the men stood up.

He was tall and muscular, with a truly handsome movie star face.

The first thing noticeable about him was his fierce, burning Pashto eyes. Almost black in colour, they seemed to pierce through my burkha.

I noticed the well-cut beard and strong arms, all in all a well rounded package. If I didn't have this odd premonition that something wasn't quite right, I could've fancied him.

Mohammazi whispered that he was Shahrokh Jalabadi.

He came closer and whispered something to Mohamamazi, whose face then broke into a wide smile.

'Nice to meet you, Miss Anna,' he said in fluent, posh English and held out his hand.

My mouth fell open. How did he know who I was? But I needed to stay calm and play along.

I pulled up my burkha to reveal my face and held out my hand too.

'And you, Mr Jalabadi.'

'Please—call me Shah. And welcome to Lashkar Gah and my home. Hopefully I can treat you to some true Pasthoon hospitality.'

There it came to me.

Shahrokh Jalabadi was Shah.

The man everyone feared. The man everyone called Afghanistan's Killing Machine. The man who was ruthless beyond words.

I was as good as dead.

31

Oh fuck! What an idiot I was!

They had known this all along and arranged me to be taken here. Fauzija and Mohammazi were in it, both probably seasoned spies. How could I've been so gullible?

My days were numbered. With no phone, no back up, I was at the mercy of the cruelest man in Afghanistan.

Formalities now over, Shah turned to his men while still speaking to me.

'Fauzija informed me about your situation when she telephoned me. Her husband is my cousin, and I am always willing to help friends of hers.'

Did he say she had phoned him? But she had no phone! I was a bonafide fuckwitt.

I quickly regained my composure. 'Fauzija saved my life. And little Mohammazi has been incredible.'

My gaze went to seek for Mohammazi but he had already joined the men, gesturing animatedly and making them laugh with something he said in Pashto.

Shah was now staring at me intently, and I felt a chill run down my spine. Was he measuring me for his evil torture regime? Was he planning to take me out and put a bullet through my heart? Or did he want to make me an example of all that was wrong with the foreign occupation by publicly beheading me?

'The people in the villages are very loyal to me,' he said in his flawless public school English.

I was too petrified to say anything and just stood there, still hoping I had got it all wrong. Chance would be a fine thing!

'As you know, this area is very dangerous for foreigners, and one mistake could cost you your life.' He pronounced the words 'your life' very slowly.

'I am aware of my misfortune, Mr Shah.'

'My family are diplomats by nature and our aim is to keep everyone happy,' he replied almost icily, his face betraying no emotion, like a true Pashtun warrior.

My arrival to his house was beginning to look more and more like a well-orchestrated operation with very sinister undertones, where everyone involved had played their part perfectly. It was almost as if I had been lured into a trap and was a pawn in a great game played between Shah and the Western government. I suspected Shah knew exactly what happened to our convoy because the scene of the incident was not far from here, and news travels fast in Afghanistan. The mountains here have eyes and ears and the tribal information highway was connected twenty four by seven. Shah had his fingers in the crusty Talib pie, after all he was in with the arms traders.

'If you want to wash and take a little rest, there is a room ready for you,' he said fiddling with his two smartphones.

I tried to look like I was in control of the situation. 'How about lending me a car to take me to the base?' I said in a slightly strained voice, although I knew what the answer would be.

'Don't worry, everything is arranged for you. In the meantime, you need some rest.'

'Is there any chance I can use a telephone?' I pointed at one of his shiny devices.

He nodded, and asked one of the men to pass a mobile phone to me. He then walked away but was still within earshot.

The London newsroom emergency number was engraved in my memory over the years. A familiar voice picked up the call, 'GNN newsdesk?' amid the blare of TV newscasts and a cacophony of excitable voices in the background. It was so assuring to hear from the 'normal' world, that I almost burst into tears. I suddenly realized how homesick I was.

'This is Anna Sanderson calling. I need to tell Phil that our military convoy was attacked two days ago and I managed to escape, but I don't know what happened to Tim, the cameraman. There was also another journalist travelling with us. Her name is Kelly. I'm safe and now in Lashkar Gah in Helmand.'

The voice at the other end went quiet for a moment, and I waited for further instructions. 'Hold on, Anna, I'll get Phil.'

A scuffling noise down the line and then Phil's familiar voice. From the corner of my eye I could see Shah hovering close by, clearly trying to listen in.

'Phil—it's Anna. I'm okay, I'm in Lashkar Gah. The convoy got fucking attacked and my phone's not working. I have no idea where Tim is...or Kelly, the other reporter who was travelling with us,' I said, as my eyes welled up.

'Anna! We've been fucking worried out of our minds! How the hell did you end up there? Are you okay?'

Shah's eyes were now burning on my face.

'Don't worry, I'm being looked after by some local guys. They say they can drive me to the nearest base soon.' I knew this was an outright lie, but I couldn't scream down the phone that someone should come and rescue me. If anything, I wasn't going to let Shah witness my fear. Stay tough, Anna!

'Hang on, Anna, how do you know you can trust these people? They could be…in with Taliban?' he was searching for words, clearly trying not to alarm me.

'Thanks, Phil, that's not the kind of encouragement I need right now,' I said, feeling irritated and frightened. 'There isn't a single military guy in sight in this shithole and I can't exactly call out "Search and Rescue" can I?'

Shah took a step closer. This was clearly not going according to the script.

'Give it to me. Your time is up.'

And with that he simply took the phone from me in one swift movement and disconnected the call. My only hope was that Phil would send out a rescue mission.

He would, wouldn't he?

Stay still my beating heart, stay still.

Shah gestured that I should go inside the house. Across the yard, Mohammazi seemed anxious to get back to his mother. I watched him and an older turbaned man tying up carpet rolls on the donkey.

Why carpet rolls? That seemed an awful long way to take a couple of carpets. I took a step closer and saw that inside the carpets were several machine guns.

Was this one of the ways in which the guns get transported to the insurgents? But if Shah was helping the Taliban, and if everyone knew I was hiding under the burkha, why hadn't the Talibs killed me straightaway and be done with it, instead of arranging to bring me here? What was the hidden agenda?

None of it made any sense to me. It seemed as if I was walking in a dark tunnel looking for a way out.

My train of thoughts was broken by Mohammazi. Despite his deadly load, he looked happy and he turned to wave at me before trotting off.

As the silhouette of his little body disappeared out of the gates I could not help but wonder what would become of him when he grew up—maybe he would have no other choice but to join the Taliban.

Despite what looked like betrayal, I felt sad that our strange friendship had come to end as the heavy gates were closed in front of me.

I turned around and saw Shah's eyes fixed on me.

A man with two AK47s slung on each shoulder, gestured me to follow him. We went upstairs to a room that was obviously meant for guests staying overnight. It was dark and smelled of stale cigarette smoke. He pulled the curtains elaborately, like in a five star hotel. Small square windows let in a little light, allowing me to inspect the room.

At first glance, it was luxurious by local standards, with its dominating feature being an Eighties-style leather and velvet sofa and a dark glass table, decorated with gold fittings. On the left side of the room was an ornately carved king-sized bed, which looked like something straight out of a Seventies porn flick.

There was a knock on the door, and another man dressed in a crisp white salwar kameez came in with a tea tray and a plate full of nuts and dried fruits. The armed guy pointed at a towel and some fresh clothes that were neatly laid out on the bed. Again, I got the sense that everyone in this house knew about my arrival.

The last couple of days and the donkey ride had left a lasting fragrance on me, so I was eager to see the bathroom. And it failed to disappoint. Like the living room, the en suite bathroom was opulently furnished with gold taps and shiny marble walls. A bathtub, shaped like a sea shell, was nestled invitingly in one corner.

I filled the bathtub with hot water (relishing the fact that there really was hot water, here in the middle of the desert) and unwrapped a bar of what looked like Russian soap. I sank my weary body into the hot water and exhaled deeply.

Afterwards, I quickly fell asleep, despite my odd surroundings, dreaming about Tim and Kelly, donkeys transporting giant shell-shaped bathtubs up mountain paths. My anxiety about Shah and being stuck in the middle of Afghan badlands was temporarily relieved by the colourful palette of my mind producing its own narratives.

I woke up crying, confused, and unable to place where I was. Before I realized, there was another man in a crisp salwar kameeez at my door with a tray of tea, naan, hard boiled eggs, and something that looked like meat stew.

'Mr Shah wants to see you in his office in 30 minutes,' the man said softly.

I ate the meal with gusto, and headed downstairs. As I approached Shah's office, I could hear muffled conversations from his room, some of which sounded angry. One voice kept on repeating 'Yaw millooon dollar Shah-jan, yaw millooon,' which meant one million dollars. Sweat began to trickle down my back—was that the price for my head?

I knocked on the door, adjusting my shirt and trying to keep my composure.

'Come in,' bellowed a voice.

Shah's office was on the ground floor and consisted mainly of rows of chairs and one giant mahogany desk with a picture of Hamid Karzai on the wall.

The room was full of bearded and turbaned men, and thick with cigarette smoke. I had obviously interrupted them because some of the men looked uncomfortable in my presence.

'Aaah, Anna, my honourable visitor. Come in, come in. How are you enjoying your stay in my humble home?' Shah was all smiles and friendly handshakes and did not let on that disagreements were taking place.

'Great. The room is very comfortable, thank you,' I replied, trying to ignore the intense gaze of the bearded men in the room.

'I'm happy to hear that. This is the only way we do things here in Helmand. It really is our honour to have you,' he went on, gesturing with his hands.

Despite his friendly exterior, something about Shah's slick manner unsettled me. He seemed very calm on the outside and his mild, almost overly polite manner, suggested a lifetime of controlled behaviour and, to a degree, insincerity. What worried me was that his face was unreadable. I knew that this man was fully capable of terrible things that torture, things the human mind cannot even imagine.

Don't freak out. Don't cry. Don't let him know that you are on the edge.

I noticed that he had a deep, relatively new scar on his left hand that looked like a knife wound. I muttered some more thank yous and sat down on one of the leather chairs. Tea was immediately poured for me.

Everything here was like a well rehearsed play, with its main man playing the part of Dr Jekyll and Mr Hyde perfectly.

'Anna, I am trying to negotiate your safe journey back to the base camp, but I am sure you understand this journey is full of dangers for us ordinary Afghans,' he started.

Ordinary! Allow me to laugh. You are anything but ordinary.

My only choice was to nod in agreement. 'I can pay you whatever it takes once I am back in London, you can have my word on that.'

He laughed. 'Are you offering me money? I could not accept money from a beautiful lady like you.' He stroked his scar and said slowly, 'It's our Pasthun tradition to look after our guests. But I also need to protect my own men.'

'If someone could drop me off nearby, I could walk the rest of the way and your men would be safe,' I responded, the desperation in my voice apparent.

Shah smiled at me. 'The road leading to the camp is one of the most dangerous in this country. You should know that better than anyone else. There the Taliban are waiting on both sides of the road, ready to kill anyone who approaches.'

'What about making a call to the camp and arranging a swap somewhere where it is safer?' I ventured, but realized how naive I sounded.

'This would unsettle my people too much. And getting a convoy to stop, even in a deserted area, is too dangerous. No one wants to take that risk. You know this,' he said patiently as if he were talking to a child.

I did. And I could feel frustration rising up in me.

'But don't worry,' Shah continued. 'We'll wait for the right time and then we'll strike.'

The way he said 'strike' made me realize I was being used as a pawn in other negotiations. Otherwise I was of no value to him, and killing me would be far easier than keeping me alive.

But what did Shah want? Was it something the military was willing to save my life for? I hoped so.

When my escort came for me, I knew my time with him to negotiate had come to an end.

32

An entire day went by in a sleepy haze. Occasionally I would get up to write notes on the few remaining pages of my tatty notebook. The tea man was my only visitor. The door wasn't locked but an armed man had been posted outside my room. Sometimes there were two of them. If I tried to leave my room, one of them would follow me.

My movements in the house were restricted to the courtyard downstairs and the main hall. If I tried to take a different route, or look into the other rooms, I felt the poke of an AK47 on my back.

My thoughts wandered to Mark and if he had any idea where I was. If he cared to know, that is. But he was one complicated cookie. The more I thought about it, the less sense it made.

I played out different kinds of reunion scenarios and dialogues in my head, but generally it went like this:

He would heroically abseil thorough the ceiling somehow (although in reality I couldn't see how because there were no visible holes. But fantasies don't care for details).

Me (looking beautiful, but slightly startled): 'Hello Mark. How are you?'

Him (looking amazingly rugged, but smiling): 'God, Anna, I have missed you so much. I love you. Will you marry me?'

Me (remembering to play hard to get): 'Will you promise not to act all weird again and not to go anywhere near that awful Shabita?'

Him: 'Shabita who? Oh, that evil woman with the fake laughter and ugly shoes? Of course I won't—you silly sweet girl. I love you.'

And so it went.

The next day a lady wearing a head scarf and a long skirt came to clean my room and brought clean clothes and some more soap and towels. When I tried to speak to her, she didn't respond, and gave me a blank look instead.

Later that day the tea man was replaced by a young, skinny boy who stared at me curiously as he put down my tray of tea and fruits. He must have been about Mohammazi's age and, again, my attempts to strike up a conversation were met with an empty gaze.

Another new day started with the call for prayer. I was not sure if it was still night when I first woke up because my sleep was disturbed by the fear of being dragged out of my bed into the deep unknown mystery—death.

I got dressed and opened the door. The guard was asleep, but there was another guard across the hallway who was wide awake. I gestured to him that I wanted a walk, and immediately the guard placed outside my door woke up.

The stairs were being cleaned by the same woman who had brought me tea the other day. She was crouched down with an ancient scrubbing brush in her hand. She was so engrossed with her work that she barely noticed me. As I took the final step, I saw something lying on the ground. It was a lipstick. I quickly picked it up and hid it under my shalwaz kameez.

Once I was safely back in my room, I took the lipstick out to inspect it. The brand was Sax—the same that Kelly always wore without fail. I remembered how she would always blabber about her and her 'Sax trade secrets'. The shade was 'blush', a sort of brown-pink, which was again Kelly's colour. Tears welled up in my eyes. But just then a thought struck me. What would Shah be doing with an Aussie lippy? Has he kidnapped an Australian journo?

Hang on. What did I just say to myself?

Could it be? No, it's not possible. Kelly couldn't be here, could she? But what was the lippy doing here at the bottom of the stairs?

I slowed down and looked behind me, where the cleaner had been. She was now gone. It was too much of a coincidence. What if Kelly was being kept here? Then perhaps Tim was here too. My god!

I started pacing around the room frantically.

Where could they be? And how could I get to them? And why the hell were we all here? I had noticed that on the left of the landing was a thick wooden door that just seemed to be leading to another wing of the house, but I couldn't be quite sure. Maybe that's where they were, and Kelly had left the lipstick on the stairs, knowing that I would go past it. Maybe the cleaner was in on it. She had to be the one who had left the lippy, because Shah's cronies would have picked it up the minute they saw it. It would be risky as hell for her, but maybe she did it. Or maybe I was going stark raving mad?

Even if they were here, this means that we were all stuck in this hellhole. And our chances of getting out were getting slimmer by the day.

I felt panic bubble up inside me.

This is it. This is how I'm going to die. In a house that has a lot of gold plating and shell-shaped bathtubs.

Nothing significant happened after the discovery of the lipstick. The days and nights merged into one another, as I slowly resigned from desperation and sadness to boredom. There were days when I would hatch escape plans, but after a while I would give up knowing that they were futile. I tried to keep track of time and kept scribbling in my notebook faithfully. I had interviewed many people who had spent time in captivity and had always wondered how they coped. Now I knew—with great difficulty. Of course, my situation was nothing in comparison to real victims. I was a silly reporter who was in trouble because of her own doing.

I left my room often, even though I was always shadowed by my minder. I made mental notes. The house was surrounded by a ten-metre wall, lined with rusting barbed wires. The windows in my room were too high to jump out from, as they didn't have a ledge or a landing that could make it easier, and the option of running out of the gate without being shot at didn't really seem inviting.

I did entertain various fantasies about finding Tim and Kelly, but deep down I started to believe that they were just pure fantasies. How could I ever escape my armed minders?

I wasn't even allowed to go and meet Shah. I thought that if only I could meet him somehow, I would talk some sense into him, or at least find out what his plans were, but each time I ventured into the direction of his office, my path was blocked by men with various firearms.

The only place the guards would not follow me into was the kitchen. A woman's world. I was quietly relieved by it. The kitchen was as big as my flat back home, and throughout the day it was a hive of activity with either food being cooked, pans cleaned, or even clothes being washed. Sometimes the women would just sit on the floor talking to each other while peeling potatoes and plucking chickens. There was never an idle moment.

The lipstick still played on my mind, but by now I had started believing the possibility that it could have been a cruel coincidence, or that somehow, or someone, was playing tricks on me.

Phil and the rest were vaguely aware of my location and that provided a glimmer of hope in this dark situation… although a newsroom full of journos was not the best option for negotiations with hardened criminals. They just couldn't let me die here, could they? Even though I was well aware that a lot worse happened in this country, and that over the years, many of my fellow journos had been shot and died in grim surroundings, I just couldn't entirely accept a similar fate for myself. Surely our government would not let us die, I kept telling myself.

The sun went down and the TV continued with its fuzzy stream of war news in Pashto, sending me to sleep with its lullaby of misery.

Every day I wished we hadn't dreamt up 'Operation Lipstick'. It was stupid, childish, and dangerous, and cost me everything I had. Guilt, sadness, and hopelessness were all merging into one giant knot inside me. By keeping me a prisoner, Shah held an ultimate control over me and I was convinced that there was a price over my head, but I wasn't sure what that was.

I tried to create little daily routines to keep myself sane. Something along the lines of tea, breakfast, and an attempt at a Pashto conversation with a staff member. I kept the TV news on with the faint hope that there would be a picture of me with the word 'missing' across the screen. Perhaps London had alerted the embassy, which meant that there would be a flock of brave SAS men on its way to rescue me. Realistically, this wasn't likely to happen. They would not bring out special forces to rescue a hapless reporter. In all likeliness, they would leave me here. After all, who was to blame for the insane journey we embarked upon, what seemed like a lifetime ago. Phil might make a token effort with the embassy but that was all.

I started to have nightmares, and often woke up sweating in the night and then lay awake, thinking of how they would finally execute me. Would I be shot? Beheaded? Left somewhere to starve to death?

I blamed myself for being so stupid and trusting these people. I should have just made my own escape instead of trusting Mohammazi and his mother. Maybe the worst thing was the realization that Fauzija, whom I trusted, had betrayed me, especially because I thought we had some sort of female camaraderie going on. But maybe she didn't have a choice—it was her and her children's lives at stake after all.

My only hope was that the British government, or whoever they had targeted, would pay up. Shah's calm and calculating manner was unsettling, and it had become evident that I could not plead with him or elicit any feeling of sympathy. If anything, I did not want to give him the pleasure of knowing how desperate and frightened I was.

33

I sat by the window, playing my usual escape fantasy in my head, when I heard male voices approaching. I sat up with a jolt when I realized they were speaking in English.

The voices grew louder, and my first instinct was to scream for help but then I paused for a second. Come on, Anna, think straight. They probably were Shah's allies, and I would only make things worse by crying out for help. After all, they must have come to the house to visit Shah, not to rescue reporters in distress.

I stood up to listen. Judging from the direction of the sound, the men had to be positioned directly below my room.

'The last time we got a straight 2,000 bucks per piece, but now they're bargaining for more.'

He spoke with a gruff American accent.

I patted myself on the back for ignoring my instinct and not calling out for help. It was evident that these men, whoever they were, would not help me.

'Don't worry buddy, Rich has promised us more deals in the pipeline,' said another voice, this time with a British accent.

This little snippet made me shoot up from my chair.

I strained my neck through the small window, trying to get a better look at the two men. This was incredible, but not unlikely. After all, I knew Shah was the conductor of vile in this part of the world, and the two men would have inevitably had to come to HQ to do their business.

The only thing visible was the tops of their heads, one balding and the other grey haired.

'Yeah, but we need to make sure that Najibullah delivers this time. You remember what happened the last time, when we had to pay off that stupid reporter chick to keep her mouth shut,' said the Brit.

What reporter chick? Who has been after this story? There could only be one person so bent—Shabita!

My god, she had been on their trail and they had paid her off. That explains the appearance of several designer handbags, fake nails, and all the botox. The girl was living it large with dodgy cash. And I suspected this gig may not be her only one. If only, if only I could prove it.

Suddenly I remembered that the voice recorder and camera in my phone were still working!

Sliding the voice recorder carefully on the window sill, I pressed record. Click. The reassuring red light came on. My hands were trembling.

'Don't worry, I saw her out of the base yesterday and she will keep her mouth shut for sure,' the American said. 'She had travelled here especially to meet us and this place ain't Costa Del Helmand, so she must have been keen to get out.'

'To be honest, mate, half a million quid is not a lot, is it? Compared to what's to come,' the Brit continued.

'The weakest link is Rich. I reckon he is close to cracking up and we can't afford that. We can take care of the business without him on the way,' the Yankee drawled.

'Don't worry, I have a plan. He is likely to have a serious accident at work very soon, it's all arranged.'

'Look, Phil, this wasn't supposed to get bloody. As much as I worry about Rich slipping up, I don't want any dead bodies.'

'Mate, don't worry. He'll just lose an arm in an accident. That's all. And no one will be able to trace it back to us, you know what this country is like. And Shah is here to help.'

The two men laughed in unison.

Photo, I had to get a photo—but how? I couldn't leave my room without my minder noticing, and any unusual activity would attract attention and alert the two men. My arm wasn't long enough to stretch the camera out of the window. I quickly glanced around my room, looking for something longer that I could attach the phone to. I needed to get pictures of their faces by lowering the camera, even by a few inches would help. Aha! I suddenly realized I was wearing an underwire bra. I quickly took off my T-shirt, ripped a hole in my bra with my teeth, and pulled out the wire.

I fished out a few elastic hair bands from my bag, and fixed my camera onto the wire. A stretched out tampon that I found at the bottom of my bag further helped to secure the equipment. I swung it about to check if it was secured tightly. It was. Who needs macho Swiss army knives when you've got girly stuff lying around. I set the camera on auto-mode to take a picture every thirty seconds, and pushed it through the window bars, positioned above the men's heads. I knew, if one of the men was to look up I would be dead, so I quietly prayed that they would not hear the gentle click of the camera. I silently wished for my hair bands to hold out and bear the burden of their precious cargo.

Just as I lowered my wire–tampon contraption, the afternoon call to prayer rang out from the nearby mosque.

My camera got to work. I carefully moved it around and reset it to take more pictures. In the end, I must have got about ten pictures. I pulled the camera back in through the window carefully, inch by inch, so as not to alert the men.

The men were still talking but, because of the call to prayer, I was unable to get a clear recording. However, I understood that the two men had come to pay Shah his share. These men no doubt needed his permission before attempting anything on his turf.

Despite this brief moment of jubilation, the hopelessness of my situation hit me hard. What good were these photos? The chances of me getting out alive from a house being used as a base for weapon smugglers was next to zero. The chances of escaping to safety in Taliban controlled area were negative. The men's conversation trailed off as they walked away from the window. I scooped up my recorder from the window sill and flicked through the photos.

The outline of one their faces could be clearly made out. The second man's face could also be seen, although it was blurry. It was a stroke of luck in a luckless situation. I replayed the conversation and was relieved to hear that the Yank's comments about Rich's hand were clear. The Brit's voice could also be heard too but fainter.

The material was explosive, and I knew I had a huge story in my hands. But the truth was that there was very little I could do while sitting in captivity. I vowed to follow up the story when, or if, I ever got out.

34

Something had woken me up. A dull banging sound—thud, thud, thud.

My eyes still half closed, I listened to the sounds of the house. It was still dark outside. The metallic banging could only mean that the maids were up and getting the kitchen ready. I contemplated not getting up. After all, what was the point? I had cried myself to sleep and was still wearing my jeans and T-shirt from last night. I felt the sobs rise inside me again. I needed to pee. Sighing, I dragged my sorry self to the bog.

I didn't turn the lights on, for wanting to remain in a semi-comatose state for some more time. I sat down on the toilet seat and glanced at my watch—3.30 am. The banging sound continued. What was it? It seemed to be coming from the kitchen quarters.

My eyes had begun to adjust in the dark and soon I was able to see. In front of me was the familiar narrow window I had stared out of so many times while planning my escape. But there was something odd happening outside. A shadow seemed to be moving outside the window.

I stared at it for a while, but nothing happened. Must have been my mind playing tricks as usual. But all of a sudden, I could see the outline of a hand.

'What the…' I stared at it in shock.

Someone or something had pushed the window open. I was too scared to get up and look for the light switch. Stupefied, I awaited my fate. The head bobbed up first. It seemed like a man's face, but I couldn't really see in the darkness.

Then I saw his face on the windowsill clearly. I wasn't dreaming.

'Anna, don't scream. It's Mark,' he whispered.

What the fuck!

If I hadn't been so terrified, our encounter would have been comical. But I was so relieved, I felt pee trickling down my leg.

This wasn't a rescue scenario I had imagined during my lonely long hours. Still, as rescues go, it was good. Fantastic even!

My hero!

A huge wave of relief came over me and I could have kissed him then there and with my jeans still around my ankles. He pulled himself into the room through the window.

He was whispering. 'We've drugged the guards, but someone else might be up. We have fifteen minutes to get you out. Pull your trousers up, love,' he said, while gently holding me close.

'But what about Kelly…Tim…?'

'Shhh…we haven't got the time to talk. I'll tell you everything later. Hurry!'

'I have to get something from the room first.'

'Anna…please…'

There was no way I was going to leave the evidence for the story and let go of the biggest scoop of my life. I grabbed my phone, stuffed it in my back pocket, and followed him to the window.

'Here, grab this,' Mark handed me a piece of sturdy rope. 'Turn your body sideways, you'll be okay.'

I'm too fat, I wanted to whine, but realized that was not the time to air my weight anxieties.

I grabbed the rope and pulled myself up on the windowsill. Mark was holding me from my bum. Talk about embarrasing situations.

'Tilt your waist to the right. Now push your top half out first, and I will help you with the rest. That's it, well done. Now take the rope and whatever you do, don't let go of it.'

Do not let go of the rope. Do not let go.

I felt a tug and as if by miracle my body squeezed out of the narrow window, sending me spiralling into the darkness. I suppressed a scream but didn't let go of the rope that was around my wrists.

'Okay, now grab hold of the ledge in front of you and inch yourself closer to it,' came an order from the darkness.

I did as I was told and seemed to somehow gain my balance. My hands were getting tired from hanging from the ropes but I knew if I let go, it would be over.

'Here,' said Mark from above, 'hang on in there. Now lower yourself down slowly.'

He held the rope, while I lowered myself down. The movies never show you how it happens in real life. My getaway wasn't really elegant or Catwoman like. I looked more like a sack of potatoes wobbling on some string.

'Only a few more metres to go,' he whispered.

Suddenly there was a flash of light and my heart stopped. Fuck.

'Don't worry, keep going,' Mark whispered.

I hit the ground like a baby elephant while he climbed down soon after, like a world class acrobat.

Something had fallen out of my pocket.

Kelly's lipstick.

'Quick—to the gate,' he whispered.

'I can't leave,' I said.

I could feel Mark's impatient stare in the dark.

'There is a chance that Kelly and Tim might be here too.'

'Just run, Anna, I promise you it'll all be okay.'

For once in my life I didn't question what I was being told to do.

We began to run, adrenaline pumping in my blood. The iron gate was open, and outside it there was light.

A light I had been desperate to see during many dark days. And in front of those flickering beams of light stood Kelly and Tim.

35

'Ladies and gentleman, as we are preparing for take-off, could I please ask you to take your seat and fasten your seatbelts,' came the stern voice of the stewardess through the tannoy.

We were on our way from Duschanbe to Athens and there we would take a flight to London.

The stewardesses' uniforms were made of heavy nylon circa 1979 with starchy collars and blue eye shadow to match. 'Tajik Air takes you higher—now and forever' it read on the back of the polyester covered chair in front of me. It made me giggle.

I sat on my seat, all belted up and glanced at the handsome man sitting next to me. I couldn't quite believe it was me, Anna Sanderson, soon to be thirty-three—the eternal singleton, sitting next to my dream guy, holding his hand! I let out more laughter.

Brimming with happiness, I could have danced my way down the plane aisle. But given the plane was an old Russian Tupolev, I didn't think this would be the most sensible of ideas.

'Let's have a little toast—to our health,' Mark said, clinking my glass.

The neat vodka burned my throat, but I savoured it like precious nectar. I leaned my head back on the seat and thought of the previous weeks. Images rolled before my eyes, like a fast forward film.

Kelly, Tim, and I had all been rescued by people trained in hostage situations, specialist guys, heroes. Like my Mark. As cheesy as it may have sounded, he was my hero. They had all information about Shah and after Phil had alerted the embassy, a rescue mission was put in place, led by local intelligence expert—Mark. The whereabouts of Kelly and Tim had been a mystery to his team since they had been picked up soon after the ambush by Shah's men. But Intel soon found out where they were. It was easier to trace me because of the phone call. Kelly had indeed managed to bribe one of the housekeepers to leave the lipstick as a sign to anyone who would be looking for her—after all, what are the chances of an Oz lippy ending up in a house in Helmand?

After our escape, we had been transported to the nearby base. All three of us, jubilant and bubbling with sheer happiness. Tim, too, seemed at ease with the fact that Mark and I were finally together. He shook hands with him and said, 'You're one lucky guy.'

On the bumpy Tupolev, Mark turned to me, smiling. I realized it was the first time I had ever seen him smile properly and look so relaxed. 'The things I've been telling you haven't all been true,' he began, his fingers lightly tickling the top of my hand.

'No shit…' I beamed back.

He started slowly, almost like tasting every word. I was suddenly filled with fear—was this when he revealed he was married?

'Come on now, Miss Cheek. I left out some bits about my job and why I was in Kabul. But there are other important things I need to tell you too.' He must have seen my expression change because he quickly added, 'It's nothing serious but I just want to be honest….my background…I was an only child and my parents were both retired academicians with high hopes for me. When I went to Sandhurst, I think both of them were disappointed that I had chosen a career in the army.'

He went on to tell me that he had done his time in the army, climbed high up the ranks, and eventually moved on to work for MI6, the British Intelligence agency, but soon left to start his own Intelligence agency business.

'A spook shop?' I asked.

'Sort of. We would take on highly classified jobs that were pretty much untraceable by any government officials because of their…ahem…sensitive nature. We've been on to those arms guys for ages and have even been paid by various European governments to bust their racket, but you got to them first. I couldn't quite believe when you pitched up in Helmand, telling me all this stuff about Rich and his gang. Years worth of work and you guys just pulled the rug from under our feet.'

'You're having me on…' I started.

He shook his head to interrupt me.

'So the whole operation back in Now Zad—Operation Zewertia—was just an elaborate cover up?' I asked.

'Yes, even the local squad didn't know our plans. That's why you got to the base, because they had no idea. But afterwards all hell broke loose, because they should have never got a journalist on board in the first place. But lucky for me they did.'

'Sorry.'

'Don't be, it was worth the trouble, just to see you in those tight leggings.' He took a gulp from his vodka and grinned.

I blushed.

Mark continued, 'But when you got ambushed I was beside myself with worry. And then that business with Shah. We had to get to you before they got fed up and fed you the bullet. You know your story will cause a storm. Chuck has already resigned because of our investigation, and has returned to the US where he will be a subject for investigation after a phone call from not so kitteny Kelly. Rich and his cronies have vanished. Most likely to Yemen, but they won't stay underground forever. We will find them,' said Mark.

'What about Shah?'

'Probably hiding somewhere in the Gulf. Truth is, it will be hard to bring him to justice. He's one slippery eel.'

'And Shabita? What happened between you two?'

'Us two? I had to stay friendly with her, although I can't

stand that woman. She had worked it out that Rich was involved in the arms deal and had decided to blackmail them. She will probably be arrested under international law.'

'So why all the secrets and lies?'

'There were those silly diplomat types that got nervous about me being involved with a reporter. After all, I do know plenty of state secrets.'

Mark explained that at Ariana's party, his co-workers weren't really who they said they were, but he was forced to take minders from HQ with him. Again to prevent him from talking to me.

I leaned closer to him and sighed. My tiredness had vanished and happiness bubbled inside me. As if the surrounding world was brand new. I no longer cared if I had stubbly underarms or greasy hair. There were more important things in life.

'Who knows what's next?' Mark said. 'It's time for me to think about my future. Maybe I can call it our future,' he said, his brown eyes looking at me seriously, those deep pools of mystery, I loved so much.

'No one has ever rescued me from a toilet before,' I said to him, giggling.

'I'm all about the romance factor,' he laughed and kissed me.

'So why did you take the risk of getting involved with me?' I said finally.

He took my hand and said with his eyes shining, 'I'm in love with you, Anna. I'm all yours—if you'll have me.'

It took a couple of seconds to sink in. This was what I had been waiting for all my life. My heart began to sing. I kissed him on his beautiful mouth and said, 'Let that be your answer.'

I wanted this moment here, on the Russian Tupolev, to last forever. But in reality I feared the plane itself may not last much past Athens.

We were now soaring above the beautiful Afghan mountains. Over the clear blue sky we clinked our glasses, which were brimming with the best drink I've ever had— lukewarm vodka; it dissolved all my doubts straightaway.

Having survived the bumpiest of life's roads, my happiness felt as breathtakingly pure as the snow-capped mountains of the Hindu Kush below us. I squeezed his hand and looked out of the window. I didn't want the dazzling white snow to melt into rivers unknown.

At least not so soon.

Acknowledgements

So many people helped me with this book and I am thankful for their wisdom.

Operation Lipstick would not have been born without Zeina Awad and Jane Meikle, who inspired me to write the book after a night out in a dodgy bar in Dubai.

Two special Kabuli friends—Satu Elo and Johanna Valenius—deserve a huge thank you for their comments and insights into Afghanistan.

Operation Lipstick would have not been possible without Trisha Bora, my editor at Random House, whose steely professionalism, helped me carve a proper book out of a messy manuscript.

I would like to thank my gang—Henrika, Riina, Hanna, Paulina, and Catherine—whose opinions and insights have been valuable throughout the writing process.

In addition, my dear friend Jessica Sallabank's feedback on my grammar deserves a mention.

A big thank you to Andrea Busfield and Sandy Balfour, who helped me with the small print.

And finally, I would like to thank my husband Joe, for his (seemingly) endless ability to laugh at my bad jokes.

A Note on the Author

Pia Heikkila is a journalist with over fifteen years of experience in international media including Al Jazeera, CNN, CNBC, the *National*, and the *Guardian*. She has lived in South Asia since 2008, and has spent time in Afghanistan as a correspondent reporting for the international press. She currently lives in Mumbai, where she covers news, lifestyle, and business stories for print and TV. This is her first book.